PRAISE FOR *STEALING*

'A dazzling mix of fact and fiction from one of Britain's leading royal commentators'

—Andrew Morton

STEALING THE CROWN

ALSO BY TP FIELDEN

The Miss Dimont Mysteries

The Riviera Express

Resort to Murder

A Quarter Past Dead

Died and Gone to Devon

STEALING THE CROWN

A Guy Harford Mystery

TP FIELDEN

THOMAS & MERCER

Text copyright © 2020 by TP Fielden
All rights reserved.

No part of this book may be reproduced, or stored in a retrieval system, or transmitted in any form or by any means, electronic, mechanical, photocopying, recording, or otherwise, without express written permission of the publisher.

Published by Thomas & Mercer, Seattle

www.apub.com

Amazon, the Amazon logo, and Thomas & Mercer are trademarks of Amazon.com, Inc., or its affiliates.

ISBN-13: 9781542017374
ISBN-10: 1542017378

Cover design by Ghost Design

Printed in the United States of America

For

Rachel and James Liddell

CAST OF CHARACTERS

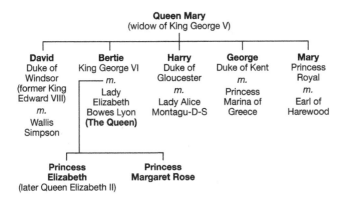

Queen Mary
(widow of King George V)

David	**Bertie**	**Harry**	**George**	**Mary**
Duke of Windsor	King George VI	Duke of Gloucester	Duke of Kent	Princess Royal
(former King Edward VIII)	*m.*	*m.*	*m.*	*m.*
m.	Lady Elizabeth Bowes Lyon	Lady Alice Montagu-D-S	Princess Marina of Greece	Earl of Harewood
Wallis Simpson	**(The Queen)**			

Princess Elizabeth
(later Queen Elizabeth II)

Princess Margaret Rose

GUY HARFORD – artist, Buckingham Palace courtier, reluctant spy

RODIE CARR – burglar, blackmailer, black marketeer

FOXY GWYNNE – American socialite, former Jean Patou model in Paris

RUPERT HARDACRE – Guy's flatmate, employed by the General Post Office

EDGAR BRAMPTON – assistant private secretary, Buckingham Palace

ADELAIDE BRAMPTON – Edgar Brampton's widow

ALAN 'TOMMY' LASCELLES – deputy private secretary to King George VI

SIR TOPHAM 'TOPSY' DIGHTON – Master of the Household, Buckingham Palace

AGGIE – Buckingham Palace clerk (secretary)

TED ROCHESTER – gossip columnist, *News Chronicle* newspaper and *Boulevardier*

BETSEY CODY – rich American socialite in London

VISCOUNTESS EASTHAMPTON – suspected Nazi spy

TOBY BROADBENT – member of the King's personal bodyguard

Life is a dream, but the dream is true

—*Sadhguru Jaggi Vasudev*

CHAPTER ONE

Outside, the streets around Piccadilly were awash with debris from the recent raid, the air tainted by the smell from burst gas mains, the gutters running with water from the fire hoses. The gradual destruction of a once-great city and the terrible news from abroad had the effect of altering personal behaviour. These days, through the patina of good manners could be seen the slow decline of ancient values, and in dark corners, in the refuges of the night, a new order was growing at an alarming rate.

Down steps still covered with plush carpet and behind heavily curtained doors, two women dawdled over the remains of their second sidecar. Both were startling to look at – the blonde in a lightly padded Betty Grable sort of way, her dark-haired companion undeniably beautiful but looking slightly odd with her old-fashioned Eton crop.

Their jewellery was expensive but big. Their clothes looked new and their high-heeled shoes were clearly still at the breaking-in stage – each had taken one off under the table. They spoke in carefully modulated tones, caution governing the delivery of their vowels.

'Another, Lem?' It was now past seven o'clock.

'No thanks, Rodie. Time for a dip.'

'No swimming pool here, ducks.' She knew perfectly well what her friend was getting at but never passed up an opportunity to tease.

'Nooo,' said the woman, who answered to Lemonade but preferred to tell people she was Claudia. 'The other. Do a bit of work.'

'Remember your manners, girl! You're in The Ritz now.'

Upstairs, the permanent residents of the fabled hotel, from King Zog of Albania to Mrs Keppel, famous mistress of King Edward VII, were preparing to move from their observation posts in the Palm Court into the dining room. An unofficial order of precedence marked their journey, with the king and his family slightly ahead of the bulky seventy-three-year-old who'd made her fortune from doing what comes naturally. Others of lesser blood followed at a discreet distance.

But down in the Basement Bar, life moved at a livelier pace, with white-jacketed old men circling like ballet dancers. Many had served here in the First War, retired, and now were hauled back for a second round of duty. For each the same rules applied: first establish the customer's place in the pecking order, then remember what they drank.

'Thank you, Your Grace, three pink gins. And Your Lordship, another whisky with water on the side? Sir Henry, one moment if you *please . . .*'

The two women idly watched this courtly dance while exchanging pieces of essential information. In their line of duty, it was vital to keep on top of the latest developments – shifts in personnel, changes of location, fluctuating tastes and desires, who's suddenly rich and who's dead.

'Can't hang on much longer,' said Claudia. 'You can stay here all night if you want to but I've got work to do.'

'Dippin'? You can forget it – it's your first time in The Ritz, Lem, you don't know the rules. Sit *down*!' Rodie grabbed the hem of her friend's skirt.

'Right time of night,' insisted the other, rising again. 'Most of these boys have been here since the sirens went. They've drunk their fill – an' a few more.'

'Listen to me, Lem!'

'No, I want to get on. I'm meeting the boxer later.'

The woman called Rodie looked around the lofty room, its ornate plasterwork as yet undamaged by the bloody conflict outside. Certainly, if you were in their game this was the right place: at the bar, at the tables, lounging round the fountain down the other end were men from the better regiments – the Guards, Dragoons and Hussars – with just a sprinkling of Royal Navy and RAF types as well. Few of them existed on their service pay, and none of them polished their own shoes. They were rich.

'Sit down, Lem, and look at me. You're talented, you've got the looks, but you've got to learn – you don't dip the Ritz Bar.'

'Don't be soft,' said Claudia, taking out her powder compact. 'They're just waiting to give it to a girl like me.' In a certain light she was remarkable-looking, and knew it.

'That's where you're wrong. Use your eyes – your *eyes*! What do you see?'

'A lot of rich men, and a lot of rich women.'

'Notice anything else?'

'Good-looking. *Rich*,' repeated Claudia, joyously flapping her eyelashes, taking in the room.

'And . . . ?'

'I don't get you.' Only half-listening, she was thinking about the bruiser from Deptford.

'Notice something about the way they're sitting?'

'Nicely. Very nice deportment, no slouching – like you always tell me.'

'And . . . ?'

'Don't follow.'

'Oh, *Lem*. The men are sitting with the men, the women are with the women.'

3

Claudia put down her compact and looked around as if for the first time.

'Oh,' she said. 'So . . .'

Her voice trailed off in a mixture of incomprehension and disbelief. The two sidecars had fogged her usually sharp perception.

'These people belong to a club you and I will never join,' said Rodie. She gazed into the innocent face, waiting for the fog to clear. 'And this bar is where they like to come. To be amongst their own, bless 'em.'

'What the two-and-sixpence are we doing here, then?' snapped Claudia. She'd progressed nicely from shoplifter to pickpocket on account of her looks, her nimble brain, and her ability to move quickly. But despite the dress she was wearing tonight, despite her colossal appeal, despite the age-old surroundings of London's smartest hotel, she still looked like a kid on the make.

'You've got a lot to learn,' said Rodie, smiling at the pianist. She was always thrilled when he nodded and played her favourite tune.

'Might still work, though,' said Lem, ever the optimist. 'I look nice, don't I? Bourne and Hollingsworth, this dress. Seven guineas!'

Rodie ignored this. 'Look,' she said, nodding her head. 'That man over there. He's called Colonel Cutie. Works in the War Office. Comes here every night looking for young officers. Not all of them are homo, but a lot of them want to get on – make sure they get the right posting, get shifted to a better regiment. Some of them want to do something daring, others want the opposite. The colonel fixes all that. And in return, of course . . .'

She looked kindly at her pretty blonde friend and shook her head. 'These chaps aren't much use to a girl like you, Lem. You can switch your headlights off.'

Through the crush emerged an athletic-looking figure in a tight-fitting civilian suit. Ignoring the blonde completely he looked down angrily at Rodie.

4

'It was you, wasn't it!'

'Don't know what you mean, Rupe.'

She clearly did.

'Guy Harford found a red rose in his office this morning. And a kiss chalked on his desk.'

Rodie burst out laughing.

'It was *you*, wasn't it?'

'What makes you think that?'

'Just the bloody damn-fool thing I'd expect from you. You fall in love with him when you've only known him two minutes, and to prove it, you go and do something like this.'

'He's *gorgeous!*'

'For heaven's sake, Rodie, what can you be thinking of? Breaking into Buckingham Palace? Burgling a courtier's office? Defacing royal property? Are you mad?'

'You look quite handsome when you get angry. Give us a kiss.'

'I should never have introduced you!'

'Darling,' said Rodie. 'He's lovely. He's single. And,' she added, waving her arm at the serried ranks of uniforms pressed against the bar, 'he's not like any of *those*. He's a painter, an artist – just think of those eyes!'

'*You burgled Buckingham Palace.* If they find out, it's Holloway for you – three years minimum.'

'Does he know it was me?'

Hardacre stared at her in disbelief. 'Know? *Know?* How many burglars do you think Guy's met? Let me be more specific – how many *female* burglars do you think he's met? Female burglars who said within ten minutes of meeting him, "I think I'm going to marry you"?'

Rodie was pleased with this. She turned to Claudia, but despite the urgent word of warning, her friend was extravagantly waggling

5

her eyebrows at a captain in the Life Guards. He stared back, bewildered.

'Pay attention,' said Rupe sternly, 'because this is embarrassing for me. Guy has one of the most sensitive jobs in the country, and your damn-fool high jinks could land him in terrible trouble. And what about me? What's he going to think of me for introducing you?'

'It was a piece of cake, Rupe. I didn't even have to go over the palace wall, just walked in when they weren't looking. You know there are half a dozen gates into that place, they don't all have a guardsman with fixed bayonet standin' around. And, honestly, the locks on those royal doors! They should be ashamed of themselves!'

'Did you take anything?'

Rodie looked indignant. '*Take* anything? Why would I do that?'

'Because, my dear, you just burgled your way into the greatest treasure-house in the country. It would be against your religion to come away empty-handed.'

'I did it for love.'

'You did it for the hell of it. You're a terrible show-off.'

There was a pause and then Claudia rose from her seat. 'I think I'll go and try my luck anyway,' she said absently.

Her fingers were itching to get inside those soldiers' pockets.

'Golden days, Guy.'

He nodded vaguely – no point in revisiting the past, it was gone. In Paris they'd been close but that was long ago, the memories now were coated with dust.

'Strange to see you dressed like this,' she said, tilting her head. 'With your hair short and shoes on your feet. Clean fingernails, too – I hardly recognise you these days.'

'Goes with the job,' he said, shrugging his shoulders. 'Just like the other did. It won't always be like this.'

'How *is* the job?' The American was trying to get her old friend to talk. 'The new apartment? What's fresh down at the Palace?'

They were sitting in semi-darkness across the other side of Piccadilly in the Berkeley Hotel. Their glasses were empty, the conversation hushed. The terrible onslaught from above had ceased but the relief that they were still alive had yet to register.

'On the whole, I'd rather be in Palm Beach,' said Foxy Gwynne jokily. 'The service is a little more attentive there. And no planes flying overhead after dark – on the orders of the Governor.'

Guy managed a laugh, and they turned to watch the waiters self-consciously slinking back to their duties. The air-raid sirens had an irritating habit of interrupting the cocktail hour, but while the staff followed orders and disappeared down to their bunker, idiots like Guy Harford and Foxy Gwynne would sit it out, eking out their drinks, hoping the all-clear would come soon.

Across the sprawling bar of The Berkeley there were a few other such couples, battle-hardened by a year of aerial attack and determined to ignore the bombers, or maybe just ready to die. The so-called spirit of the Blitz was not always what it appeared.

'You know I always thought you'd stay on there, in Montparnasse,' Foxy said, urging him to talk. 'You were stuck on Nina, admit.'

'She preferred Lydia. And anyway, it was you I wanted.'

'Sorry, Guy, that was never a possibility.'

'It might have been. When I painted your portrait.'

'*Pas du tout*, I just eyed you that way so the picture would be interesting.'

She looked at him differently from the way he looked at her. What he saw was a vision untouched by war, a light bob of her head tossing away the fear as if it were a fly in summer; the merest irritant. She was every artist's dream of the perfect model.

She, in turn, saw a changed man. Gone were the baggy linen shirts, the long hair, the paint-splattered fingernails, the languid drawl. In their place was a man in standard courtier kit of black jacket and waistcoat, striped trousers – though his tie was, she thought, set deliberately awry and with a clumsy knot even a sailor couldn't have invented. Despite this, he looked smooth, urbane, organised.

With a vague air of apology their waiter wafted over to pour fresh cocktails. They'd ordered them an hour ago but Hitler had intervened.

'How are the wedding plans?' Guy didn't care much, but he didn't want to talk about the past.

'Beginning of December. I won't send you an invitation.'

'I may be in foreign parts by then, anyway.'

'Not with that dodgy heart of yours, darling. And anyway, I thought you'd had enough of abroad.'

'You can never tell.' He was always irritated when people reminded him of his infirmity, and especially if they mentioned the disaster in Africa. He shifted in his chair as if preparing to go.

Foxy laid a hand on his sleeve. 'Not yet. There was something you were going to tell me.' She settled comfortably back in her chair as if there wasn't a war on. She was dressed in Schiaparelli, a faint green silk which looked almost white in the low light, accentuating the glorious red crown of her hair. A waft of something tantalising hung in the air.

'It's Edgar Brampton. He shot himself.'

'*Ed?* I can't believe it, Guy – why on earth? Where?'

'In his office. Well, our office really.'

'In the Palace? In Buckingham *Palace?*'

8

Guy shrugged. 'I daresay if it comes to an inquest, which I very much doubt, he'll have been found elsewhere. At home, perhaps. Or in a wood somewhere.'

'This is ghastly, Guy!'

'Yes, a dreadful shock – terrible. All I can say is I'm glad I wasn't the one who had to tell Adelaide.'

She nodded. 'It would have been awful for you, she's such an old friend.'

'I wonder how she'll take it. Heaven knows why she married him, not her type at all.'

'Wait a minute,' said Foxy, suddenly grasping the significance of what he'd just told her. 'What do you mean, he'll have been found elsewhere?'

Guy shrugged. 'A slight rearrangement is felt necessary.'

'You mean he'll be found off the premises, so to speak?'

'Perhaps. I couldn't say,' he replied, looking round the room. There was nobody near enough to hear their conversation.

'Surely they're not going to trundle that huge great body of his back into that tiny little house? With Adelaide and the children there?'

'No,' said Guy, 'they're in Oxfordshire, been there for the past couple of months – the Blitz and all that. But the Palace has to do something – you can't have a suicide on royal premises. As it is, he was only found this morning and already they've washed the blood off the walls and straightened things up.'

Foxy sucked at her cigarette. It made her cough.

'Why? Why did he do it?'

Now the all-clear had sounded, the room was filling up with people who'd been caught outside when the sirens started. You could always tell when they entered a room, those who'd been caught near a bomb blast – they walked awkwardly, as if on thin ice. With this steady influx came a rise in volume as the survivors babbled their experiences before swiftly ordering a second drink.

'Why? I don't know, Foxy, I have no idea. There was some stupid talk about him and the Queen, but that was just people's imaginations – I mean, Ed and Her *Majesty*! Agreed he was handsome and very attentive, but I don't think they were ever alone together. He'd been in her brother's regiment, you know – I think that may have had something to do with it.'

'Good Lord,' said Foxy. 'Nobody ever mentioned . . .'

'That's because there's nothing to mention. Ed had the charm when he wanted but I don't think he was ever the type to misbehave.'

'But have you thought of this,' said Foxy, drawing up her legs under the chair, 'even the merest hint of scandal . . . it could be seen as treasonable.' War made you accept a loss very quickly, and she was savouring the delicious possibilities of Ed and Her Majesty closeted alone together.

'Don't be absurd, Fox,' he snapped, reaching forward and taking one of her cigarettes. 'I wish I hadn't mentioned it. It's top secret, as you can imagine – I'd rather you forgot all about it.'

She smiled winningly and waved a finger at him. 'And it's you who's having to go round and clean up? Metaphorically, of course – that's your job?'

He leaned back in his chair. 'I don't know, Fox, they had to give me something to do. But they don't trust me, they keep me at arm's length. Tommy Lascelles looks down his nose at me, and the only time I see Their Majesties is when they're going off somewhere and need an extra hand with the bags.' He drained his cocktail.

'I thought you were the Palace's unofficial conduit to Fleet Street.'

'Well, that too. They give me the jobs nobody else wants to do. I mean, did you know – as an American I suppose you wouldn't – but there are people there called the Sculptor in Ordinary for Scotland, the Deputy Clerk of the Closet, the Clerk of the Green Cloth, the Purse Bearer, the Mistress of the Robes . . . An impossible list of impossible people! Each with a colossal sense of their own importance, and all of them battling for preferment as if they were shipwrecked and struggling for the last place on the lifeboat.'

'You're joking, of course.'

'If only. There's the Travelling Yeoman, the Page of the Chambers, the Assistant Yeoman of the Plate Pantry – dozens and dozens of them. D'you want me to go on?'

'Are you sure you're not making this up?'

'Gospel, I promise. But, Fox, they all want recognition. From Their Majesties, of course, but also from beneath. They think somehow they're of the blood royal. There are dozens of them and I've been given the job of separating the warring parties.

'Oh, and then there's the fuss over transport. Harry Gloucester is a real nuisance about what kind of car he's given, and I spend my days arguing with the Crown Equerry over whether it's the Humber or the Daimler to take him off to see his popsy. Really, Fox, don't they know there's a war on?'

'How many times have I heard that said,' answered his companion wearily. 'Let's have one more, shall we? Then go on to Ciro's?'

'No, darling, I have to go back to the office. I'm waiting for a call from Ted Rochester – he said he'd telephone through at eight.'

'That old warhorse? Is he still alive? I used to see him in El Morocco when we were in New York, oh, donkey's years ago. Is he still scribbling that column for the *Morning Post*?'

'The *News Chronicle* now. I'm to give him the news about Ed Brampton.'

Foxy looked startled. 'You're actually going to tell him that an assistant private secretary committed suicide in Buckingham Palace?'

'Well, no, not exactly. Accident cleaning his gun. At his Chelsea home. Had hoped to return to war duties and was obviously preparing himself for the off.'

'With that wooden leg of his?'

'Most people don't know about that. First War hero eager to get back into action and so on and so forth. Ted will be thrilled to break the news, and the rest of Fleet Street will follow his lead.'

'Won't he know it's a lie? Won't he care?'

'Darling, he's a *journalist*. In wartime you take what you're given and are grateful.'

'Good Lord, Guy, what a rotten lot! How can you be party to something like that?'

He rose to his feet. 'Foxy, since you're about to marry an earl and presumably stay in this country for the duration, you may as well get used to one thing. The sock has been pulled inside out. What was criminal once is now legitimised, what was lawful has now disappeared into a very dark hole and may never be seen again. Nothing's as it was.' He took a deep breath. 'See you at Ciro's in an hour.'

CHAPTER TWO

In the morning light, Buckingham Palace looked grey and dispiriting. Gone were the bearskins and cheerful red tunics of the peacetime guard; in their place a regiment of Canadians, their smartly turned out but drab battledress doing little to cheer the famous frontage with its tragically ruined face.

Guy Harford walked the length of the black-painted railings, absorbed by the events of the previous day. The morning papers all carried an account of the tragic death of Major Brampton, MC – Ted Rochester's exclusive in the *News Chronicle* had been spotted by its rivals and followed up in their later editions. Nowhere was it even hinted that the courtier had taken his own life, nor that it had been on palace premises – nor, especially, was there a breath of gossip about Ed Brampton and the Queen. In a news flow overwhelmed by events from abroad, the story was sure to evaporate within twenty-four hours.

The policeman at the Tradesmen's Gate nodded as Guy strolled through but didn't salute. As an artist, not a military man, Guy's languid bearing did not invite the raising of an arm, so a curt nod sufficed. He wandered into the Royal Mews and unlocked the door to his office.

'Would you like me to change the water? Your floral tribute?' It was Aggie, the clerk he shared with Ed Brampton – *had* shared.

'No thank you.' He could sense without turning that Aggie was peering over his shoulder to see if another kiss had been chalked on his desk. It was she who'd discovered the rose yesterday.

'A note from Tommy Lascelles. I was just going to put it on your desk.'

Guy groaned. The King's deputy private secretary did little to hide his contempt for Guy – the North Africa business clearly remained fresh in his mind – but on the other hand, he seemed ready to recognise his skill at getting things done. In his pre-courtier days Guy may have been a useless spy, but at the Palace he was swiftly becoming invaluable.

'What's in it?'

'Top secret, it says.'

'Aggie, you steamed open the envelope. You know what it says.'

She didn't even blush. 'You're in charge of Major Brampton's funeral. Guards Chapel – one week from today.'

Guy turned to face the secretary. 'A religious service for a *suicide*? What will the Lord Almighty think?'

'The Lord Almighty counts for nothing round here, Mr Harford. Far greater is the word of His Majesty's deputy private secretary.'

'Does the King know, by the way? About Edgar?'

'Doesn't want to.' It was remarkable, Aggie's grasp of what was going on.

Guy sat down at his desk. The rose was big and slightly blowsy, deep red and with a glorious aroma, like an overbearing woman's perfume. He inhaled deeply and opened the buff envelope.

Inside were detailed instructions on how to get rid of an unwanted royal problem.

First, visit the widow, describe to her the sad accident. Reassure her that a pension will be paid and imply, without saying so, that if she asks no awkward questions the children's school fees would be covered as well.

Next, post an obituary in the smarter newspapers, focusing on Edgar Brampton's urgent desire to return to combat duties, without mentioning the artificial leg.

Third, liaise with the palace police and the Household Brigade padre to ensure the smooth delivery of a body to the small-scale but fitting military funeral.

Fourth, wrap the whole thing up and dispose of it. Neatly.

Fifth, please tell the Clerk of the Green Cloth to stop telephoning the Palace. And sort out the Duke of Gloucester's car!

Aggie had gone back to her little office in the anteroom next door. The day was warming up, and through the open window you could hear the approaching drumbeat of the guard detail who'd marched the short distance from Wellington Barracks. Once, there would have been a band, horses, gold braid, shining helmets. Today there was merely an arid crunch of boots.

'I'd better go and see the old boy. What sort of mood's he in?'

'At breakfast he completed *The Times* crossword in record time. Should be safe.'

Guy wandered out of the Mews and across the gravel to the Ambassador's Entrance. There were strict rules against palace personnel walking across the inner quadrangle, but it was the quickest route to his boss's offices. The place was so vast you needed a motorbike to get about.

The deputy private secretary's office was, in its own way, a sort of Throne Room. Certainly, Tommy Lascelles was as important as any king and knew more about the business of ruling a nation than either the present incumbent or his brothers. Arriving at the hallowed portal, you knocked and waited. After a considerable pause, you might be allowed to enter.

'The Brampton business, sir,' Guy began. 'I think first I should go round to his house in Chelsea. I'm assuming that's where the body will need to be found?'

'I have no idea what you're talking about,' said Lascelles, tugging at the stiff collar constricting his neck. 'I believe you know Mrs Gwynne.'

Guy nodded. In an instant he grasped the instructions he'd just read did not constitute grounds for a conversation, and that further negotiations on the disposal of poor Edgar's body would be conducted through a lesser being. Just like the King, the deputy private secretary knew all about Ed – but didn't want to know.

'Mrs Gwynne is, I think, a close friend of the Duchess of Windsor?'

'I believe so.'

'Is she in touch with her?'

'I have no idea, sir.' This was not strictly accurate – only last night in Ciro's, Foxy had been describing in hilarious detail the two old friends' last telephone call.

'I just want you to know' – the perfectly manicured moustache bristled – 'if the Duke ever succeeded in making a friend, he never managed to keep them for any length of time.'

'Well, I do see . . .'

'The very devoted service given him by his members of staff he appreciated so little he could only reward them with rank ingratitude.'

'Yes, I think we . . .'

'When it came to the parting of the ways, he stood there tragically and pitifully alone. It was an isolation of his own making.'

I wonder what the old fool's getting at, thought Guy. And how long will this take, it's awfully hot in here.

'I just think you should pass that along. We're trying hard to shut down lines of communication to the ex-king, except through this office. Despite the fact he is in Nassau – when he's not gallivanting round the United States – every time he hears some new titbit of information he's sending communiques and telegrams and making a frightful nuisance of himself, insisting he should come home. Much the best thing if he doesn't know anything. At all.'

'Are you saying he's a security risk, sir?'

'You're not a complete idiot, Harford, what d'you think?'

'I . . .'

'Now, this Mrs Gwynne. I've told Lord Sefton to keep his mouth shut but he says it's his future wife who's in contact with the Duchess, he has no say over her just now. I don't know whether he's being difficult or whether that really is the case, but since you see so much of her, please tell her to shut her trap.'

How did you know I see her? thought Guy. Are you having me watched?

Aloud he said, 'She's an American citizen, sir.'

'She'll be British soon, once she marries Sefton. Till then, tell her to shut up.'

'Is that all, sir?'

'Off you go. I'm busy!'

Guy wandered out. Not for the first time his artist's eye took in the lavish, theatrical decor of this more public part of Buckingham Palace. It was dressy and extravagant, just right for impressing visiting potentates, but somehow, in the middle of war, pointless and just a bit farcical. Too much paint, too much gilding, you had to have faith for it to work. Shaking his head slightly, he moved quickly down the stairs.

Outside, work continued on repairing the devastation caused by the Luftwaffe's bombing raid the year before. Cloth-capped handymen leaned on their shovels while others chatted by a tea urn set up in the palace yard. They're in no rush, thought Guy, so why am I?

The bus growled its way down Buckingham Palace Road towards Sloane Square. Everywhere among the grey buildings of Victoria and the pink-bricked houses of neighbouring Chelsea was evidence of a nation at war, from the tin hats and gas masks to the Anderson shelters and the intense looks on the faces of passers-by. Away from the lethargy of the Palace, there seemed an urgency among the populace to get out and achieve something.

The small terraced house in Markham Street, a white stuccoed cottage in the Chelsea style, was intact, alert, as if waiting for his visit. Palace rules dictated that you left a spare set of keys with the Master of the Household in case of emergency, but when Guy tried the latchkey it didn't work.

He made his way down the street to a break in the terrace and walked up the back alley, but though he was able to turn the back-door key in the lock, the door was bolted.

'Can I help?' barked a military voice. The question clearly did not mean what it said – there would be no help forthcoming from this person, an ancient neighbour who evidently did not like the look of him.

'Er, I'm a friend of Major Brampton,' said Guy. 'I'm sorry to say there's been an accident.'

'Oh,' said the man. 'Well, you won't find him here. They all cleared off to Oxfordshire. Can't say I blame them – I'd go myself if I could.'

'No,' said Guy, '*Major* Brampton.'

'Yes, him too. They've all been gone two or three months.'

Guy looked up and down the back alley. A black cat lay on top of a wall but otherwise it was deserted. 'Look,' he said, 'my name's Harford. I shared an office with Major Brampton at . . .

well, I expect you know where he worked . . . but as I understand it, Mrs Brampton and the children went to her father's home in Oxfordshire while he remained in town. Here,' he added with emphasis, pointing at the back of the house.

'You're mistaken. When Mrs Brampton left, he stayed on for a couple of days. But I didn't see him after that.'

'Look,' repeated Guy, 'there's been an accident and I've been sent here just to . . .' But he did not complete the sentence. He'd been dispatched to check the coast was clear so that, if necessary, Ed Brampton's body could be returned to the house at night to be 'discovered'.

No need to share that. 'I've just been sent to see all's in order.'

'Hmm,' said the man, unimpressed.

'The major didn't leave a key with you? As neighbours sometimes do?'

'Do you have any identification?' said the old boy aggressively. His regimental tie glinted threateningly in the sunlight.

Guy fished out his Buckingham Palace pass. It changed everything.

'Augustus ffrench-Blake,' said the man, with the slightest of bows. 'Fifteenth Lancers. Well, I *was* in the Fifteenth . . . the last show, don'tcha know. The Prince of Wales came to inspect us. Never seen such a tiny feller.'

'Key?' said Guy.

'Ah. Go back round to the front and I'll meet you at the door.'

Guy retraced his steps, and by the time he reached Brampton's house the old soldier was already standing there.

'Doesn't work,' said Guy, after pushing the key in the lock. 'Are you sure this is the right one?'

'It's a Chubb. We have Yale.'

'Well, it doesn't work,' said Guy crossly. 'He can't have changed the locks?'

19

'I wouldn't know.' The old boy was losing interest.

'May I use your telephone?'

Colonel ffrench-Blake's house was crowded with gilt furniture and huge mirrors – reminders of a grander past – and hung with oversized oil portraits of soldiers long dead.

'Adelaide?' he said into the mouthpiece. 'It's Guy Harford. May I come to see you this afternoon? I'll drive down, could be with you by teatime.'

Though the widow answered, her words were vague. Guy deliberately didn't ask whether she'd been told the truth about Brampton's suicide or had been fed the official line. It was better to wait till he saw her.

He turned to thank the colonel. 'And you're certain that Major Brampton hasn't been here in the last couple of months?'

'Completely. The walls of these houses aren't that thick – you tend to hear movement. All went quiet a couple of days after the family left. What's happened to him?'

'I'm sorry to say he has died.'

'Oh,' said the soldier, knowing not to inquire any further. 'Well, I'm sorry to hear it. He was a good fellow – for an *infantryman*.'

St Walke Episcopi boasted neither pub nor village hall, and the lane leading to it was so narrow Guy passed the turning twice. When he finally entered the village he found a single street pointing towards a large stone gateway. Round a curve in the drive came the sight of a grey-stone Palladian mansion with a pony cart under the portico and two small children playing on the lawn.

Adelaide Brampton greeted him with the wave of a duster. 'Tea's ready.'

'Adelaide, I'm so sorry . . .'

'I'll tell you straight away, Guy. It's a shock, of course it is, but things weren't going well between Ed and me. If I hadn't come away because of the bombs, there would have been some other reason.'

'I'm sorry, I . . .'

'He was a dear fellow, and brave of course. But not what might be described as a family man. He was married to the job, not to me. I had a call from the Lord Chamberlain's office, they said the Palace would make all the arrangements – I don't seem even to be allowed the job of putting him to rest.'

'I came to make sure you were all right and to let you know about the funeral.'

'Oh? It won't be here in St Walke?'

'Guards Chapel. A week today.'

'Good of you to let me know, I might have turned up at the wrong church otherwise,' she said bitterly.

'I'm sorry, Adelaide, we all do what we're told. It's the only way things work in wartime.'

She gave him a cold stare. 'He was *my* husband, not theirs. They didn't even tell me where he died.'

'Ah. Well . . .'

'Will he be sent off as a Catholic or as Church of England?'

'They're not terribly keen on incense, those chaps.'

'Well, I don't suppose it'll make any difference, he never went to church.'

'There'll be a firing party. You know, a ceremonial volley and all that.'

She gave him a sour look. 'Pretty tactless in the circumstances, since he ended up with a bullet in his head. And isn't there going to be an inquest? Since his death was supposedly accidental?'

They haven't even told you about that, he thought. Is it the war – or is it palace protocol – that gives us all such bad manners?

'I don't know. So many formalities seem to be dispensed with these days. Can I ask you . . .'

'Yes?'

'What were Ed's plans, after you came with the children to Oxfordshire? Was he going to live at his club?'

Adelaide looked surprised. 'No – why would he do that when we have a perfectly good house in Chelsea?'

'It's just that . . .' said Guy, 'I went round there this morning. Saw your neighbour, the colonel. We both tried to get into the house but something had happened to the front-door lock. And the colonel told me that he hadn't seen Ed since you moved down here.'

'That's odd.'

'Very odd, Adelaide. You don't mind my asking these questions, do you?'

'Go on.'

'In the office, all appeared normal. I wasn't close to Ed, as you know, but we got on pretty well. He didn't say he'd moved out of the house. The key he gave to the Master of the Household was the same as the one you gave Colonel ffrench-Blake – but it wouldn't work. What I'm asking, Adelaide, is where had Ed been for the past three months?'

'Another woman?' suggested Adelaide, with a wan smile. 'But, Guy, I don't think so. You know who he was sweet on.'

'Oh, you'd heard that.'

'He never talked about anybody else. HM this and HM that – I won't say it was an obsession . . . though maybe it was.' She shook her head.

'Still doesn't solve where he's been for the past three months.'

Adelaide thought for a moment. 'There is one thing.'

'Yes?'

'We spoke on the telephone, oh, once or twice a week – he's not a great letter-writer. He was very upset not getting that job.'

'Which job? He didn't tell me.'

'Private secretary to Harry Gloucester.'

Guy raised his eyebrows. 'Oh? I didn't know there was a vacancy.'

'There was. But the powers that be said under the circs they couldn't allow his name to go forward.'

'What circs?'

'Him and the Queen.'

Guy laughed. 'There's nothing in that!'

'Isn't there?'

'Oh, Adelaide, he was just a devoted courtier. If she was sweet on him it'll be because he does – did – his job efficiently and they would sit around and talk about her brother. His regiment, the Black Watch, all that. Nothing more.'

'Sure?'

'She's the Queen, Adelaide!'

'Mm.' She looked away. 'Anyway, he was upset, he thought he could straighten Harry Gloucester out. The man's a complete chump, you know.'

'He is the King's brother. You don't "straighten out" a royal duke.'

'You don't know the half of it. And just think, Guy, if anything happens to the King, Harry Gloucester will be Regent – he will sit on the throne.'

'That's not going to happen.'

'Well, *he* seems to think it might. It's astonishing how much he needs protecting from himself.'

'And Ed was going to do that?'

'He talked a lot about it. How the King has got the Duke of Windsor wishing he was back on the throne – still trying to throw his weight about even though he's thousands of miles away. The Queen is always complaining about it.'

Guy nodded. 'I know.'

'And then his younger brother just as eager to see if the throne will fit his big fat bottom. I shouldn't be surprised if he doesn't sneak into the Throne Room sometimes and just sit there, trying it out for size!'

'All this backstabbing,' said Guy, shaking his head, 'when there's a war on. Unbelievable.'

'Tip of the iceberg. Remember, Ed had been in the Palace since the Abdication. You've only been there . . . ?'

'Six weeks. Had to get away from . . .'

'Tangier. I know. There was quite a lot of talk when you first turned up. What went wrong out there? How did you end up in the Palace? You're a painter, not a courtier!'

'It's a long story.'

'Well, you can tell me over dinner.' Adelaide poured more tea, then walked over to the window to call her children in from the lawn.

'There's something very odd about all this,' she said over her shoulder. 'The Gloucester job was pretty much guaranteed. Then, suddenly, it wasn't. The Lord Chamberlain's office . . . they told me he'd had an accident with his pistol.'

'That's right.'

'You're sure about that?'

'Yes, as certain as I can be. I didn't actually see the . . .'

'It's very strange, Guy.'

'Because?'

'Because he didn't have a pistol. After he retired from the army, he handed it in. Guy, he *didn't have a pistol.*'

CHAPTER THREE

'So you see, Rupe, it's a bit tricky.'

'Why don't you get the police to do it?'

They were sitting in the flat they shared above Victoria bus station. At the best of times the place was dreary, but once the sunlight had gone it became almost oppressive. The mood was lightened by a few small canvases Guy had managed to salvage in his flight from the ghastly Tangier business. His sunset over the Gates of Herçules was particularly fine – and hung, slightly crooked, over the leaky gas fire.

The rooms were damp and so were the sofas they sat on, but in wartime you do not choose your accommodation; it chooses you. Similarly, you do not choose your flatmates, especially when you've been parachuted back into London with your tail between your legs.

Rupert Hardacre claimed to be a postman, but even at first glance it was easy to see he was more than that. The clothes in his wardrobe, the people he met, the unexplained absences all pointed to something else, and yet, each morning, he put on the uniform and peaked cap supplied by the General Post Office and disappeared at dawn.

Conversationally, much of their individual lives was off limits. Occasionally they would discuss a problem on the tacit understanding that it would be immediately forgotten. In general, their common ground was a discussion of the whisky they were drinking, and how to get more.

'So,' prompted Rupe, 'the police?'

'Can't involve them because Edgar's death simply cannot become a police matter. A tragic accident, no call for Scotland Yard to be poking their noses in.'

'So what you're saying is . . .'

'What I'm *saying* is my people, the powers that be, want the option of being able to plant Edgar's body back in his house in Markham Street so he can be "found" there. My job this morning was to make sure there was nothing in the house which would compromise that – but I couldn't get in. Somebody's changed the locks.'

'Why would they do that?'

'I have no idea, and I don't care – maybe the lock just got jammed, I don't know. All I know is – I can't get in the house, and by tomorrow morning they may well want to plant Edgar's body there. They can't leave it too long, after all. Anything rather than it being found on palace premises.'

Rupert stretched his long legs and looked at the ceiling. 'You're asking my advice?'

'Of course.'

'There's only one solution I can think of at short notice. But you won't like it.'

'Anything.'

'Rodie Carr.'

'I don't . . . really . . . I couldn't possibly . . .' Guy spluttered. He could not summon the words to express his horror.

'She's the only person I know, and certainly the only one you know, who can get through a locked door just by looking at it. Take what she did getting into your office, *and* there were police and armed guards all over the place.'

'No, Rupe, no! She's a criminal! Come to think of it, how do you even *know* someone like that?'

'In my line of work' – a wintry smile – 'you meet all sorts.'

'When you introduced me to her in the pub the other night I simply couldn't believe it. The woman's a blackmailer, a black marketeer and a burglar, for heaven's sake. She should be in jail!'

They'd been sheltering in The Grenadier, hidden in a Knightsbridge cul-de-sac, during yet another bombing raid. The pint-sized black-eyed girl had been in a corner, laughing and having a ball, but the tales she told were not victimless.

'Look,' said Guy, 'I don't judge anybody. I lived in Tangier for over five years – there are precious few rules there, and no laws to speak of – certainly no morals – but I've never encountered someone like her. She's without a single scruple.'

'Is that so shocking?' said Rupe, pouring them both another shot. 'The world is changing. We live in an age of legalised murder – is what she's doing worse than that?'

'And then she said she wanted to marry me!'

'She's very beautiful, Guy.'

'For heaven's sake. Preposterous!'

'If the deadline's dawn tomorrow, she's your only hope.'

Guy swallowed the whisky at a gulp.

◆ ◆ ◆

Rodie stood on the self-same step occupied by the ancient colonel only a few hours before, only this time the door was wide open.

'What kept you, Rupe?' she whispered, but her big eyes were looking out for Guy. 'Come on in!'

Markham Street was in complete darkness, but inside the house a small light shone from a candle on the hall table. From down the road a hoarse voice yelled, 'Put that light OUT!'

'Get inside,' ordered Guy, and all three crowded into the narrow hall. He shut the door quickly.

'Move quietly,' he warned. 'The man next door can hear. In fact, why don't you two just go and sit in the kitchen while I check around? And make sure the curtains are drawn before you switch on any lights.'

The house was roomier on the inside than its cramped exterior suggested. He made his way upstairs aided by the feeble light of a torch and stepped into the front bedroom. The house smelt musty, the air in it still, suspended; it took no time for Guy to conclude that what the colonel said was true – nobody had lived here for many weeks. He had no idea what he was looking for, but, pausing to pull together the curtains, he switched on the overhead light and looked about.

'Did you think any more about my marriage proposal?' Rodie had crept silently up the stairs on plimsolled feet and was standing in the doorway dressed from head to toe in black.

'Your workaday outfit, I see,' said Guy dismissively. She did look extraordinarily beautiful. 'Why don't you get a proper job?'

'I'm probably better off than you are,' she retorted. 'And who's to say what a proper job is these days? What are you doing sitting behind a desk in that dusty old room in the back end of the Palace? Rupe said you come from Tangier.'

'Look,' said Guy, 'this is no time to be exchanging curriculum vitae. And you can damned well put those down, for a start.'

He'd noticed that in one gloved hand Rodie had a small gilt travelling clock and in the other an ornate silver box.

'Nobody'll miss 'em.'

'For heaven's sake!' he hissed. 'We're in the house of a man who's killed himself. We don't know the circumstances, but it's a tragedy. To many, he was a wonderful, kind, generous chap, and he's dead.'

'Wonderful, kind, generous – and with no need for these any more,' said Rodie, oblivious to the tragedy which hung over the house.

'Do you have a brain?' said Guy. 'If so, use it! The man who lived here disappeared from this house a couple of months ago. He was coming into the office every day, but he never came home at night. I'm looking for a letter, a note – something – which might tell me where he was when he claimed to be here.'

'If I were you, I'd try his desk, then,' snapped Rodie. 'You won't find too many clues in a bedroom.'

They went downstairs. Rupe was already in the small room beyond the kitchen which Ed Brampton had used as his study. The desk was open, and Rupe was neatly collating and piling the papers inside.

'I've had a look through but there's nothing helpful here,' he said over his shoulder. 'Couple of unpaid bills, begging letter from his sister, some palace bumf which by rights should never have left his office. That's about it.'

Guy was astonished. 'You've done all that? You're not a burglar too, are you, Rupert?'

The man turned round with an enigmatic smile. 'There are many departments in the General Post Office. Not all of them employ people to shove letters through somebody's front door.'

'Well, I didn't suppose you . . .'

'Guy,' said Rupe, 'do you have *any* idea what you're doing here?'

'Well, since you put it like that, no. I felt I had to get into the house just to make sure all was in order. Then I thought there might be a clue as to where Ed had been staying before he shot himself . . .'

'You're sure he did that? Shot himself?'

'What d'you mean?'

'Nothing,' said Rupe, turning back and closing the desk. 'There's a small safe in the wall behind that picture.'

'My turn!' whispered Rodie joyously, and slid across the room.

'Wait, wait . . . Hold on a minute!' said Guy, running his hands through his hair. 'This is supposed to be a house-cleaning operation, not a full-scale burglary.'

'Won't be a jiffy,' whispered Rodie, her ear against the combination lock. Guy looked on helplessly – as a mission leader he was a failure, with his two underlings completely out of control, robbing him of all initiative.

The safe door offered little in the way of self-defence and soon they were poking in its murky interior. 'Are they rich?' said Rodie, sifting through a pile of small leather boxes. Her nimble fingers were opening the catches and evaluating the jewels within.

'Come away!' hissed Guy. 'That's private property! This is disgraceful!'

Rodie turned round to look at him and slowly smiled. She was doing it just to irritate him. 'Don't you think I look nice in this?' she teased, stringing a heavy diamond necklace round her black polo neck.

'For heaven's sake!' spluttered Guy. 'Put it back and let's get out of here. We've achieved the main objective. The rest can wait.'

Rupe led the way.

'Incidentally,' Guy said to Rodie, 'how did you get into the house, as a matter of interest?'

'That'd be telling,' she said as she gave him a peck on the cheek.

' . . . and a great friend of the Duchess of Windsor, of course.'

'We won't talk about that, if you don't mind.'

'How are they getting on in the Bahamas? We hear so little these days.'

'No, Ted, no!' Foxy protested. 'You're interviewing me because I'm marrying Lord Sefton. You're not interviewing me about my friends. If you were, we'd be here all day.'

They were drinking coffee and looking out of the window at the activity going on below in Hyde Park. The thick turf of Rotten Row had been dug up to make way for trenches, while further away a platoon of troops was hauling down a vast barrage balloon. The drab grey wasteland was dotted with khaki figures.

Ted Rochester took up his silver propelling pencil and dabbed again at his notebook. 'Tell me about Paris, then.'

'It was hilarious. In New York I won a competition to become a model for Jean Patou. I thought I was going to be in the movies, but then this came along. He whisked a bunch of us off to France on the *Berengaria*, we were an overnight sensation!'

'No surprise, with those looks,' said Ted. Like all gossip columnists, he could lay it on thick.

'Well, we certainly put the local girls' noses out of joint. But after all the press calls and the publicity and the photographers, it became rather boring. I was supposed to walk around Patou's showroom modelling the gowns for his rich customers, but it was all rather demeaning – such vulgar women. So fat. And the hours, my dear, dawn till dusk – and beyond!'

'So you became a painter.'

'Doesn't everyone in Paris? That's when I met your friend Guy Harford. Only he's a serious painter, Ted, a genius – have you seen his work? I'm going to try to get him an exhibition now I'm here in London.'

'I gather he has his hands rather full at the moment,' said Ted.

'Does he?' Each knew more about Guy than they were saying.

'So you painted.'

'And watched. All good painters watch as much as they paint. They sit outside cafés observing – looking inside people, *searching* inside them, to discover what lies behind the face, what's hidden in the heart. It's what makes Guy so good – he's like a detective that way. If you haven't seen his pictures, you must.'

'I will. Get that exhibition going.'

'We used to bump into all the greats – Derain, Max Ernst. At the Café de Flore we'd see Picasso, he always sat at the same table by the door. But then Guy inherited that little house in Tangier from an aunt, and off he went.'

'That would have been when?'

'Six or seven years ago. I think he'd be there still but for . . .' Nobody talked about why Guy came home.

'Then you married,' continued Ted. His article was for *The Tatler*, whose readers would want to know about the Vanderbilt connection.

'Yes, dear Erskine, the sweet boy. He was the brother of an old friend from the New York days – Kiki Preston, d'you know her? – but we were too young. Paris was brimming with Americans, I just picked the wrong one.'

'So now you're marrying an English lord.'

'The dearest man alive.'

'And very rich.'

'Don't be coarse!' said Foxy, not displeased.

'Who's a close friend of the Duke and Duchess also.'

'I really am NOT going to talk to you about the Windsors, Ted. You're a snake, bringing the conversation back to them all the time.'

'If it wasn't for them, you and Hugh wouldn't have met. Did you know the Germans have captured the *Nahlin*?'

'Our love-boat, no doubt you would call it! Yes, I did, as a matter of fact.'

'That does surprise me,' said Rochester, not surprised at all. 'It hasn't been announced. I was keeping that as a special treat for you.'

'There are ways,' said Foxy, her red hair shining in the grey light. 'The Nazis didn't get the cocktail shaker, though. It's in Nassau with the Dook.'

'Our ex-king, rich as Croesus, pinching a trinket off someone else's boat? Now that's a good story, Foxy!'

'Don't you dare.'

'You're fond of them, aren't you?'

'Difficult people. But yes.'

Rochester got up and walked to the window. 'Not everybody's convinced we ended up with the right king. The present incumbent is doing his best, and of course *she's* a pillar of strength, but . . .'

'What are you saying, Ted? Kick old Bertie out of the Palace, bring back the Duke of Windsor?'

'Well, he wouldn't say no, would he?'

'I have no idea. But in the middle of a war?'

'War or no war, the old rivalries go on – think of the Tudors, Foxy. Harry Gloucester fancies his chances too, I hear.'

'That's absurd. The man's a fool.'

'It's true, though. Another bomb drops on Buckingham Palace – pouf! – and King George VI is no more. Who's going to pick up the crown from the rubble?'

'Princess Elizabeth, of course!'

'She's *fifteen*. Overnight Harry will become Prince Regent – and once he sits on that throne there'll be no budging him off it.'

'In the middle of a *war*?' Foxy repeated.

'Who else? He's the next in line, there's no other choice. Let me ask you another thing – did you know Edgar Brampton?'

'Adelaide's husband? No, not particularly. I only met him a few times. I saw he'd died – you wrote something in the *News Chronicle*. Poor Adelaide – she was an old friend of Guy's, you know.'

'I know.'

'I get the impression she was rather sweet on him.'

'I heard Edgar was going to become Gloucester's private secretary,' said Ted, uninterested in Adelaide. He had a way of making a question sound like a statement.

'Really?'

'Hugh may have heard something.'

'Well, I won't ask him, if that's what you're after. You journalists are terrible rats – I thought this was supposed to be an article about a sweet old New York girl marrying an English lord whose family goes back – how d'you say? – to William the Conqueror. Instead you're trying to squeeze private information out of me!'

'We're a nation at war,' said Ted, turning to face Foxy. 'We're at war, we glean information where we can. This business at the Palace is unsettling, and the death of Edgar Brampton is a serious loss – he was probably the only one who could restrain Harry Gloucester.'

'Well, you won't get anything out of me. Back to asking me about Paris.'

But Ted Rochester's mind was far from the City of Light.

CHAPTER FOUR

'Better watch out,' said Aggie, picking up some fallen petals, eyeing the wilting rose with disfavour. 'Shall I throw this away? It's past its best.'

'No,' said Guy, after a moment, 'I think I'll keep it. Watch out for what?'

'Topsy. He's a terror.'

'Who?'

'The Master of the Household, dear. You call him Sir Topham Dighton, I call him what I like. Of course, Topsy's been up at Balmoral since you arrived, but now he's back you'll know it. He likes to stick his nose into everyone's business, then he goes and whispers to the King. A sort of unofficial spy.'

And not the only one, thought Guy. 'Do I have to report to him as well?'

'Not really. Just keep on his good side.'

'I'll do my best.'

'I wonder,' said Aggie, shaking her head. She had a stiff permanent wave and favoured floral dresses.

'Did you by any chance take Major Brampton's diary away?'

'Diary? No,' said Aggie absently. 'I expect it got swept up by the chaps who cleaned this place up after . . .' She didn't finish the sentence.

'I don't think so,' said Guy. 'It was still in his bookshelf over by the window yesterday – I noticed particularly. Rather nice green leatherette cover. Now it's gone.'

'I didn't even know he kept one.'

But you did, Aggie, you did – and I bet you know what was written in it. 'I'm going over to the Guards Chapel to talk to the padre.'

A blue-battledressed footman opened the door without knocking, and with a vague air of condescension nodded at Guy. 'Harford, is it? The Master would like to see you. Now.' He turned on his heel and sauntered off, not bothering to shut the door.

'They get worse,' said Aggie tartly. 'That one should be with the Royal Fusiliers in Egypt, but he says his mother's dying and he's her only relative. Anyway, off you go. Privy Purse entrance, up the stairs to the first floor, second on the left. I'll have the tea on when you get back.'

'Thank you.'

'Don't tell him anything you wouldn't tell your mother.'

Guy marched down some steps and through the byways and corridors which made up the underground village supplying the needs of the royal palace. He passed painters' shops, wine cellars, food stores and carpentry cupboards, all playing their part in the maintenance of the place. He checked his watch as he reached Dighton's door; it had taken a full eight minutes to reach his destination. He knocked and entered.

'Aha!' barked the silver-haired figure standing four-square in front of a vast marble mantelpiece. 'The Tanja Man!'

'Harford, Sir Topham,' Guy confirmed stiffly. He thought he'd managed to put the Tangier business behind him.

'Hertford, yes. But I shall call you Tanja Man,' responded the Master curtly. He must be well over seventy, thought Guy, but obviously age does not mellow everyone.

'City of sandals and scandals. I was there in '22 with Lord Bute. Aha. I expect you know him.'

'Well, as a matter of fact . . .'

'You're here under a cloud, Tanja Man,' went on Topsy, not requiring an answer. 'This is just a friendly warning, nothing official. Do as you're told, keep your nose clean, and there's a job here for life. Step out of line, gum up the works, and I'll have you in the Tower of London cleaning out the latrines.'

'Thank you, sir.'

'Aha. You're dealing with the Brampton affair.'

Guy looked out of the window. The rooks were circling St James's Park like enemy bombers. He didn't immediately answer.

'I said, the Brampton affair,' barked Dighton.

'You'd have to talk to Mr Lascelles about that, sir,' replied Guy, remembering Aggie's warning. 'It's, er, unofficial.'

'Edgar was my wife's cousin once removed. We have a family interest.'

'Absolutely.' Guy compressed his lips in mute refusal.

'I warn you, Tanja Man, I require the fullest cooperation from types like you who sneak into the Palace through the back door, shirking their military duty. Hah. Dodging the column.'

'You'll see from my medical record, sir, that . . .'

'Oh, yes, yes, yes! Obviously the dissolute life of a painter in Morocco has rendered your heart completely useless. You should have taken more care, but I suppose all those drugs people take out there . . . Now, get out, and write me a full report on everything you've done. Mark it "Top Secret", make only one copy, deliver it by hand to this office.'

'If that's all, Sir Topham . . .'

'Next Friday morning,' barked the gnarled old courtier, fishing into a waistcoat pocket for his snuff box.

The long journey back to the Royal Mews gave Guy the opportunity to review his situation. The foul-up in Morocco was hardly his fault, though it suited everyone concerned that he should take the blame. After his arrival back in England and sitting behind a Foreign Office desk for three interminable months when nobody spoke to him, the job at the Palace had been fixed. He may have taken the blame for what went on in Africa, but at least he was being looked after.

Up to a point. He hadn't been sure when he shut Topham Dighton's door that he didn't hear the word 'scum' – and now, pushing open his own office door, he was confronted by a bulky figure in Coldstream Guards uniform, one foot on his desk and drinking his tea.

The officer half-rose from his seat, then plonked down again. Artists – painters – did not warrant the courtesy of a formal introduction.

'Toby Broadbent, Coats Mission. I won't shake hands.'

Guy looked over the captain's shoulder and saw Aggie making saucer eyes, as if to say, 'You're in trouble.'

'Been asked by the Master to look you over.'

'Make yourself at home,' said Guy, but the irony was lost on the soldier. 'I've just been to see him.'

'I've got your file here,' said Broadbent heavily. 'Says you caused a diplomatic crisis in Tangier. The Americans and the French and the Germans and the Spanish all at each other's throats. Had to be airlifted out, get you out of trouble double-quick.'

'That's roughly correct, if a trifle one-sided.'

'Well,' said the soldier, breaking into a forced smile, 'you sound like our sort of fella. We like people who make life difficult for others.'

'The Master doesn't.'

'Ah well, he's been here since the First War. Failed to move with the times.'

'Who exactly *are* you?' said Guy, unsure whether to trust Broadbent's sudden switch of mood.

'Coats Mission. We're here to protect HM and the rest of the family. Down to the last bullet and the last man. Won't go into the details, but in case of an invasion it's our job to spirit them away.'

'And it's your job, Captain, to decide whether I might pose a threat to His Majesty?'

'Can't be too careful. That's rather nice,' he added, pointing with his chin, 'though I'm not much of a one for art.'

Guy glanced at the unframed oil painting on the wall opposite, a faded memory now. 'The Grand Socco,' he said. 'It's a kind of souk. Depending on your point of view, either the filthiest place in the world or the most exciting.'

'Never been to Tangier,' replied Broadbent. 'Old Topsy says most of the people there should be in jail.'

'I daresay he's right. That's what makes it interesting.'

Broadbent turned over the pages of the bulky file before him. 'I see you were recruited by Teddy Dunlop.'

Is this going to be the full interrogation, thought Guy. Are they going to take me away to a darkened room and beat it out of me? Is this forced jollity just a ploy?

'I wouldn't say 'recruited', it was more a question of being press-ganged. Franco's men marched into Tangier, and the Foreign Office was caught on the hop. They needed extra manpower quick and I happened to be there.'

'You'd been living in Tangier for six or seven years?'
'Yes.'

'I gather you'd made a reputation for yourself as an artist.'
'It's a city built on seven hills. The light there is remarkable.'

'You made another reputation for yourself, Mr Harford. As possibly the worst spy ever recruited by MI6.'

'Have another cup of tea,' said Guy, masking his irritation. He did not like the man's supercilious tone.

'So here you are, put on special duties at the Palace – but really, you know, old chap, that's our area. The Coats Mission is the outfit to protect the Crown, not chaps from civvy street.'

'I won't get in your way.'

The sunlight from the window illuminated the medal ribbons on the guardsman's chest, a tiny riot of colour amid the broad sea of khaki. He's brave, thought Guy, and confident – but not very bright. I wonder what he'd have done when they came through the door with their guns cocked – would he have tried to shoot his way out? Or do what I did, use his wits?

The captain turned over a couple of pages. 'Now, tell me about Edgar Brampton.'

'No thanks,' said Guy firmly. 'You need to talk to someone whose office is closer to the Throne Room than this one is.'

'Don't muck me about. Our job is to protect HM. We need to know everything.'

'Not from me.'

The captain pushed his teacup aside. 'Look, this is a shocking state of affairs. Major Brampton – decent chap, wrong regiment of course but a decent type – killing himself on royal premises. You know there's a law to stop that sort of thing, don't you?'

'I don't think you can apply the law retrospectively. When a chap's dead, not even His Imperial Majesty can bring him back to face justice.'

Broadbent's cheeks went pink. 'The Royal Verge, dammit!'

'The royal . . . what?'

'Wouldn't expect you to know. Nobody's allowed to die within royal palaces. The area in and around the palaces is called the Royal

Verge. If they do croak, it's a matter for the *royal* coroner, not some local quack with a taste for spreading unwanted gossip. Royal coroner sews things up tight and nobody's the wiser, but he prefers the body off the premises.' He pronounced it 'orf'.

'I find that faintly absurd, don't you?' said Guy. 'I hear a chap was killed when the Luftwaffe bombed this place last year – did they cart him *off the premises*? Simply because he wasn't permitted to die within palace walls?'

'Is that what you've done with Major Brampton? Whisked him away somewhere?'

'I might have.'

The Coldstreamer gave him an icy stare. 'I don't take kindly to impertinence. No place for it in a royal palace. We're here to protect His Majesty, we use everything in our power to ensure his safety and well-being. D'you understand?'

'Perfectly.'

'This business with Brampton. We need to know. It's unsettling. We. Need. To. Know.' He thumped the desk with his fist as he spoke, and Rodie's rose in its jam jar shed a few more petals. 'And I can tell you, Mr Harford, you'll find life pretty uncomfortable until we do. Understand?'

'Perfectly.'

That's two enemies I've made in a morning and it's not anywhere near lunchtime, thought Guy – not bad going.

Aloud he said, 'Will you be coming to the funeral? Next Thursday, Guards Chapel. All are welcome.'

The captain snorted, got up, and banged his way out of the room.

Rupert said he'd forgiven Rodie but he wasn't sure. He suspected she'd gone back and lifted a small but important piece of jewellery from Edgar Brampton's safe – he could tell by the smile on her face. And the fact she insisted on buying the drinks.

They were sitting in the back bar of The Grenadier public house just behind Constitution Hill, and Rodie was yapping away about some rich relations who may or may not have existed. She kept on bringing the conversation round to Guy, but Rupe kept deflecting it.

'Strange that a man like that never married.'

'Tell me some more about Mrs Elkins and her Daimler.'

'Does he have any money?'

'I doubt it. Painters never do. Was it *her* Daimler, or did you steal it for her?'

'I could make him rich, Rupe! Think what a great combination we'd make!'

'Forget it. He likes blondes.' Rupert had no idea what Guy's preferences were, but he was embarrassed by the sudden and unexpected burden he'd placed on his flatmate.

'Here he comes!' cried Rodie, black eyes shining. The assistant to His Majesty's deputy private secretary was elbowing his way through the crowd to where they were sitting.

'Whisky awaits,' said Rupe, pointing. 'How did it go?'

'A hell of a day. Kicked around like a football all morning, and then the Markham Street business this evening.'

'They get the body into the house OK?'

'There was an air raid on so everyone was indoors.'

'Did they remember to bring the wooden leg with him?'

'Ha ha, very funny.'

'Who gets to discover the body?'

'The palace police. They'll have been worried when he didn't turn up for work, if you get my meaning.'

Rupert scratched his jaw. 'But surely that's a job for the Metropolitan Police?'

'They do exactly what they're told when it comes to the Palace.'

'I suppose,' said Rodie speculatively, 'once the body's been found and they've taken it away, the house will be empty?'

'Don't even think about it!' snapped Rupe. For heaven's sake, she'd had the emeralds already!

Rodie gave an angelic smile and looked up into Guy's face, begging his blessing. 'Nobody would notice, would they, darling?' she breathed. 'If I popped in for a look-see? Nobody would mind?'

'Are you completely mad? My colleague's dead, he has a grieving widow, and his children have lost their father. And you're thinking about burgling his house?'

Rodie's features slammed shut. 'Don't you know there's a war on?' she snapped. 'If a bomb hit his house there'd be nothing left anyway. Have another drink and loosen up.' She got up and made her way towards the bar.

'What happened this morning?' asked Rupert.

'Hauled over the coals by a senior courtier, then interrogated by the army. This is off the record, Rupe?'

'Of course. Was it the Coats Mission lot who questioned you?'

Guy sat back in his chair in wonderment. 'I thought you worked for the GPO. I can't imagine how you could possibly *know* such things. And by the way, don't take that answer as a confirmation.'

'At the Post Office we don't discriminate,' said Rupert with an enigmatic smile. 'We push letters through anybody's letterbox, be they high-born or low.'

Guy scratched his head. 'Everyone seems anxious to know what I'm doing about Ed Brampton. I don't get it.'

'I take it you're not telling *everyone*.'

'Nobody. Apart from you, the postman,' grimaced Guy, 'and that's probably a treasonable offence. Old Topsy Dighton threatened me with the Tower of London.'

'He'd know all about that. Several of his family, over the centuries, have parted company with their heads there.'

'You *do* seem to know a lot about my business. I must remember to ask about yours.'

'Oh,' said Rupert, a wry smile flitting across his face. 'Stamps, parcels, mailbags, that sort of thing. Sealing wax and string. All very dull really.'

'Just tell me this. Why are we suddenly graced with the presence of Miss Rodie Carr? She's done her job, must we now celebrate with her? I mean, I'm delighted she got us into Ed Brampton's house – though I'm still mystified as to why the keys didn't work – but must she now follow us about like a puppy?'

'She's very decorative. In her peculiar way.'

'And completely without scruple. Back in Tangier, people could be many things – and they were, Lord knows – but I don't think I've come across such a trickster. So completely without a moral compass.'

'She's a rare and valued asset. You have no idea the hell of trying to find, in the middle of a war, a burglar you can trust.'

'Trust?' said Guy, as the black-eyed Rodie eased her way through the crowd, back to their table. 'Trust? Look at her!'

They both did. There was something about the way she walked, balancing a tray of drinks, twisting and turning and deftly avoiding the sharp elbows and sudden lurches a late night in an air-raid pub can occasion, which gave her tiny figure immense authority.

And then there was her face. Guy could see what Rupert meant.

'It's not late,' Rodie said, a little flushed as she plonked the drinks down. 'We could go dancin'. Get a taxi down to Hammersmith Palais' – she said it 'Pally' – 'and pick Lem up on the way. Make it a cosy foursome.'

The two men looked at each other. Guy raised his eyebrows to Rupert, and Rupert spoke for them both.

'I don't think you quite understand,' he said. 'Guy works for . . . well, you *know* who he works for. Lovely as you are, Rodie, he can't be seen with people like you, people with a criminal record.'

'I never went to jail!'

'Only because it was a first offence. And how many have there been since then? Don't you see?'

Rodie looked like a three-year-old who'd dropped her ice cream in a puddle.

'Snobs,' she said bitterly. 'You're just snobs, the pair of you! You don't mind usin' my God-given talent to do something which should rightly land you both in the dock – but you can't be seen out dancin' with me.'

Rupert nodded genially. 'The way of the world, Rodie, the way of the world. Now, why don't you hop away and pick some nice gentleman's pocket?'

CHAPTER FIVE

It's remarkable, thought Guy, how resourceful people can be in wartime. It was only a few short hours since he'd overseen the carting of poor Ed Brampton's body back into his Chelsea home. Now the body had been 'discovered', the next-door neighbour squared, the place tidied up, and the dead courtier taken away again to a place of rest prior to the final oblations.

Now Guy was back in Ed's drawing room, sitting with Adelaide over a cup of tea.

'There's no sugar. Sorry.'

'I prefer it this way.' The usual wartime white lie.

'The King wrote to me, a very charming letter. I was surprised – Ed worked at the Palace for ages, but their paths never crossed.'

'HM has a reputation for graceful behaviour.'

'The point being that His Majesty is a very jealous sort, and I never expected such a kind gesture.'

'Jealous?'

'Oh yes. Ed, you know, and the Queen. There was a terrible fuss over Kenneth Clark.'

'The Keeper of the King's Pictures?'

'Handsome, but an exceptionally vain man. Used to go around the place saying, "She's in love with me" – meaning Her Majesty.

And for all I know she may have been – he's a frightful show-off and ladies' man, and she's a bit susceptible. But there was an explosion one night at Windsor, the King got into one of his rages and there was all hell to pay.'

'Good Lord. Biscuit?'

'He really *is* jealous. It didn't help that Clark could barely conceal his contempt for His Majesty – an exceptionally stupid man, I think he said. So one way and the other he was probably Public Enemy Number 1 at court.'

'Same old story with Ed, then?'

'Well, Guy, I *was* surprised, I must say. Whatever went on between Her Majesty and Clark, everyone knew that Ed had a tremendously soft spot for her. No, actually I'd say he was *in love* with her. And probably it showed, he was such an idiot. And if *I* – who never get invited to the Palace – knew all about it, you can be pretty certain the King did. Anyway, I thought it was a lovely gesture and I shall treasure his letter.'

Guy got up to pour more tea.

'You know, there are a lot of question marks around Ed's death, Adelaide. I wonder how much you know – or want to know, come to that.'

'Of *course* I want to know – he was my husband for twelve long years. He's dead, we don't know how or why. I'm his wife, for heaven's sake!'

'I've been told to keep my trap shut.'

'And that includes me?'

'Apparently.'

'It's disgusting.' She thought for a moment. 'OK, here's the deal – I'll tell you about the Duke of Gloucester if you tell me about what's been going on here. In my house.'

Guy thought guiltily about the break-in, the search through the rooms, the rifling of Ed's papers, the missing emerald brooch, and whether some resourceful hands had since put it back in the safe. 'I'm stuck,' he said. 'Under orders, not sure how much I should say except that really I should say nothing. What do you want to know?'

'Did he kill himself?'

'That's a difficult one.'

The widow looked up fiercely. She had a fine face, almost a perfect English rose with her thin blonde hair and pale complexion, though war, or something, had robbed her of her bloom. But her cornflower eyes were still magnetic.

'You've just given me the answer,' she snapped. 'Ed was a brave man and a good soldier. Granted he was a fairly useless husband but that's not the point – his life shouldn't end this way, in mystery, skulduggery, tossed away like a dead game bird. This story about him cleaning his gun . . .'

'Look at me,' said Guy. 'Look at me, and promise you won't repeat this. Can I trust you to do that, Adelaide?'

'All right.' She screwed up her face as if awaiting a slap. 'He was killed?'

'Probably.'

'I knew it.' Her hands were twisting in her lap.

'The Palace works in mysterious ways. He was found in his office. Pistol on the floor, that's all I know. Next thing, his body is whisked away and brought here. Can't have a suicide – or whatever it is – on royal premises.'

'I knew it! I knew it, when I walked into this house. There was no sense of . . . violent death, d'you know what I mean? It may sound silly but I can sense these things, Guy. I knew it didn't happen here.'

Quite a lot did happen here though, thought Guy, after he'd gone. Including pinching your family jewels.

'So what happens now?'

Guy looked at his tea, untouched, going cold. 'Ed will be given a hero's send-off at the Guards Chapel. You will be the grieving widow. The Palace will send its best men to bid him farewell, and that'll be that.'

'Will the best men include that odious snake Dighton?'

'The Master? I imagine so. Wasn't he related to Ed?'

'In a vague sort of way. He got Ed the job at the Palace. You know, Ed was wounded so badly in the First War he found life difficult – he'd been reduced to being a Kleen-e-ze salesman. Selling shoe brushes door-to-door. If it hadn't been for Daddy, we shouldn't have had a roof over our heads.'

'Poor man. I had no idea.'

'Dighton saved Ed's bacon – but then never let him forget it. He'd have Ed doing all sorts of dirty jobs for him – spreading rumours, blackening people's names, all sorts of things that were absolutely against Ed's own principles. He was very upright, Guy.'

'You could tell that at a glance.'

'Topham Dighton is *not*. I suppose he thinks it's his job to protect the Crown, but actually he's not much more than a jumped-up hotel manager for Buck House and Windsor Castle – he just loves intrigue, and of course he's been there so long nobody can get rid of him. I think the King detests him.'

'Well, I daresay you'll put on your best smile for him at the funeral.'

'Naturally. There are the school fees to think of – I expect the Privy Purse to cough up for those.'

She's tougher than she looks, thought Guy.

'And then that'll be the end of the matter, Mr Courtier? My husband?'

'Strictly speaking, yes. My orders are to close the whole thing down as soon as possible. He's had a good write-up in *The Times*, and that should be enough to satisfy most people's curiosity.'

'Nobody seems very curious about the pistol. The one that killed him, the one he didn't own.'

'No, they don't. What can I say, Adelaide? It's not a time for questions.'

'Did you like him, Guy? You shared an office with him, even if only for a few short weeks.'

'You and I have known each other since our schooldays, we're the same generation. Ed was that much older, it was difficult to get to know him. I was surprised to hear you'd married.'

'He was a wounded hero. I took pity on him. *Did* you like him?'

'We were very different people. I've never been in the army.'

'What I'm trying to say is – did you like him enough to want to do something about this or are you just going to let it go? Are you going to turn your back on what happened – in his office, with somebody else's pistol – are you going to let somebody *murder my husband* and get away with it?'

'Well,' said Guy uncomfortably. 'When you put it like that . . .'

The women sat in comfortable companionship, two aliens caught by war in an elegant apartment overlooking Grosvenor Square. 'I preferred it when Joe Kennedy was still here,' said Foxy Gwynne, looking out on to the US Embassy. 'Sociable, a wonderful ambassador. Gave great parties, did a remarkable job in preparing for the war. I'm not sure about the new man.'

'Kennedy didn't think much of Britain's chances, though – that was the big strike against him. I saw Winston just before he became Prime Minister, he was talking hot and strong about what he called "our special relationship".'

'Naturally. His mother's American.'

'So Kennedy didn't fit in any more, he had to go.'

'What'll happen to Kick? I heard she's going to marry the Marquess of Hartington.'

'Joe made her go home with him, but she'll be back – she's fallen in love with England.'

'*And* with a man who one day will own half of it!'

'While *your* future husband owns the other half!'

Foxy Gwynne laughed and rang the bell. 'What'll you have?'

Mrs Granville Lee Welch Kendall Cody III, a very rich woman by virtue of a succession of shrewd marriages, smiled and said, 'If this was New York I'd be ordering a Manhattan, in honour of Lady Randolph Churchill.' Her diamonds glittered in the lamplight. 'As it is, I suppose it'll be the usual gin and orange. Though it's disgusting, isn't it? Sticks to your teeth.'

'Oh, go on. You love being in London, Betsey, in the thick of it.'

'Granville has important work to do here.'

'And you have important people to see.'

'Oh, George!' she laughed. 'He's like a puppy dog, follows me about wherever I go. Writes me letters, sends me flowers. I've never been wooed by a prince before.'

Wooed, thought Foxy, that's a good one. After all those husbands.

'He's bored though,' said Betsey. 'Thinks he's undervalued. I keep telling him he's doing a grand job, but he wants more. Says he's snipped enough ribbons to last a lifetime, made the same stupid speech a thousand times, wants something that's a bit more of a challenge.'

'He's extremely popular.'

'He knows that. But, darling, he said to me, "All that handshaking. It broke my father's hand once. *And* the Duke of Windsor's. It'll be my turn next." He wants to get away from the crowds and do something more political – he's very keen on forging Anglo-American relations.'

'Well, he seems to have put that into practice with you, Betsey. Quite energetically.'

'Ha ha! I'm giving a dinner for General Knox again next week – will you and Hugh come? I daresay my young princeling will look in – I want him to meet the general.'

'That would be lovely, let me know when. Now, in return, I want you to think about my friend Guy Harford.'

'I don't think I ever met him.'

'He's only just back from Tangier. Working at Buckingham Palace now in some tiresome job which I think will only cause him headaches in the long run, but Betsey, he's a gifted painter. You have so many friends here – is there a gallery you know which might stage an exhibition of his work?'

'Harford, did you say? Tangier?'

'Yes, does it ring a bell?'

'It does now. Wasn't there a dreadful schemozzle – everybody threatening to shoot everybody else, even though it's neutral territory? I had General Montgomery to dinner the other night, he made a terribly good story out of it.'

'Sounds like Guy!'

'It was a complete disaster. Tangier's supposed to be neutral, a place where the Allies and the Axis meet, in the same way those soldiers played football with the Germans in the First War. Finely balanced diplomacy, Monty called it, with everyone trying desperately hard to learn everybody else's secrets while at the same time not putting a foot wrong. Unique in the world. Until your friend Guy went and did that.'

'What exactly is the "that" that he's supposed to have done? He's never said.'

'Oh, I don't know,' said Betsey evasively, 'I can't have been listening.' She was looking across the room at her sable coat, relic of a bygone age, slung across the back of a chair. She shivered. 'These British summers, darling. Sometimes I wish I was back in Charleston.'

'No, you don't! You're the queen of London, the biggest socialite our mighty American nation has ever produced. You reign supreme, and you love it.'

'Amazing what good a few ol' greenbacks can do in times of trouble!'

'You make everybody happy with your parties. And now there you are, helping your prince find a better job for himself. Selfless! May I ask, does Granville know about him?'

'Oh darling, he's so busy with his airplanes and his diplomacy and his hands-across-the-sea. No time for romance.'

'Your prince on the other hand . . .'

'No time for anything else, Foxy!' Her laugh tinkled across the room.

'So can you help Guy?'

Betsey flapped her eyelids at her friend. 'Are you two . . . ?'

'Certainly *not*! I'm engaged to be married! It's just that he needs a boost. The Tangier business took it out of him rather and, really, he shouldn't be reduced to pen-pushing at Buck House.'

'I'll see what can be done,' said Betsey. 'And now I want to talk about Wallis and David.'

'Yes?'

It was an unspoken competition between the two well-connected women – Foxy had known the Windsors longer, but did Betsey know them better? The age-old one-upmanship among those close to royalty was no different in wartime England than it had been in Tudor times.

'I'm glad they're safe, though the job they've got is a terrible snub. I just worry, stuck out there, miles from anywhere, that it'll be the undoing of them.'

Foxy lit a cigarette. 'I spoke to Wallis on the telephone a few weeks ago when they were in Palm Beach. She seemed pretty chipper.'

'All the time they're in America, yes. But they're back in Nassau now and she's hating it. He's in a rage because everyone's been ordered not to call her Your Royal Highness, while she hates the house – she told Nancy Carew "the dining room looks like a ski hut in Norway". *And* she's taken down the portrait of the King – that didn't go down well.

'They've been there for a year. They were allocated a certain amount of money to do the place up, and she spent a quarter of it on a dining table – a *table*, my dear! And then he keeps threatening to come back to London.'

'I heard that,' said Foxy, nodding. 'Hugh says he's making the Prime Minister's life a misery over this HRH business, and he feels the Bahamas can govern themselves – they don't need him, and he could do much more for the war effort back here in Britain.'

'I like them both,' said Betsey, 'but they're living in a dream world. He wants to come back and play at being a field marshal – the King's never going to allow it.'

'It's more than that. He wants his status back. Five years ago he was king and emperor, the world at his feet; now he's like the mayor of some coal-mining town up north. I definitely get the impression he believes that if Buckingham Palace is bombed again, and the King is killed, he'll get his old job back. That's the real reason he wants to come home. To stay close.'

'I'd say Wallis prefers Palm Beach. No blackout, no air raids, no saluting. Plenty of champagne. *And* they curtsy to her.'

'What do you think, then? She won't come back with David?'

Betsey Cody smiled. 'On the contrary, I think she will. She'd *love* to wear that crown!'

CHAPTER SIX

'Ah, Aggie. Can you spare a moment?'

'Will it take long, Mr Harford?' Aggie slowly looked up from the letter she was reading. She had moved into Ed Brampton's desk, a far more imposing affair than her modest workstation in the anteroom.

'You never told me that Major Ed was related to Sir Topham.'

'Everybody in this place is related to someone or other. That's how it works here.'

'Not me.'

'You may not be related, Mr Harford, but *somebody* put in a good word for you. Otherwise you wouldn't be here.'

'I don't think so. But you? You're related?'

'I'm below-stairs,' came the tart response. 'We get our jobs from the Labour Exchange.'

Aggie was wearing a luminous shade of blue which caught the light a certain way, making Guy think of the strange turbaned Englishwoman in Tangier, the one whose tame peacock came each morning to lie on her eiderdown like an exotic bedspread.

'Come on, now – tell me about Ed Brampton and the Master . . .'

'Like I say, *everyone's* related. The fellow who had Topsy's job before him was Sir Derek Keppel – lovely old man, he was. His brother was married to Mrs Keppel – you know, the old king's poppet.'

'The one who lives at The Ritz?'

'Mrs K occasionally puts her nose round the door here at the Palace too, but Kingy doesn't approve. Doesn't want his grandfather's piece of stuff lording it around the place – which she'd do, given half the chance. She treats this place like a second home – knows all the footmen, gets them running errands, earwigs all the gossip then goes and blabs it back at The Ritz. She's a pain in the backside.'

'Well, I don't suppose . . .'

'Then there's your boss, Tommy Lascelles. His cousin's married to the Princess Royal. And the Master of the Horse, old Beaufort, he's got Queen Mary staying with him at Badminton – his wife's the King's cousin. And so on.'

'Fascinating, Aggie, but what I actually want to know is, what was it between Ed and Sir Topham? What sort of jobs was Ed asked to do – given he wasn't actually supposed to be working directly for the Master of the Household?'

'Well,' said Aggie, 'I could tell you a thing or two, but if you want the full story, it's in that diary of his, wherever it ended up. Why do you want to know?'

'Orders from above,' lied Guy.

'I'd find the diary if I were you. Meantime here are some more orders from above – a note from Tommy about your extra duties.'

'Extra . . . ?'

'It may take some time to replace Major Ed, and while we're waiting, everyone has to do their bit.'

'Go on,' said Guy gloomily, 'you may as well read it out.'

'The most important is King Haakon.'

'Mm?'

'He's a hero. He was forced out of Norway last year by the Nazis and came to stay here for a bit. King George is very kind – when Haakon arrived he had only the clothes he stood up in, so HM lent him anything he needed from his own wardrobe. He's charming, very nice to everyone.'

'What am I supposed to do with this throneless paragon?'

'Meet him at the Privy Purse door and give him his laundry.'

'His . . . *laundry*?'

'He likes to call round for it himself.'

Guy looked up. 'He collects his own washing? A king?'

'He don't mind. Major Ed was told that it's a security thing – His Maj doesn't want people knowing where his laundry is sent to, it would give his address away. The Germans want him dead because he refused to abdicate, so he has to be very careful. But I don't think it's that – he just likes looking in, and if King George is free they have a drink together.'

'Good Lord. And so I . . . ?'

'Collect the laundry from Tom Jerram – that's the King's valet – and take it over to the Privy Purse office. Wait for King Haakon to arrive, hand it over, say something nice, escort him back to his car.'

'And I call him . . . ?'

'Your Majesty, obviously.' Aggie said this with a superior tone; it was clearly *her* office now. 'You've got a lot to learn, Mr Harford. Some of it can even be quite fun.'

'Anything else?'

'Princess Elizabeth and Princess Margaret.'

'Ah.'

'Major Ed would look after them when they came into the Palace, which isn't very often – Windsor's far safer. While they're hanging about waiting for the Queen, Princess Elizabeth likes to visit the horses in the Mews. That was Major Ed's job.'

'I don't know anything about horses,' said Guy with alarm.

'Don't worry, they do. Lots.'

'Anything else?'

'There's a note here about the Duke of Gloucester's car. Have you done anything about that?'

'For heaven's sake,' snapped Guy irritably, 'why doesn't the chap take the bus like everybody else?'

'I see you won't be applying for that job, then. The one Major Ed was after.' It went without saying that Aggie knew all about Ed and the Duke of Gloucester job.

'Anything else, perchance?'

'Just Charlotte.'

'Charlotte?'

'The parrot.'

This is ridiculous, thought Guy. At this moment, if things had gone differently, I could be sitting on the side of a mountain in my dusty land far away, paintbrush in hand. Instead, here I am being treated like a subaltern in a fashionable regiment with nothing better to do than please the colonel's wife and pour the drinks. Laundry, horses, cars – and now a parrot. All this – and squaring away a murder, of course.

If that's what it was.

'Go on.'

'She's become a bit of a nuisance. Used to belong to old King George – he picked her up in a bar in Port Said, I daresay he was tipsy at the time. Anyway, Charlotte was his lifelong companion – he loved her more than he loved Queen Mary, I reckon. She'd sit on his shoulder while he was doing his State papers, and when HM went down to Cowes for the regatta, she'd go too.'

'And no doubt was awarded the Order of the Garter for services to His Imperial Majesty.'

Aggie pushed up the spectacles drooping on the end of her nose and looked at him sharply. 'You won't get very far here,

Mr Harford, if you take that tone. We all push in the same direction at the Palace, 'specially in wartime.'

'I should have thought animals came under the aegis of the Royal Mews. Anyway, what am I supposed to do with it?'

'Not it, *her*. She's currently housed with the Gloucesters, but they're moving around rather a lot at the moment and she's become just one thing too many. You're to find her a new home.'

Guy rose from his desk. 'When I took on this job,' he said, shuffling up a few papers, 'I had no idea that my diverse range of talents could be put to such comprehensive use. Remarkable! I'm going over to the Guards Chapel.'

The walk eased his frustration. He stepped through the traffic on to the pavement of the Victoria Memorial and then turned right in the direction of Wellington Barracks. At the far end stood the glorious Greek temple whose role for the past century was to bid farewell to old soldiers – some killed in action, most merely extinguished by old age. In another life I would be sitting at an easel painting this, he thought, the light is perfect today.

As he entered by the west door his nostrils filled with the smell of charred timbers, the result of a Luftwaffe firebomb attack the previous winter. But the interior, with its alabaster, marble, mosaics and stained glass, seemed above all conflict: immune, still, and gently glowing.

'Oh, it's you,' growled an unwelcoming voice. 'What are you doing here?'

It was the bulky Coats Mission officer, Toby Broadbent, seated in a pew towards the rear of the chancel.

'Came to visit the padre,' replied Guy. 'And you?'

'A private moment,' said Captain Broadbent vaguely, though he didn't look the godly type.

'Have you seen him anywhere?'

'He's saying his prayers. Come outside, I want a word with you.' Broadbent rose and took his elbow roughly.

'I'm rather busy,' replied Guy, irritated at being manhandled.

'Won't take long.'

The two men halted under the soaring Doric columns of the portico and eyed the immaculate parade ground before them.

'Didn't want to mention such things in a house of God,' said Broadbent stolidly, 'but people I've been talking to are expressing concern about you.'

'I can't imagine why.'

'The company you keep. You're not really one of us, are you?'

'If by that you mean I am not a serving soldier, you would be correct.'

The captain, a good head taller than Guy, leaned forward and fixed him with a look of distaste. 'I know that! I'm not talking about that – I'm talking about the people you know, the people you mix with.'

Guy looked away. In the distance a small platoon of men were displaying their parade-ground skills. 'I really don't think that's any of your business,' he replied mildly, thinking, is this about Foxy and her friend Wallis Windsor? Only the other day Tommy Lascelles had described her as 'a shop-soiled American with a voice like a rusty saw', though surely she couldn't be that bad or she wouldn't be a friend of Foxy's.

'Look,' said Broadbent through gritted teeth, 'my job is to pre-serve the life of the King. We don't want people hanging round the Palace who keep the company of common *criminals*.'

'Don't know what you're talking about,' said Guy.

'People are keeping an eye on you, Harford.'

'Evidently.'

'You've been seen with a woman who is part of a gang. A *gang* – burglars and shoplifters, people who'd knife you soon as look at you!'

'I don't think that . . .'

'If there isn't a knife handy, they'll just shove the glass you're drinking from in your face.'

'I really *don't* know what you're talking about.' He started to make his way back inside the church.

The captain grabbed Guy's elbow again. 'Yes you do! Rosemary Carrigan! She's part of a gang who call themselves the Jellied Eel Brigade!'

'I know nobody of that name,' said Guy truthfully.

'Lives at the Elephant and Castle, Gurney Street. Known associates include a smash-and-grab man called Johnny Jackson, a bare-knuckle fighter called Ruby Sparks – that's a man by the way – and a drug dealer called Billy Chang . . . D'you want me to go on?'

'What's this all about?'

'You were seen with her the other night, no point in denying it.'

'Are you saying, Captain, that I – an assistant private secretary at Buckingham Palace – am under surveillance?'

'*Everyone's* under surveillance,' said Broadbent grimly. 'There's a ruddy war on, hadn't you noticed? You were in The Grenadier public house with her. She put her arm around you. Rosemary Carrigan.'

'Ah. That could be somebody I know by another name. But if what you say about her . . . associates . . . is true, I have no knowledge of that.'

'Just a pretty tart, then, eh? Out for a good time with her?'

She's bit more than that, thought Guy, and a lot cleverer than you for a start. 'That's rather offensive. She's a friend of . . . a friend.'

'Not the way it looked. It looked like you and she were . . . having fun.'

'No harm in having fun, Captain, even you. We may all be dead tomorrow.'

'She's a common *thief*! She's a blackmailer! She's a black marketeer! I daresay when she can't steal something to sell, she sells herself – we can't have that kind of person associating with people employed at the Palace!'

'That's not . . .' Guy burst out angrily, but stopped himself.

'A *burglar*. Who, in a country at war, breaks into people's homes and steals their belongings!'

Just as well you don't know she broke into your wretched Palace, thought Guy, as easy as blinking – so much for your protection of the sovereign when Rodie Carr can waltz in, pick the lock on my office door and leave a rose on my desk. Then wander out again without a single challenge. I expect she could have put tin tacks on the throne if she'd wanted to.

'Well, I'm going to tell Tommy Lascelles about this,' said Broadbent hotly. 'He needs to know the kind of people he's employing these days. Unless . . .' he added.

'Yes?'

'Unless you tell me what's going on over Ed Brampton. Then perhaps we can forget about your little indiscretion with that . . . *tart*.'

◆ ◆ ◆

The whisky bottle was its usual near-empty self. A tepid sun wearily put itself to bed while heavy buses clanked and banged their way out of the coach station beneath.

'So you see, Rupe, delightful though she is, I can't see Rodie again. It's just too complicated.'

'*Bless my buttons!*'

'I agree she's a wonderful distraction, but it's pretty obvious I'm being watched. Perhaps what we . . .'

'*All's well! All's well! Where's the Captain?*'

'Oh, shut up!' snapped Rupert Hardacre. 'For heaven's sake, Guy, how long are we going to have to put up with this?'

'Charlotte? I rather like her, actually. Anyway, I can soon put a stop to that.' He rose and lifted a heavy tapestry – embroidered with a fanciful coat of arms featuring an African grey parrot wearing a crown – over the cage. A muffled grunt came from within, then silence.

'They don't ask for much, just a little conversation now and again,' said Guy encouragingly. 'You'll get used to her.'

Rupe crossed his legs aggressively. 'I'm sure there's something in the rental agreement about having pets on the premises.'

'It won't be for long. Sooner or later I'll have to go down to Gloucestershire – I may be able to palm her off on someone there. Anyway, how's everything going in the world of the General Post Office? Raided any interesting mailboxes recently?'

Rupe looked at him sharply. 'That's not what we do.'

'Just joking,' said Guy. 'Curious though, that in this world of "Careless Talk Costs Lives", you seem to know everything I do, while I know nothing at all about *your* job.'

'Best to leave it that way.'

'Understood,' said Guy, slightly crossly.

'However, I did learn something today which may be of interest,' Rupert went on. 'Tell me first, though – what's the state of play with your dead body?'

'He's still dead. The funeral's on Thursday.'

'After that?'

'What d'you mean?'

'I mean, is that the end of the matter?' said Rupe. 'Or are you supposed to be investigating what actually happened? How on earth did you even get involved in this ridiculous charade of placing a dead body in an empty house and then discovering it?'

'I've been told to mop things up and leave them shipshape. Quite soon, if I've done everything according to orders, people will have forgotten Ed Brampton ever existed.'

'Apart from the widow and children.'

'Oh, you know about them too,' said Guy archly. 'You really do know everything.'

'QED. There were photographs of them all over the mantelpiece when we dropped in the other night.'

'Ah. Yes.'

'I just wondered if you're planning to take things further.'

'My boss says no. But Adelaide wants to know what happened – of course she does.'

Rupe got up and stretched, wandered over to the window and looked up into the darkening sky.

'How much do you feel obliged to do her bidding?'

'She and I have known each other since we were children. I hadn't seen much of her in recent years but she's a very fine person – I feel I owe it to her to find out what I can.'

'Even if she might be upset by what she learns?'

'I wouldn't know. Until I find out something, I won't be able to judge.'

Rupe had his eye on a trio of Spitfires streaking westwards across the London skyline. 'Have you heard of Lady Easthampton?'

'I don't think so.'

'Her husband is heir to Earl FitzMalcolm. Some friends of mine have had their eye on her.'

'Friends in the Post Office?'

'In a manner of speaking.'

'Been peeping through her letterbox?'

'Oh, grow up. I'm just going out for a breath of fresh air now. You may find some useful bedtime reading in your room. See you later.' Rupert swallowed the last of his whisky and wandered out.

Guy refilled his glass and walked the few paces over to the small room containing a single bed, wardrobe, dressing table and little more. There were cracks in the ceiling from a recent bombing raid, and the window overlooking the bus station forecourt was streaked with dirt. The wallpaper had mostly faded from a startling orange to a more acceptable umber, but there was still evidence here and there of the original atrocity. For a moment Guy's thoughts turned to the small house covered in bougainvillea, with its shaded courtyard and tinkling fountain, its light, airy studio, and the promise each day of another exquisite dawn.

He turned away from the window to find on his bed an anonymous brown folder. Propping himself up on his pillows, he opened it to find a single sheet of paper – a carbon copy of what appeared to be an official report, but lacking attribution, signature, or identifying letterhead.

He read:

ZSUZANNA 'SUZY' GERTLER

aka VISCOUNTESS EASTHAMPTON

This person, born in Hungary but more recently domiciled in Poland, arrived in the UK on 4 July 1935.

She appears to be the long-term mistress of Edward Stanislas Zeisloft, a Pole who made his fortune selling arms to both sides during the Spanish Civil War. Zeisloft was based in London but left at the outbreak of hostilities; his present whereabouts are unknown.

Despite this regrettable alliance, since arriving in the UK Lady Easthampton has been on familiar terms* with the Soviet ambassador, on affectionate and intimate terms* with the Turkish ambassador and others, while one of her closest friendships* has been with Prince Habib Lotfallah, who has ambitions to become king of Syria. Other contacts include an army officer at the War Office and a cook employed by Randolph Churchill, son of the Prime Minister.

Reports from our contact in Paris in early 1940 suggest that Zeisloft is either a German agent or double agent. He is very rich and has been providing Lady Easthampton with a considerable amount of money.

Upon arrival in this country, Lady Easthampton, who is an attractive woman, quickly made her way into society circles, though it is not clear how she achieved this.

She came to our attention because in 1937 she was heard to say she wanted to marry 'a wealthy Englishman' and encouraged Sir Hugo de Lys to propose marriage. However, she rejected his proposal because in the meantime she had become acquainted with the elder son of Earl FitzMalcolm.

Ambrose Easthampton carries the courtesy title of Viscount Easthampton but, despite his background and education, is an undischarged bankrupt and dependent upon alcohol.

It is understood their marriage in 1938 was one entirely of convenience. Lady Easthampton, or more correctly Zeisloft, paid Lord Easthampton £500 to secure the marriage, and he is now in receipt of a substantial allowance from them both.

Lady Easthampton is a highly sophisticated woman, having engineered a place for herself in society in order to go about her principal business, which is spying for the arms trade.

The Home Secretary has ordered that she be placed under close scrutiny in preparation for a detention order under Rule 18b.

TOP SECRET	CPW/OR
RESTRICTED CIRCULATION	2/1941
INITIAL AND RETURN	pp. DHRTA

A few moments later there was a tap on Guy's door.

'Better than *A Book at Bedtime*?' smiled Rupe, nodding at the radio.

'Interesting enough,' agreed Guy, levering himself up. 'I imagine there must be quite a few of these adventuresses hanging around London.'

'None quite like this,' said Rupe. 'It's easier to penetrate the British upper classes if you're foreign, especially from a land where not many people have travelled. And being an outstanding beauty is no hindrance – she has a particular fondness for provocative necklines. No, what makes her different is the people she's targeted, and why. She's ruthless, cunning, colossally ambitious – exceptional.'

'Just the kind of person in need of the tireless scrutiny of the Post Office.'

'Very funny. Would you mind giving me that back now?' Rupe reached out a hand.

'Any more? I'm not ready for bed yet. A few more stories about London's Mata Haris might put me in the mood for sleep.'

'Oh Lord,' said Rupe, taking back the folder, 'I see the penny hasn't dropped.'

'What d'you mean?'

'Why do you think I left this for you?' said Rupe, shaking his head in wonderment. 'Major Brampton. And Lady Easthampton. Do you get it now?'

'Oh,' said Guy. 'Oh.'

'You never read this.' The door slammed.

CHAPTER SEVEN

The windows on one side of Markham Street had blown out, yet oddly the houses themselves seemed untouched. As Guy walked gingerly up the street, his feet crunching and clanking the glass shards underfoot, he thought about his pledge to Adelaide Brampton. In the short time he'd known Ed he had not altogether enjoyed his company, and actually when he came to think about it there'd been too many intervening years for him to feel any close link with Adelaide either.

Yet here he was, sticking his head in the lion's jaws, stumbling into trouble, just when he should be concentrating on the job at hand and thanking his stars he'd escaped that dreary quotidian of the Foreign Office. Life at the Palace was decidedly peculiar, yet it had its own rationale, its own momentum, and the job everyone was doing there to keep up the nation's morale was remarkable.

The King, the Queen, and especially the young Princess Elizabeth shone like a beacon of hope in these dark days; and if others who sheltered behind the palace railings were less admirable, that was understandable: lordly, inflexible men they were, fearful of being projected into the real world. Guy had come from a place where life was rarely led by the rules, and if his eccentric contribution was a help to the war effort, who was he to complain?

But why – crunch, crunch – were his feet taking him back to the scene of the crime? Did he even know what he hoped to achieve coming here this evening? Were those shadowy figures from the Coats Mission on his tail – and if they *were* tailing him, why?

He looked over his shoulder but the street was almost deserted. The only people he could see were down the other end, absorbed in the business of sweeping up last night's bomb damage. Someone looking out of a front-room window gave him an uninquisitive look, and a woman with her hair tied in a scarf walked past giving him a dazzling smile – hardly the action of an undercover agent, surely?

He finally arrived at the Bramptons' house. This side of the street remained untouched, such was the arbitrary effect of bomb blast – if you turned your back on the windowless terrace opposite, it was almost as if there was no war – the sky was bright, the air warm and still, the sparrows chirping in the gutters and chimney stacks.

His thoughts returned to Rodie, her face ablaze with anger and humiliation. Where she comes from, he concluded, the nature of friendship is different. That night, in the dark, breaking into Ed's house, had made them equals – all criminals together – so why *shouldn't* they go dancing together, as everyone else did in these beleaguered times?

But where Guy came from, friendship took longer to develop, longer for the barriers to fall. You never said outright what you thought about a person, but gradually edged your way towards it. You did not say 'You're gorgeous' or suggest after a first meeting that you should marry – it just wasn't the way with the people he'd grown up with.

And yet isn't that why he loved the life of Tangier – even with its double-dealing, its hidden vices, its disregard for the conventions? Why *shouldn't* Rodie say all those things?

Because she breaks the law, he reminded himself. Because she lacks the capacity to tell right from wrong. Because she steals from people. Because she says, 'When I want something I take it.' He shuddered at the thought.

He felt in his pocket. Just before her outburst Rodie had handed him, with some pride, a latchkey – 'Just in case you want to go back,' she'd teased. Being a bit of an expert, she'd managed to fix the jammed front-door lock and had a copy made. It was as if she'd given him a secret love-token instead of the illicit means to open Ed's front door.

'Where did this . . . ?'

'Easy when you know how,' and as she passed the key over her hand closed on his. 'Don't lose it, darling,' she'd whispered.

Guy glanced once more over his shoulder as he let himself into the house. When he'd broken in before he had no idea what he was looking for; now he had a clearer purpose. He walked through the front hall and was making his way towards Ed's study at the back when he stopped in surprise. On the floor by the foot of the stairs leaned the portrait of Ed which Adelaide had painted when they were first married: cheeks bronzed by the sun, hair disarranged by the wind, a cream flannel shirt crumpled, the wounded soldier seated on a bench smiling up at his portraitist. It was a very different Ed to the one Guy had shared an office with.

Distracted to find this memento of happier times so randomly abandoned, he wandered into the drawing room. A glance told him that Adelaide had been hard at work before returning to the country, removing photographs and the selection of pointless objects with which the English upper classes cover their polished surfaces. Previously this room had looked cluttered, now it looked almost bare – as if Rodie had come back and helped herself.

And yet Guy knew this to be the work of Adelaide – the portrait told him that in an instant; no burglar worth his salt would give it a second look. Was she taking everything back to St Walke Episcopi, or was this the erasure of a husband of twelve years from her life?

Guy shook his head and moved on through the house to Ed's study. Unlike the denuded drawing room, it was in exactly the same state it had been when he, Rupe and Rodie had visited.

I've become a criminal, he thought. I turned up my nose at dancing with a girl because she breaks into people's houses, but am I any better?

He pushed the thought to one side, glanced round the tiny room and pulled down some files from a shelf.

Don't get distracted, he told himself, you're looking for one thing and one thing only – a single clue. But as he opened the top file to find a series of memos signed by Tommy Lascelles, he knew this was a job which could take a very long time.

He shuffled through the carbon copies of replies and suddenly there was another tranche of memos, this time from Sir Topham Dighton. Quite what they were doing at Ed's house when they should be under lock and key at the Palace, Guy could not fathom. Almost certainly they'd offer up information as to what Ed was doing clandestinely for his second master at the Palace – but this wasn't what he was looking for.

An hour later, as the air-raid sirens wound up to their nightly hysterical wail, the files had dwindled to a single unopened folder. Guy wandered into the drawing room and poured himself a whisky. He'd read his way through Ed's domestic bills, the letters from his club, his regiment and his school, the correspondence with his wider family. The file he'd saved till last was a random collection of cards, letters, telegrams and other ephemera, which were clearly gathered together in this way because they were of the most significance, personally, to the dead man. Here, surely, was what he was looking for!

But fifteen minutes later Guy was no wiser. He drained the whisky and made a decision – he'd have to take away the palace file, the one with memos from Lascelles and Dighton; it contained too much information to be absorbed while his adrenalin levels were running high and he was waiting any second to be discovered by the nosy colonel next door.

Such an action was fraught with danger – if he was spotted as he made his escape, or got run over in the street, or any one of a number of other eventualities in the crazy possibilities of wartime night, he'd be found in possession of documents which should never have left Buckingham Palace. Questions would be asked about where and how he'd got them, which would almost certainly lead to the discovery that he'd broken into Ed's house – not once, but twice. And that could quickly lead to accusations of him consorting with a known criminal – Rodie Carr, or whatever her name was – all of which would put an end to his life as a courtier and could well put him behind quite a different set of railings.

He poured another whisky while he weighed up the options, his eye scanning the room while he thought. As a diversion he reached over to the bookcase to see what Ed's reading habits were. Military history, obviously, was his preference, followed by the works of John Buchan, Conan Doyle, and Edgar Wallace. They summed up the mind of a man who was not Adelaide's equal, war hero or not, Guy thought.

Turning away, his eye fell on a volume of photographs by the Bauhaus artist Moholy-Nagy – *not* something Ed would have picked up at Foyles or Heywood Hill or wherever he shopped. Must be Adelaide's, he thought.

As he took the book from the shelf his trained eye took in the geometric art and surrealist photography which marked the author out as a pioneer of new thought and vision in art. As he leafed through, a large envelope dropped out and fell to the floor.

Bending to pick it up, Guy felt from its thickness that inside were letters or notes – whatever they were, he thought, finally he'd found what he was looking for.

'I had the strangest dream,' said Foxy. 'Buckingham Palace had been bombed – again – only this time the King did not survive.'

'Happens all the time,' said Guy. 'You transfer your own anxieties on to the heads of others. You're probably worried about Hugh.'

They were lunching in Claridge's, its wide marble floors as polished as in peacetime, the waiters perhaps less so; but even here the portions were small these days.

'Oh, Hugh's all right. Swanning around the House of Lords wearing his colonel's uniform.'

'You can send me an invitation to the wedding if you like.'

'No, Guy, no. I don't think Hugh wants the old Paris crowd there – you're all a bit of a rabble, you know. And anyway, he's not that keen on you. He says he saw something erotic in that portrait you painted.'

'As intended. I didn't realise he had such an artistic eye.'

'Now, now, don't be jealous!'

'Let's change the subject,' said Guy crossly.

'I was telling you about my dream. The King was dead, and there you were in the Throne Room wearing a Garter Sash, a chestful of medal ribbons, and with a flunkey waiting nearby to put the crown on your head.'

'Were you my queen?'

'Stop it. I could see behind you the Duke of Windsor, the Duke of Gloucester, the Duke of Kent – all the King's brothers, ganging up like Brutus and his chums, ready to knife you in the back.'

'Understandable in the circs. They have a greater claim to the throne than I.'

'And then,' said Foxy, not to be deflected, 'something else happened. They all turned on each other and started stabbing each other furiously – blood everywhere, darling. It was horrible.'

'Who won?'

Foxy twisted in her seat crossly. 'You're not taking me seriously! They all wanted the throne, don't you see? They were glad their brother was dead and they all wanted to assert their right to rule the Empire.'

'Well,' said Guy, 'there may be some truth in that. Of course I know nothing, but I listen closely to what Queen Aggie tells me – she may only be a clerk, but she knows everything.'

'Tell me,' said Foxy. They had finished lunch and were waiting for coffee It looked like it was never going to come.

'It goes like this. As the senior royal brother, Windsor wants to come back here to take up the crown if Bertie bites the dust. You more or less told me that yourself.'

'But Princess Elizabeth . . .'

'Too young to have any leverage.'

'Even with that redoubtable mother behind her? You don't know what power women can wield when they try!'

'Pay attention. Gloucester – he's the hidden danger. He hates the Duke of Windsor for umpteen different reasons and thinks that, having abdicated, he no longer has any reasonable claim. Harry Gloucester is officially the Regent Designate, and if King George dropped dead tomorrow, he's the one who'd sit on the throne.'

'Yes, you told me that. What about dear Prince George, sweet man? Surely he has no ambitions?'

'There you're wrong. At the time of the Abdication he was seriously considered for the throne if Bertie couldn't face up to it – and you recall Bertie weeping on Queen Mary's shoulder when he realised he'd have to be king. They did psychological tests on Bertie to see if he could withstand the strain – and they warned George that if he didn't pass, he, George, would get the throne. Nobody wanted Harry Gloucester wandering around with a crown on his head.'

'Man's a buffoon,' said Foxy, nodding.

'Steady on – he did some heroic stuff in France at the beginning of the war. And he's a soldierly type – just right for a nation at war.'

'And in peacetime? King Ass-for-Brains?'

'The trouble with you Americans, you believe everyone at the top of the tree has to be a genius. Sometimes we get by very well on much less.'

'You were saying about Prince George.'

'Well, he may look sweet and unassuming but he knows he's king material. Did you hear that Poland secretly offered him their throne when the war's over?'

'What?'

'Perfectly true. General Sikorski saw him only the other day – I get all this from Aggie by the way, nobody else tells me anything – and he made him the offer.'

'I don't believe it!'

'And then Princess Marina wouldn't mind a leg up. Never forget that she's more royal than anyone in the Palace – both her grandfathers were kings, which can't be said of any of the present lot at Buck House. Aggie says the Queen's jealous of her – hates the fact that she's blue-blooded *and* knows how to wear her clothes. And so Marina has no sympathy for the Queen and, I think, would love to upstage her.'

'Well, that's all very fascinating, but the truth is that Princess Elizabeth will be the next sovereign.'

'I wouldn't absolutely count on that.'

Across the room there was a mild flurry as a large lady rose from a table and vaguely wandered off into the main lobby followed by a gaggle of anxious-looking women. Despite her dowdy clothes she carried a surprising air of authority.

'Poor old Queen Wilhelmina,' said Guy. 'How she must miss Holland.'

'There are worse places to be when you've been kicked out of your country. She came down to dinner in her dressing gown the other night,' said Foxy, 'so she obviously feels quite at home. Prince Bernhard is proving a bit of a handful though – up in his suite, in the blackout, he saw someone on the opposite side of the street had left a light burning. Instead of telling someone, he took out a tommy gun and fired through the window. I don't think he'll be doing that again after the talking-to he got.'

Guy smothered a laugh. 'For an American you seem to know an awful lot.'

'Hugh tells me.'

'You ought to write a gossip column.'

'Ted Rochester's your man for that. You should have seen the vicious swipe he had at Noël Coward the other day – just for lunching here with a few friends. All boys of course – but no call for writing it the way he did.'

'We ought to go. Tommy Lascelles doesn't take kindly to his staff eating lunch.'

'Is that the time? I have a meeting of friends of the American Red Cross. Just in case we come into the war, we gels want to be prepared.' She gave the word an upper-class inflection as a joke against herself. 'We've got a committee – Betsey Cody's the chairman, naturally, since she's going to pay for it all – and we've got our eye on some premises near Trafalgar Square. I want you to come and meet her, she could be a good friend to you.'

'I'm a bit busy at the moment.'

'Find the time. Bye!'

They said their goodbyes in the doorway of the restaurant, but as Foxy gave him a fleeting embrace, over her shoulder Guy spotted a figure dressed in aquamarine silk, the tiniest of straw hats balanced on the back of her urchin haircut. She was sitting in the lobby with a startling blonde who was applying scarlet lipstick as if rationing had never been invented.

'Oh God,' he groaned, scuttling sideways like a spider towards the side entrance. But it was no good – Rodie had spotted him.

'Guy.' More a statement than a greeting.

'What are you doing here?'

'This is my friend Claudia.'

Guy nodded but made no attempt to shake her hand. 'What are you doing here?' he repeated. 'In Claridge's?'

'It's a free country, ain't it? My money's as good as anybody's round here. And unlike *some* – she nodded at an ancient dowager walking past – 'I pays my bills.'

She looks different when she's not dressed in her work outfit, thought Guy. She may have an effortless ease in these clothes, but she still looks better in burglar's dungarees.

And all of a sudden he realised he had to paint her.

'Must go,' he said. 'Extremely busy.'

'See you in The Grenadier, then,' said Rodie sarcastically. 'The pub. You won't mind talking to me in there, will you – you *snob*!'

'It's not that. I . . .'

'It's OK,' said Rodie. 'Lem and me are extremely busy havin' a cup of tea – and then we're going shopping.' There was a ravenous look in her eye as she said that, and then she started laughing.

'Shopping?' said Guy, baffled.

''Sright – the kind where you don't spend no money.'

'For heaven's sake,' hissed Guy, '*shoplifting*. You're a disgrace!'

'You didn't say that the other night when . . .' She gave him a sidelong smile.

At this, Claudia suddenly looked at Guy with new interest. Her initial once-over had been perfunctory – here was a man who clearly had to work for a living, no private income, however handsome. Now Rodie was talking about an evening out with Guy – maybe there was something there after all. But before Claudia could switch her headlights on, her friend swiftly changed the subject.

'I hear you got a parrot for company. Does it tuck you up warm at night and make you a nice breakfast?'

'I . . .'

'Pretty queer companion if you ask me. You should try harder, get out more.' She was clearly still nettled about the Hammersmith Palais. She turned to Claudia. 'Guy's an arty type, you know. Paints pictures. Quite good, so they say.'

'What are you doing in a place like this, then?' asked her friend insolently. 'You don't look much like a painter to me, right shabby most of 'em are. Shouldn't you be in a smock, daubing away somewhere?'

Guy looked with dismay down at his formal clothes, then back at her. 'Well, I have a day job. So I'm not doing much at the moment, and anyway, I don't have a studio.'

Claudia snorted. 'A painter without a studio? Like a pianist without a pianna!' she jeered. 'Why don't you get one?'

'She's right,' said Rodie. 'Why don't you get one?'

Why not indeed, thought Guy. Because I'm too busy covering up crimes, at the same time risking my career trying to uncover them again. I'm busy making my neck ache by bowing to the eminences I meet at the Palace, even if they're just there to collect their laundry. I'm busy trying to persuade an ex-Patou model not to marry a belted earl because I don't think it will work, and anyway, I might want to marry her myself. I'm busy trying to think how I can make a proper contribution to the war effort, instead of turning up to an office each day in a jacket and pinstripe trousers.

'They're rather difficult to find just now, and besides, I don't think I can afford one.'

'You seem to be doing all right,' said Claudia, nodding towards the restaurant. 'Who was that you was lunching with?'

'Yes,' said Rodie, eyes narrowing. 'Who *was* it?'

'Someone I knew in Paris. Look, I really have to go.' He paused in thought for a moment, then said, 'A word, Rodie.'

'Yes?' She smiled a dazzling smile and got up.

Turning his back on Claudia, Guy whispered, 'I know you're having fun, but you ought to be careful in this place. It's full of the crowned heads of Europe who have nowhere else to go now the Nazis have kicked them out. The security is tight – there are police and . . . others . . . everywhere. Watching. You want to be careful what you're doing or you'll find yourself in jail.'

'We just come for a look round,' said Rodie, all innocence. 'Coming to The Grenadier tomorrow?'

'I really . . . I don't know how to say this, but . . .'

'Then don't say it. Just come – nine o'clock. And don't be late.' She looked hard at him.

'Then we'll go dancin'.'

CHAPTER EIGHT

'You see, the camera never lies. You look so . . . *distinguée*.'

'So I should,' said Foxy, squinting slightly in concentration. 'D'you know how much that dress cost?'

'Not something that should ever worry you,' laughed Ted Rochester. He'd brought round a sheaf of black-and-white prints for the future countess to choose before his article appeared in *The Tatler*.

'I'll leave the rest if you'd like to keep them. What a star you were back in the Paris days, modelling with Monsieur Patou.'

'You can drop the soft soap, Ted. What do you want?'

The journalist coughed. 'I heard your friends Wallis and the Duke set the cat among the pigeons in Palm Beach when they were there.'

'Did you now.' Unencouragingly.

'They've hooked themselves up with someone decidedly iffy – Mrs Donahue, who inherited F. W. Woolworth's millions. *Not* one of us, I think.'

'Ted, you're a journalist – nobody's one of you. You're the least trusted profession in the world.'

'Ha ha. But do you know this woman? She's been trying to buy her way into society for years, but the old guard won't have it. She has this colossal mansion on South Ocean Boulevard and a hundred servants, but the harder she pushes at society's door, the more it remains firmly shut.'

This got a frosty reception. 'As a matter of fact, it was my future husband who introduced Wallis and the Duke to Mrs Donahue. She's a very generous host. And has a rather fine singing voice, so there! What a terrible snob you are!'

The journalist stepped back uneasily. 'Just trying to find an angle, Foxy. The Windsors always make good copy, but there has to be an angle.'

'They're back in Nassau now. Why don't you write about Wallis working tirelessly for the Red Cross?'

He smiled and shook his head wearily. 'That's not what people want to read. Since the Abdication there's no point in trying to write nice things about them; readers only want to hear they've grown horns and will soon disappear through the gates of Hades, never to return. The Duke's sucking up to known Nazi supporters in Nassau – and now, when he's allowed to escape to the mainland, he ends up the prisoner of a woman whose fortune comes from a five-and-dime store.'

'Woolworths? I shop there myself.'

'No, you don't. You're just saying that.'

'Well, I might.'

'Anyway, the Palm Beach *we* know, Foxy – the old families – the Amorys and the Munns, the Phippses and the Stotesburys, are all in a tizz. Of course they want Wallis and the Duke as guests in their house – but does it mean they have to invite that old witch Jessie Donahue along too?'

'I imagine it does. Good for Wallis, I say. I'm fed up with people looking down their noses at her.'

Rochester picked up the photographs and put them in an envelope. 'It's not just the English. Joe Kennedy told the Queen – I have this on the highest authority – that when he was invited to dinner with Wallis, he refused to go, saying, "I know of no job that I could occupy that might force my wife to dine with a tart."'

'Tart? From a Kennedy? That's rich!'

'If you'll permit me to say so, Foxy, your country's ambassadors don't know the meaning of diplomacy. After the Paris man, Bullitt, came here, he said all sorts of rude things – he sent off a note to President Roosevelt saying "The King is a moron, and the Queen is an excessively ambitious woman who's ready to sacrifice every other country in the world in order that she might remain Queen Elizabeth of England."'

'Outrageous!'

'He said it, not me – I don't know what Her Majesty can have done wrong. Bullitt himself described the King as a rather frightened boy and likened the Queen to one of his golf caddies up in Scotland. And he talked about "her cheap public smile".'

'I think somebody else said that.'

'Who?'

'Her sister-in-law. Not everybody adores her.'

'That's as maybe, but she's the only queen we've got and she's doing a grand job,' said Rochester. 'Your people ought to leave her alone. Anyway, let's talk about Guy.'

'What about him?' Foxy instinctively felt that, with Ted Rochester, every conversational gambit was a leading question. He had snakelike charm and ratlike cunning and didn't mind if it showed.

'This business about Ed Brampton seems to be taking up a lot of his time.'

'Oh . . . I don't think so,' followed by a silence. 'I think he's just generally busy. War work, you know.'

'Look,' said Rochester, suddenly urgent. 'Word gets about. Guy has been toiling round the clock on getting the Brampton business squared away. There seems to be a lot more effort going into giving

Ed a big final send-off than should be accorded a chap who, after all, should know one end of a pistol from the other.'

'Not necessarily, Ed was a fine . . .'

'The preparations – the whole buzz around Major Brampton's funeral – seem disproportionate, Foxy. I'm a journalist, it's our job to sniff the wind.'

'And what can you smell?'

'I find it hard to believe his death was an accident. And if it wasn't, what was it? Brampton was close to the Queen, we know that. Could he really have killed himself – if so, why? Or was it something else – something to do with Her Majesty?' He looked fiercely at Foxy. 'Because if it wasn't an accident or suicide, something very strange has occurred. And even in the midst of war, we have a right to know.'

'Don't you have anything else to write about?'

'That's what people always say when you're close to uncovering the truth.'

'Well, you won't be uncovering it from me. Even if I knew the answer to your questions – which I don't – I wouldn't tell you, Ted, are you mad?'

'You're close to Guy . . .'

'He's a friend of yours, too.'

'Not like you, though. After all, in Paris you and he . . . you know . . .'

Foxy stood up and glared. 'That's the trouble with you journalists!' she snapped. 'You hear something and want to believe it's true, so in your minds it *becomes* true. There was nothing between me and Guy in Paris – not like that, anyway. We were very close and he's, well . . .' Her voice drifted off.

'Too poor, is that it?' said Rochester wickedly.

'That's enough!'

'Sorry, I didn't mean that.' He did. 'But, you know, Edgar Brampton was a good man, decorated war hero and all that. A great support to the Queen. As such we should know what happened – I gather there isn't even going to be an inquest.'

'Why can't you be satisfied that it was just an accident?'

'Because when Guy called to tell me Brampton had died, he didn't make a very good job of it, frankly. Of course I ran the story in my newspaper more or less as he'd dictated it – but, you know, I didn't believe him. He was anxious and upset, it didn't ring true.'

'As it happens I remember that night very well. We'd just sat through a blitzkrieg, bombs falling everywhere, you're thinking all the time "Is it me next? Is it my turn now?" Nobody's in a right frame of mind after something like that.'

'Have it your way,' said Ted. 'I just have a feeling he wasn't telling me the truth – not the whole truth, anyway. If I knew where Brampton's widow was now, I'd go and see her.'

'Oh, I wouldn't do . . .' started Foxy, and then stopped herself.

The journalist said nothing but looked at her. Then: 'London may be crumbling and tumbling, our way of life may be in shreds and tatters, we may not be here tomorrow. Even if we are, who knows who'll be in charge, Churchill or the Führer, or Vera Lynn maybe? But while we struggle on and don't give up, there's such a thing as law and order.'

He picked up a pen and began to spin it between his fingers.

'If Edgar Brampton didn't die by accident – and what seasoned army officer who went through the whole of the First War with pistol in hand *would possibly allow it to go off next to his brain* – then it can only be one of two things. Suicide or murder. If it's murder, the public has a right to know. Even in the midst of war, we can't allow people to be bumped off – whether they live in a palace or in the Old Kent Road.'

Foxy thought about this for a moment. 'What do you want me to do?'

'Talk to Guy. Maybe I can help. He has this terrible job at the Palace, so I imagine he's been given the responsibility of sweeping it all under the carpet. He's only been back in Britain five minutes and knows next to nobody. On the other hand, I have a large number of contacts in the police and . . .' – he paused – 'elsewhere . . . and maybe I can help him with whatever it is he's got to do.'

'I can tell you, Ted, that all he's got to do is make sure the funeral goes off OK.'

'You say that. I somehow don't think it ends there.'

◆ ◆ ◆

Guy stood at the back of the Guards Chapel, watching. From long experience he'd learned that the congregation at a funeral says more about the recently deceased than any number of fine words launched from the pulpit.

The choir – boys only, the tenors and basses were away at war – sang 'The Strife is O'er, the Battle Done', and Ed Brampton was finally consigned to his maker.

The front of the chancel was filled with Adelaide's sizeable family, and a respectable cross-section of the Buckingham Palace hierarchy including Tommy Lascelles, Topsy Dighton, and the Keeper of the Privy Purse, Sir Ulick Alexander. Further back were a few dog-eared survivors of the First War, a pall-bearer detail from his old regiment, and a couple of officers from the Coats Mission including the tiresome Toby Broadbent.

But Guy's eyes were scanning the crowd's less obvious figures, guessing at their identity, watching their body language, hopelessly looking for clues.

I'm not much good as a detective, he thought; to be successful surely you must first learn the trade, and I haven't. I don't know who I'm looking for and I don't know how to look.

As the congregation filed out he caught Adelaide's eye but, as she was surrounded by family, all he received in return was a perfunctory nod. There'd be time to talk at the drinks party she'd arranged – but what had he got to tell her?

That her husband had been associating with a traitor?

'Did Foxy give you my message?'

He started. He hadn't seen Ted Rochester in the chapel but suddenly there he was – charming, suave, and as always, just a bit too pushy.

'Yes. She wasn't quite sure what it was about, and neither am I. May we talk some other time? I'm nominally in charge of this show.'

'I hear you're in a bit of a tailspin over Ed's death,' lied Rochester – he'd heard nothing of the kind.

'I don't know what you mean.'

'The suspicious circumstances.' This was sufficiently vague for the reporter to sound as though he knew what he was talking about.

Unversed in Fleet Street trickery, Guy replied, 'They may look suspicious to you, but they don't to Tommy Lascelles. What's good enough for him is good enough for me.'

'If there's something that needs to be cleared up, I have friends in all sorts of places who can be of help.'

'I've no idea what you're talking about. And thanks for the offer, but it's all under control.'

'Ah!' cried Rochester. 'So there *is* something!'

'Don't you have anything else to write about?' said Guy, irritatedly setting off for the funeral reception.

'Someone else said that to me last night,' came the self-satisfied reply. 'I'll repeat my answer to her – people always say that when you're close to uncovering the truth.'

'There's no truth to uncover. See you around, Ted, you won't be welcome at the wake.'

◆ ◆ ◆

Later that night, Guy and Rupert were jammed in a corner of The Grenadier. He'd ditched the mourning clothes and was wearing one of his Tangier shirts in pink linen.

'That's a bit bold,' said Rupe, handing him a whisky.

'Oh, shut up. I'm fed up with the whole business. I don't know how much longer I can stick it at the Palace.'

'What now?'

'Topsy Dighton, the Master of the Household, had me upstairs after the funeral and gave me his opinion on how it could have been done so much better.'

'Ah well. All over and done with now, though?'

'Not exactly. In fact, far from it. That file you showed me the other night.'

'I have no idea what you're talking about,' said Rupe with a steely smile, his eyes quickly scanning the pub.

'What? Ah, yes . . . yes,' stumbled his apprentice. 'Of course not. Well, to put it another way, I read something very interesting about Lady Easthampton. As a result, I went back to Markham Street and popped my head round the door.'

'How did you get in?'

'Rodie made me a key.'

Hardacre laughed out loud. 'And after all you've said about her! Anyway, why the visit?'

'I was looking for something, anything. If you'd been around I would have asked you to come along for the ride.'

'I've been busy.'

'Well, as it turned out I managed perfectly well without you. And found what I was looking for – thanks to your file; I wouldn't have known what to look for otherwise.'

Rupe winced at the mention of the file but let Guy continue.

'There was an envelope containing a handful of letters and cards signed "S" and "Suzy". Your friend Lady Easthampton.'

His flatmate looked around uneasily. 'We really shouldn't be talking about this in a pub, but what did they say?'

'Very little. Most were about making appointments to meet. Spattered with kisses and endearments but nothing actually suggesting an affair. And there was a book of photographs she'd given him which she'd signed. I brought them all back to the flat – you can have a look if you like.'

'What sort of dates were they written?'

'Well, they peter out about the time Adelaide took the children off to stay with her father. If you recall, the old buffer next door said that it was around then Ed disappeared and the house was left empty.'

'When did the correspondence start?'

'Some time towards the end of last year. The words she offers in them are a bit of a come-on, if you know what I mean, but there's nothing else in there. Though,' added Guy archly, 'I daresay the GPO, being experts on letters and cards and suchlike, will be able to read more into them than I have.'

'Ha ha. Your round.'

Guy waded through the crowd to the bar, and while waiting to be served found himself looking around to see if Rodie had arrived. He hadn't exactly agreed to go dancing when they saw each other in Claridge's, but the shirt must have been put on for a reason.

'So what do you think?' he said to Rupe when he brought the drinks back. 'Suzy Easthampton, I mean?'

'Well, if I were a betting man, I'd say she was up to her old tricks. She's spent the whole time since she got here from Poland sucking up to increasingly influential people. You can actually track her upward path from the odd MP through the Cabinet to the House of Lords and – eventually – ending up as the wife of a lord herself. She's had affairs with all of these men, I imagine, but if they were asked they'd claim they'd never heard of her.'

'I assume they *have* been asked?'

'In a manner of speaking.'

'And?'

'And it means the authorities don't have anything on her – her hands appear to be clean, and yet they know she's associated with this man Zeisloft who is working for the Germans.'

'Why don't you . . . er . . . why don't the authorities pick her up?'

'She's disappeared. That's to say, nobody's seen her since just before your colleague's unfortunate death. I'd say,' said Rupert, looking up at the ceiling, 'that what you've discovered could be of great use.'

'How?'

'Careless talk costs lives, old chap. Haven't you read the wall posters?'

'This is ridiculous,' said Guy. 'We can't go on talking like this. You don't work for the General Post Office, Rupe, and there's no point in pretending you do. We've been living in that flat too long for you to want to keep it up.'

'Let's go for a walk,' agreed Rupert, nodding. 'It may be incredibly noisy in here but there's always someone listening.'

They wandered out into the summer night, Guy casting one last glance around the pub to see if the small form of his burglar friend was seated somewhere. For once, there was silence in the skies and they wandered off into Belgrave Square, with its wide pavements and large stone houses. The place was deserted, save for a pair of policemen on their nightly beat.

'You've gathered I work for the government,' said Rupert. 'I guess it's pretty obvious. I'm going to leave you to guess which arm, but whatever your guess it's sure to be wrong. I let you have that report on Suzy Easthampton because it's our belief she's been trying to reach a certain target. You've seen the pattern of behaviour since her arrival in Britain – working her way up the social ladder – and I have to say she's done remarkably well to have got as far as she has. I think we have to put that down to the fact that she's sexually attractive – and that she has a powerful brain to go with it. She senses men's vulnerabilities and knows just how to play them.'

'I can't see that poor old Ed Brampton was such a good catch, if what you say is true.'

'Let's sit here.' Rupert pointed to a wooden bench within sight of the two bobbies. He lit a cigarette and went on, 'It wasn't Ed she was after, it was the Duke of Gloucester.'

'Gloucester? Why him, for heaven's sake?'

'You have to go back a bit, Guy, to understand this. Have you heard of Operation Willi?'

'No.'

'No reason why you should. This time last year the Nazis attempted to kidnap the Duke of Windsor and encourage him to work with Hitler on a peace settlement, or – if Hitler invaded Britain – to put him on the throne in place of the present king.'

'What? He'd never agree to something like that! Surely it can't be true!'

'There's more to it than that – but basically they thought they could buy him off. They put aside fifty million Swiss francs as bait.

It didn't work – and Windsor was sent to the Bahamas, where he's acquiring a nice tan.'

'And representing our interests.'

'You might say that. Anyway, Windsor is out of the way. But the Duke of Gloucester is not, he's most definitely here – and, we learn, very restless. He's a bit of a handful and the powers that be don't quite know what to do with him.

'We think that Lady Easthampton had been given the task of getting to know the Duke in order to work the same magic trick on him as they did on Windsor – only with better luck this time.'

'Explain the logic.'

'If Hitler invades, King George will either be locked up or shot. Harry Gloucester will be given the throne and ordered to sweeten the populace and keep them from revolting.'

'That's just incredible. It wouldn't work – people wouldn't stand for it.'

'Wouldn't they?' said Rupert. 'Look at the Channel Islands. Hitler's done a pretty good job there of subduing the populace. All you have to do is starve people, cut off their water and electricity, chuck a few in jail and shoot anybody that doesn't like it. It's not rocket science.'

'So what would be the point of King Harry if Hitler's ruling the country?'

'Maintaining the status quo. Keeping the natives quiet. If you pluck a new king from the existing royal house, people sooner or later will fall into line behind him.'

'I can't see that happening.'

'It's not what we think, it's what *they* think, and they're convinced they nearly pulled it off with the Duke of Windsor. Look at that visit to Germany just before the war, even raising his paw in a Heil Hitler salute.'

'To my certain knowledge, Harry Gloucester was blown up in France last year – by the Luftwaffe. I doubt he feels that warmly towards Herr Hitler after that.'

'You're wrong. You have only to read that series of articles in *The Week* about his German sympathies. And you can bet your bottom dollar he'd feel warmly about the prospect of the throne beneath that ample bottom of his.'

'Well . . .' Guy was about to tell Rupe the rumours of Gloucester's ambition circulating in Buckingham Palace, but then said, 'Look, this really isn't the place to talk. Let's go back to the flat, you can take a look at those Suzy Easthampton letters, and then maybe we can work out some rules of engagement. I'm just as bound by secrecy as you are.'

'Well, yes. I think you might be able to help me,' said Rupert, rising and nodding towards the police constables, who were going for a stroll.

'And I think you might be able to help *me*,' said Guy. 'Is there any whisky left, d'you think?'

CHAPTER NINE

There was a problem finding a shilling for the gas meter. Neither man had the right coin in his small change, though by the end of their search the kitchen table was covered in a sprawl of half-crowns, florins, sixpences and threepenny bits.

'Try the cup on the dresser.'

'OK, got one,' said Rupert, taking it down from a shelf. 'Oh, I nearly forgot, this is for you.'

He fished in his pocket and handed over an envelope.

'From?' said Guy, but he knew. The energetic scrawl, quirky and malformed, said it all.

He peeled it open to find two tickets to the Hammersmith Palais. On the back of one, the same hand had written 'Next Monday. 10 p.m. You've got my ticket too, so don't be late.'

No signature.

'I thought she was coming to the pub tonight. She was certainly threatening to.'

'*Bless my buttons. Give us a kiss!*'

'Ohh . . . put a sock in it!' rasped Rupert. 'How much longer, Guy?'

'Charlotte? She's just pleased to see us. Been alone all day – it's no way to treat a parrot.'

'*All's well! All's well! Where's the Captain?*' Charlotte edged along her perch and gave Rupert a venomous stare.

'All I can say is, I hope it won't be here much longer!'

'Rodie,' reminded Guy. He surprised himself with the mention of her name.

'Yes. She's working for me tonight.'

'Good Lord, really?'

Rupert opened a bottle of brown ale – 'All there is, I'm afraid.'

'I'll have a cup of tea.'

'So, as you say, the moment has come when we lay our cards on the table,' said Rupert. 'You've known, roughly speaking, what my job is more or less since you moved in here, only you're too much of a gentleman to come out and mention it. Obviously I know what you do. But not the details. It'd be pointless, and highly irregular, to have a full exchange of information between us, but it appears we might be able to help each other out. On that basis, are you prepared to break open the Official Secrets Act and let a few home truths come fluttering out?'

'In return for a similarly guarded breach of the rules?'

Rupert nodded and smiled.

'Go on, then,' said Guy. 'You go first.'

Rupert went over to the blackout curtains to make sure no light was escaping into the summer night. 'I don't think it would take a genius to work out that if Ed Brampton hid away a number of letters from his Hungarian lady friend, and those letters all pointed to a series of meetings, that something was going on between them.'

'Yes,' said Guy, 'but before you go any further, my understanding – from my clerk and from his widow – is that if Ed had eyes for anyone, it was the Queen, not some raven-haired Mata Hari, if that's what she is.'

'The Queen? Do you mean . . . ?'

'No, absolutely not. I think he was a bit besotted, that's all. We'll never know what she thought of him – she sent some lovely flowers, by the way.'

Rupert nodded vaguely. 'Suzy Easthampton's plan was to sleep her way to the top. Why she did it didn't seem to make any sense up until you discovered those letters – but now we have her and Ed Brampton in the same room, it makes everything much clearer.'

'If I understand it correctly, she's been in England since 1935,' said Guy, shaking his head. 'That's a long time to wait about to pull off something like this.'

'It may not have been like that in the first place. Remember, her boyfriend is an arms dealer. Maybe the original brief was to get close to a Cabinet minister or two during all that sabre-rattling before war was declared and see what developed from that. Then war came . . . and suddenly Zeisloft, if that's his real name, has an incredibly valuable asset to sell to the Germans – he owns an undercover agent, in place in London, mixing with the crème de la crème. Operation Willi has gone phut, but now here's another bite at the cherry. Our Suzy is directed to get as close to the Regent Designate as she can. So she turns her headlights on Ed, and away we go.'

'So how can I help? Do you want me to alert the King, through Tommy Lascelles?'

'Too soon for that – there's no concrete evidence. An adventuress turns up on our shores, finds herself a useless drunk of a husband who happens to be a lord, and that's it. But there *is* something else you can do.'

'Yes?' Guy was feeding Charlotte a piece of apple through the wires of the cage.

'Go and talk to Adelaide Brampton. You know her quite well, obviously.'

'And say what? You thought your husband was in love with the Queen but in fact it was a Hungarian spy all along?'

'Wives have a way of knowing things. She'll tell you more.'

Guy thought about the abandoned portrait in the hall.

'Well, I can certainly ask her. The whole thing comes full circle, really. And this is maybe where you can help me, Rupe.'

'Mm?'

'Adelaide's angry at the cover-up over his death. Tommy Lascelles wants the whole matter squared away and forgotten, and to the best of my ability I've done what he asked. But old Dighton – the Master of the Household – he's kicking up a fuss. My clerk told me that he and Ed had a very strange relationship, given that Ed was supposed to be working for Lascelles – Dighton would get him to do errands which had nothing to do with his official duties. There was a diary with the various things he did for Dighton, but that's gone missing.

'Then there's the question of what he was doing with a gun, since he didn't possess one, and how an experienced army officer could make the mistake of accidentally putting a bullet into himself, sufficient to cause his own death.

'And then there's the mystery of what happened to Ed in the last weeks of his life. The moment Adelaide retired to the country with the children, he shut up the house in Markham Street and disappeared – where did he go?'

'Maybe he was with Suzy Easthampton.'

'I assume you were having her tailed?'

Rupert looked embarrassed. 'Well,' he said, 'not exactly. And, you know, there's a war on. We were keeping an eye on her, but maybe not that close an eye. Not all the time. There are others.'

'Well,' said Guy, 'it seems to me you need to find out what's happened to her, while I talk to Adelaide and see if she's got anything to say about Lady Easthampton. Don't you have any idea where she might be?'

Rupert drained his beer.

'Her husband lives in a small house on the River Thames at Bray. Then there's the family estate in Perthshire – thousands of acres. If Lady E's disappeared up there we'll never find her. Well,' he admitted, 'not easily.'

'I've got something to add which I hope won't go any further,' said Guy. 'And in order to get something from Adelaide, I really need some help.'

'Go ahead.'

'As you know, until that last-minute reversal Ed Brampton was about to be promoted to become the Duke of Gloucester's private secretary – a good step up for him, but actually quite an important appointment from the Duke's point of view as well, because he needs a safe pair of hands to look after him. Tommy Lascelles told me the other day the Duke's always agitating for a bigger job – "We have to find something for him to do, he's becoming quite restless," he said.

'Though he rather looks down his nose at me, I think he was sounding me out to see whether I wanted to take the job on – I think they're a bit desperate. But Ed was the man who would have sorted him out, made him do his best for King and country and all that, not me.

'Why, then, was he suddenly dead? It wasn't an accident, Rupe, I'm sure of it. And then Sir Topham Dighton keeps pushing me to do something more with the investigation, but I've been thinking about that, and I ask myself whether in fact it isn't a devious trick – Dighton thinks I'm such a bumbling idiot that I'm sure to muck up any inquiry into Ed's death.'

'Why d'you say that?'

'Well, he keeps going on about what happened in Tangier. He calls me – in that supercilious way of his – his Tanja Man. He clearly thinks I'm a complete buffoon.'

Rupert gave a snort of laughter. 'Have some beer. I think you'd probably better tell me about Tangier.'

◆ ◆ ◆

A mile away in a windowless, airless basement room beneath the Air Ministry, a young Royal Air Force officer stood vaguely to attention with a vacant expression on his face.

Sitting opposite, three oldish men with many rings decorating their uniform sleeves looked down on him with ill-disguised contempt.

'A complete disgrace!' said one vehemently. 'Here we are, in the middle of the world's greatest conflict, and you go and do this!'

The young officer looked straight ahead, saying nothing.

'Of the three armed services we are the most courageous but the least regarded. We won the Battle of Britain but still we face an ingrained prejudice. We at the Ministry are doing our damnedest to try to correct that balance – to get rid of the prejudice! – and then this happens.'

Another, older, man joined in the assault. 'This is nothing short of a court martial offence which should put you behind bars and have you dismissed from the service. And after your very decent show in Spitfires, too. It's shameful!'

The third man, sitting between the other two, brought the proceedings to order. 'Flight Lieutenant Haskins,' he intoned, 'you are accused on two counts, the first of breaching the rationing regulations, punishable under the provisions of the National Security Arrangements. This offence carries a maximum of six months' imprisonment.

'Second, you are accused of bringing the service into disrepute. The offence means the forfeiture of your commission and your dismissal in disgrace from the Royal Air Force.'

'Permission to speak, sir.'

'Go ahead.'

'Will you be court-martialling Queen Mary as well?'

'What?'

'I understand she holds the rank of Honorary Colonel of the Queen's Own Rifles. I looked it up. The offence I'm accused of therefore undeniably includes another officer. And I ask myself why I am standing here, alone, unrepresented. Is this actually a court martial?'

The air vice-marshal sitting in the centre replied, 'I warn you to take care, young man. Remember your precarious position! In answer to your question, this is a *preliminary* hearing. To ascertain the facts of the case. To, er, limit the damage it may cause the service.'

The accused took this in, then said, 'I wonder if I may sit down?'

'You may not! Stand to attention!'

'I hope you don't mind,' said Haskins mildly. 'I've got a sore knee.'

'Oh, get him a chair!' the AVM irritatedly ordered a guard standing by the door. 'Now tell us in your own words what happened.'

'I was coming back to camp from Chipping Sodbury, but my transport let me down,' said the officer, leaning back comfortably. 'So I was thumbing a lift. I wasn't having much luck when up drew this large Rolls-Royce and the chauffeur told me to hop in. Well, I wasn't going to say no to that!'

'What happened then?'

'I didn't recognise her at first, I'm not much of a royalist to be honest, but gradually it dawned on me that the old lady in the car was Queen Mary. She made me sit next to her and was all chummy and nice – apparently she quite often takes pity on servicemen thumbing lifts, and it was my lucky day.

'She started asking me about my war, and I told her about being shot down over the Channel in my Spitfire and how,' he said resentfully, 'I was now only considered ready for the scrapheap. "A burned-out case", they called me.

'She asked what I was doing now and I told her. "The best they can find for a chap with eight enemy kills and a Distinguished Flying Cross is to give him the kitchens to manage," I said, and at that she got frightfully interested – not in my DFC, mind, but the kitchens.

'"Do you ever get any sausages?" she said, and I told her of course we do. "We don't have sausages at Badminton," she said. "I love sausages. Can you get me some sausages?"

'What could I do? She's the queen – well, she used to be – and it was an order. I went back to the camp and had a think about it. It's not difficult to move the rations around a bit so I got hold of a few pounds of sausages and took them over to Badminton. A big place, it is, a duke lives there and . . .'

'Get on with it!'

'I was told to introduce myself to someone by the name of Coke, a sort of ADC to the Queen. Well, I can tell you, this chap was embarrassed. He realised straight away it was a breach of regulations; he said to me, "She's always doing this. She goes to people's houses and we come away with items of furniture. She's a ruddy magpie! And now this," he says, "this really is bad. Can't you take 'em back?"

'I told him I'd already "lost" them in the accounts book and it would draw attention if I brought them back. "Give 'em to Her

Maj and God bless her," I said. "Hope she enjoys 'em. You're starving her here, do you know that?"

'He thought that was very funny and told me what they'd had for dinner the night before. A right old bean-feast.'

'Did you take any money from him?'

'Ten shillings. He insisted. Said I was to put it in the mess fund if nothing else.'

'Did you?'

'No, actually. I went into the officers' mess, bought a round of drinks, and raised a toast to the royal family.'

'He took money,' said one of his inquisitors to the chairman. 'Another offence.'

'Permission to speak,' said Haskins.

'Yes,' came the weary reply.

'Surely the offence is with Her Majesty? She instigated the . . . crime, if that's what it is. I'm just a junior officer acting on orders from a senior officer who also just happens to be a queen.'

'Did you get the impression she'd done this before?'

'I have no idea. No harm done, though, surely? It was a lot of sausages but we have a thousand men on the base, it was a drop in the ocean. She's got a bit of a cheek, though – she asked me when my day off was and told me I was to report to the house and volunteer for what she called "wooding" – chopping down trees and the like. I told her I had my hands full in the kitchen. She's a rum one, that.'

'Let me explain something to you, Flight Lieutenant,' said the air vice-marshal crisply. 'If this gets out there'll be all hell to pay – the royal family using their influence to breach rationing laws, and having a good tuck-in at the same time as the rest of the nation is practically starving. It's just the sort of thing the *Daily Mirror*, or that frightful chap at the *News Chronicle* – what's his name, Rochester? – would love to get their teeth into.'

'It's not likely to get out, though, is it?' said Haskins. 'It being the royals?'

'Why do you think you're here?' barked the senior officer. 'Somebody reported you to the RAF Police. That same somebody could just as easily pick up the telephone and dial a number in Fleet Street.'

'And so they ought. Jolly good story,' said the young pilot, only half under his breath.

'Flight Lieutenant, your actions risk bringing the Royal Air Force into the gravest disrepute. The light-hearted way you approach this scandalous breach of the law is deeply regrettable. Were it not for your distinguished service during the Battle of Britain . . .'

'Yes?' said the officer, sensing – as he'd sensed at ten thousand feet, when he saw the Messerschmitt raiders turn tail and skedaddle eastwards, mission vanquished – that the threat had passed.

'Were it not for that service I should have you arrested. As it is, you will be posted to Canada, where you will instruct whippersnappers like you how to fly a Spitfire properly. Dismissed!'

'Righty-o,' said Haskins, and wandered out without so much as a salute.

CHAPTER TEN

'You've never been to Tangier?'

'No.'

Guy thought of his abandoned house smothered in bougainvillea and surrounded by fig trees like huge umbrellas, the light at dawn, and the long, seductive sunsets. 'It's not everyone's cup of tea – pickpockets and counterfeiters and everybody changing foreign currency as fast as they can. Intriguers and spies and very rainy in winter. Very much an acquired taste.' He could have said: It is paradise to me and I would happily die there.

'A bit dicey now, though.'

'Only up to a point. The Spanish marched in and took control in 1940 and declared it a neutral city; that's to say, it's *they* who run the place, and everyone else – the Germans and British, the Italians and French – are all expected to be on best party manners.'

Rupert lit a cigarette. 'How did you come to – how shall we say it – work for our government out there?'

Guy looked up at the canvas on the wall. The sunset he'd painted, going down over the Grand Socco, looked a lot like Turner but with deeper, more passionate colours.

'There's a remarkable British colony out there – everybody knows everybody, and mostly they all get along together. The doctor is a dour old Scotsman called Harry Dunlop, but it's his wife,

Teddy, who's the life and soul of the party. By coincidence she's also our top spy there. Once the war got under way, every single nation worth its salt turned up in Tangier because of its strategic importance – it dominates the gates of the Mediterranean, you see, only nine miles of water between it and Europe. So if you want to invade anywhere, you pass right by our door. First step in your plan for world domination is to set up an embassy or legation in Tangier and spy on all the others.'

'I thought the capital city was Rabat. Surely the embassies are there?'

'Nobody seems to take any notice of that. The kind of people who turned up in Tangier once war was declared weren't interested in diplomacy, but they did pack an awful lot of cloaks and daggers in their suitcases.'

'But why you? Don't tell me our government has so few trained agents that they had to haul you in off the street to help out!'

'It wasn't quite like that. Just before war broke out I was painting away quite successfully and had an exhibition in the El Minzah Hotel. A chap who called himself Henri d'Orléans came into the gallery one day and bought two.'

'Orléans? Isn't he . . . ?'

'Obviously, as an artist you know if someone buys a picture, they like your work – but if they buy two, they *love* it. So I took the trouble to go over and talk to this man and we got to know each other. I thought he was rather grand, the way he talked, and yes, you're right – it turned out his title was Comte de Paris, and if France still had a monarchy, he'd be King Henri VI today.'

'This is where you got your taste for royalty, Guy!'

'Very funny. He lives in a place along the coast called Larache, and he invited me down there to paint some exteriors of the house. When I got there he'd come and sit and talk while I painted, but he only seemed to have one topic of conversation – the restoration of the monarchy in France. He thought it was extraordinary the way the House of Windsor had managed to cling on after the Abdication – "In my country, King Edward would have been guillotined" – but he felt the coming war was sure to alter things in his favour.'

'But they haven't had a throne in France for a hundred and fifty years! He can't honestly think it's ever going to come back.'

'He thought that if France was overrun by Germany, like in the First War and the Franco-Prussian war, his people – wanting strong leadership and fed up with the politicians – would rally behind him. He still believes that to this day.'

'What an extraordinary encounter. But what happened, how did you get pulled into becoming a government agent?'

'Well, I finished the paintings and came back to Tangier. I was having dinner with Dr and Mrs Dunlop and, naturally, told them what I'd been doing. Teddy – Mrs Dunlop – arranged to come round to my studio the next day to look at some of the sketches, and that's when the whole mess started.'

Rupert had taken out a small notebook with a 'GPO' stamp on its cover. 'D'you mind if I make a note?'

'As long as it doesn't compromise what I'm doing at the Palace.'

'For my eyes only. Go on.'

'Teddy Dunlop swore me to secrecy, then told me I could be of immense assistance to the British government. She said that officially Britain could have no contact with someone like the Count of Paris because he basically wants to overthrow the French Republic – who just happen to be our closest allies in this war. On the other hand, he has a huge following in France. If the Vichy government falls, and the people decide they don't want de Gaulle, that's Henri's chance to grab the throne. And he will if he can – remember those bloody riots in Paris only six or seven years ago, when people were on the streets demanding the return of the monarchy?'

'Several people were killed, I seem to remember.'

'Well, it shows the level of feeling, and Henri d'Orléans believes he can benefit from that. Teddy Dunlop told me that if he becomes King Henri, they want him in their pocket. So does everyone else, of course, and the general feeling is he'll give his friendship to the highest bidder.'

'Sounds like a trustworthy sort of chap.'

'He's French, Rupe, what do you expect? On the other hand, you have to see it from his perspective – he wants his throne back. There has to be a line of communication between him and London, one strong enough to airlift him away should the need occur. In the absence of anything more concrete, I, apparently, was it.'

'You became the go-between.'

Guy nodded. 'We'd got on very well while I was down at Larache, and Henri said his son needed painting lessons. He was only six but very talented, and his father wanted an established artist to bring him on. So back I went to Larache and became court painter to the French throne – ha! – plus the Count's unofficial contact with the British government.'

Rupert was scribbling something in his notebook and didn't look up immediately. 'Did he mention the Cagoule?'

'That bunch of thugs? The men who've pledged to put him back on the throne? He pretends he doesn't know what they're up to, but he told me enough to make me think he does. All too clearly.'

'They're bankrolled by Mussolini. Technically, therefore, your Henri's the enemy.'

'Rupe,' said Guy, 'if there's one thing I've learned since this war began, it's that there are ten different kinds of enemy. Some are more enemy than others. With people like the Count of Paris, who could be our greatest ally tomorrow, you have to screw up your eyes, blank your mind, and erase the word from your vocabulary.'

'Humph,' growled Rupert. 'So then what – you're staying down the coast with the Count and his son, passing back what you learn to this Mrs Dunlop. What went wrong?'

Guy sighed. 'He was happy with the arrangement – he wanted Britain to be his friend as much we wanted to be his.'

'So what happened? You fell out with the Count?'

'He fell out with me. Everything was going smoothly, and once war was declared he wanted to enlist in the British Army. But then in 1940 he thought the evacuation from Dunkirk – leaving France to face the future alone – was the grossest possible betrayal. He called on his followers to support the Vichy government, so once again, he is our enemy.'

Guy went on: 'By this time, Tangier was filling up with legations and embassies and consulates. The Germans and their hangers-on commandeered the Rif Hotel; our side stuck to the El Minzah. The two places were stuffed with double agents who took money from both sides for telling basically the same story – just hopping from one bar to the other, then back again. And of course everyone's room was being turned upside down; it was chaotic. Then the Americans came in, sending a dozen men calling themselves vice-consuls but who were nothing of the kind – they were spies. Rather superior material to our own lot, intellectually and experience-wise, and so Teddy Dunlop persuaded me to cosy up to them, painting being an innocent-looking sort of profession to their eyes.'

'And?'

Guy sighed. 'It was a hot night, and I was sitting with one of them, a man called Don Williams from Cincinnati, in a café near the Rif Hotel where the Germans hang out. To cut a long story short, I suggested he infiltrate a group of evacuees from Gibraltar, boys with rather too much drink inside them, and see whether he couldn't get inside the hotel when they went in.

'A high-ranking German military attaché was there – Colonel Reiner – and with him some popsy from Berlin who's said to be close to Hitler. She started making scathing remarks about the Allies, and one of the Gib boys got up, walked over, and smacked her in the mouth. There was a spectacular brawl, blood all over the place, and Williams got caught up in it. When they discovered he was American – well, let's put it this way, the fine diplomatic balancing act so carefully crafted by the Spanish was on the brink of collapse. The Germans had captured – or "arrested" – Williams, and were leaning on the Spanish authorities to have every other US citizen kicked out of Tangier.'

He gave a derisive laugh. 'It was put to me that the whole course of the war could have altered if the Spaniards hadn't taken a firm hand, and of course I – the innocent British artist – carried the can for the whole damned incident. I have to tell you, Rupe, the whole thing appalled me. I'm a painter, not a spy. But it looked like a British agent had deliberately put the cat amongst the pigeons, pushing a US diplomat into a brawl involving a high-ranking Nazi officer. Whitehall using any tactic it could to drag America into the war. It wasn't like that, but somebody had to take the blame and it was me. Teddy Dunlop had me airlifted out to Lisbon that night, and I was sent home for a carpeting at the Foreign Office.'

Rupert leaned back in amazement. 'But, Guy, you weren't employed by them!'

'As far as they were concerned, I was. What's more, when I got to Whitehall, instead of apologising for getting me into this mess, they claimed I'd done it deliberately. "How can we possibly trust the word of someone who appears to live so well on no money? Who have you been seeing, who have you been talking to? Are you a double agent, like everyone else in that fly-infested hole?" All that kind of nonsense! I didn't want to leave Tangier, Rupe – it's my home, for heaven's sake – but I had no choice. And once I was in the hands of MI6 or the Foreign Office, or whatever you want to call it, I was their property.'

'Reliant on them.'

Guy sighed. 'Yes. Then after a bit they realised it wasn't my fault. They'd made a huge fuss, threatening me with jail or the firing squad, whichever was my preference, but now they didn't know what to do. So instead they offered me a job. I had no money – everything I had was back in Tangier and I'd come home to a country at war and with no idea what to do with myself, so I said yes. They found me this flat and . . . wait a minute, Rupe . . .' Guy's voice faltered. He paused for a long moment before speaking again. 'The thought has only just occurred. I was given this flat by the Foreign Office . . . but they said I would have to share it.'

His flatmate smiled and shrugged his shoulders. 'It was lucky that I was just looking for a place myself at the time. We . . .'

'You know,' said Guy slowly, 'the timing – it seems strange. Your suddenly turning up like that. Almost as if you'd been sent by somebody to keep an eye on me. *Spy* on me. Now, why on earth should someone in so lowly a position like me need to be kept under observation?'

'I wouldn't put it quite like that,' replied Rupert smoothly. 'But you certainly need looking after. You shouldn't be allowed out alone at night.'

◆ ◆ ◆

The great hall of the National Gallery in Trafalgar Square echoed mournfully. Stripped of the great paintings of Van Dyck and Velázquez, Holbein and Raphael, its walls were now bare but for the occasional token canvas, and its grandeur seemed suddenly overblown and pointless.

Gas masks over their shoulders, Foxy Gwynne and her American friend paid their shilling entrance fee, filed in between the gilt-topped marble pillars and sat down. They were there to hear the great Myra Hess play her lunchtime concert.

'Mrs Churchill,' whispered Betsey Cody, pointing. They could just see the back of a stern, angular hat belonging to the Prime Minister's wife. 'Randolph came to dinner the other night – what a bore that man is! But he gave me an idea.'

'And the Queen,' interrupted Foxy, also pointing. 'With that supercilious Sir Kenneth Clark practically sitting in her lap!'

'From the look on her face, I don't think she minds in the slightest.'

Both twisted their heads round as they waited for the great pianist to ascend the platform. Myra Hess's lunchtime concerts were an oasis of calm and a celebration of normality; the sandbagged room with its uncomfortable canvas chairs was crammed with civilians, uniforms, and a sprinkling of schoolchildren.

'Oh,' said Foxy, 'and over there, Guy's spooky friend Rupert something-or-other.'

Betsey looked at the roneoed concert programme and wrinkled her nose. 'Scarlatti. Bach, Schubert, Brahms,' she said in a bored voice. 'Why not something livelier?'

'Cole Porter? Noël Coward? I don't think she plays those. We can go to the Café de Paris for that.'

Betsey shot her a look.

'Oh, Lord. All those dead, an absolute tragedy – you forget so quickly these days!'

'Not me. I lost a few good friends that night.' Both women, recalling the bomb which had demolished the restaurant only weeks before, pushed out their chins and looked straight ahead as the famous pianist took to the stage, a uniformed man following to turn the pages for her. The music began.

They lingered once the concert was over, wandering back to the entrance through a series of abandoned side galleries where empty gilt frames hung eerily on the walls.

'I had a thought about your friend Guy,' said Betsey. 'You asked about an art gallery, and my dear rich friend Mr Gulbenkian will provide it. He has a share in a gallery off Piccadilly and was going to show Rex Whistler's war paintings, but with Rex off with the Guards in France, he's had to resort to a load of prints in the window which nobody's interested in. I told him about Guy's portrait of you – it truly is magnificent – and Gulbenkian said, "That's what we need! We need faces – wartime faces. Famous faces and private faces – war workers, ARP people, the ladies in the East End with their hair in curlers. And the smoke-blackened firemen – as well as the rich and the famous, of course. Nobody's done a show like that, and it'll make your friend's name!"'

'Well, I don't think he has many portraits at his disposal. He left most of his work in Africa.'

'He'd better get cracking, then!' exclaimed Betsey. 'He could start off with Pamela Churchill. She was there at dinner with Randolph the other night – the life and soul of the party, my dear, dazzlingly good-looking. They say the Prime Minister envies his son more than a bit!'

They laughed.

'And if Guy did a good job of Pamela, who knows – maybe old Winston would let him into Number 10 to paint him as well.'

They paused at the top of some marble stairs. 'I don't know,' said Foxy guardedly, 'he did that portrait of me because, well . . . let's say he has to be inspired. He doesn't usually do portraits, more huge seascapes and skyscapes.'

'Are you saying he's *not* a portraitist?'

'I'm the most famous person he's painted,' laughed Foxy, 'and nobody knows who I am.'

'Famous Paris model! Soon to be the Countess of Sefton!' Foxy sensed that, despite her riches, her friend was envious of this last part.

'This is very sudden. He's working flat out at Buckingham Palace just now and there are some odd things going on there, Betsey, only I can't say what.'

'Well, Gulbenkian was very clear. He's keeping the prints in the window for the summer because it's not a time when people want to wander round galleries. But come the autumn he wants an exciting new show. Don't say I don't try hard on your behalf! Invite us both to dinner next week.'

'I won't do that,' said Foxy. 'Hugh wouldn't like it – Guy, I mean.'

Betsey raised an eyebrow. 'OK, well, tell you what I'll do. I'll invite Guy and Pamela – Randolph's going back to war and she'll be at a loose end. If she likes Guy and he can see a portrait in her, then he'll have got off to a flying start.'

'The poor lamb,' said Foxy. 'He came away from Tangier in such a rush he didn't even bring his brushes with him.'

'I daresay the Lord will provide,' said Betsey confidently. 'And there's a room we don't use in the roof of our apartment – that can be his studio if he hasn't got one of those either.'

'You *are* generous, Bets!'

'And why not. Only one thing.'

'What's that?'

'Pamela Churchill. Guy's not to fall in love with her like he did you. She's taken.'

'Well, obviously. She only got married a couple of years ago. And there's the baby.'

'No, no, you don't understand. She's got a boyfriend, darling. Name of Harriman.'

'*Averell* Harriman? President Roosevelt's special envoy? He's old enough to be her father!'

'Anything's better than that beastly Randolph, darling! But just in case – because she *is* a bit frisky – you just tell Guy to behave himself.'

'Poor lamb,' sighed Foxy. 'And he's so in need of love.'

CHAPTER ELEVEN

The train steamed slowly to a halt with a squeal of brakes and an angry puff of smoke, but though the carriages were full, Guy was the only person to alight on to the small platform. There were no signs to identify this anonymous stopping-place, but the guard put him right: this was Badminton.

The journey had been long and uncomfortable, but had provided plenty of opportunity for Guy to go over his meeting with Tommy Lascelles the previous day.

'Treason!' the courtier had barked, angrily polishing his spectacles.

'Beg your pardon, sir?'

'Treason, Harford, treason! That's what the newspapers will call it if it ever gets out.'

'Sorry, sir, I don't understand. Who has . . . ?'

'Communicating with the enemy is a treasonable offence, Harford. Surely you know that!'

Guy started guiltily. Was the whole business with the Count of Paris and Mussolini now about to rebound on him? Hadn't he gone through enough anguish with the dust-up over the American spy and the Nazi general's mistress?

'The Count of Paris is both our enemy and our ally, sir. It's a difficult situation . . .'

'Paris? I'm not talking about Paris!' snapped Lascelles. 'It's Queen Mary I'm talking about, Harford. The King's mother!'

'I don't quite follow.'

The courtier calmed down a little as he reset the spectacles on his nose. 'Of course you don't, dear boy,' he said. 'Come and sit down. Cup of tea?'

'Er, well . . . thank you.' Guy fingered his collar uncomfortably.

'I am sending you on a mission which requires tact, diplomacy, and an iron will. Are you equal to that?' The old boy was leaning forward with an earnest look on his face.

'Of course,' said Guy, thinking, why me? I'm the one who does the parrots and the laundry – great missions requiring grown-up thinking aren't assigned to people like me. Unless . . .

'The matter,' said Tommy, offering the sugar bowl, 'is both simple and highly complicated. In a nutshell, it may be said that Queen Mary has been breaking the rules and communicating with the enemy.'

'Good Lord.'

'She doesn't seem to realise that the articles of war apply to her as much as they do to everyone else. That, of course, is understandable – in her time she has been empress of half the world, as well as queen consort in these isles – she's a woman to whom nobody has ever said no. She is decent, honourable, committed to this country winning the war, and believes in doing her bit. It's just that nobody can tell her that she's got to stop writing to her German relatives. It won't do, Harford, it just won't do!'

'Who's she writing to?'

'All sorts. She's related to half of German royalty, and to many more who are not royal. Heaven knows how she gets the letters away from these shores – pigeon post, I shouldn't wonder – but she does. There's a coterie of friends who are so devoted to her they'll do anything – including, in this case, risking imprisonment and disgrace – to accede to her wishes. It's got to stop, Harford!'

'Surely His Majesty . . . the King . . . he's her son – can't he have a word with her?'

'I don't know how effective that would be. He may be king, but to her he's just another of her sons. He's not the one to tackle her.'

'Well, sir, surely you yourself . . .'

Lascelles looked at him sharply. 'I maintain a professional distance,' he said defensively. 'I can't be seen to be accusing His Majesty's mother of treason.'

'But you just have, sir.'

'Don't be more of an idiot than you already are,' came the withering reply. 'My job is to choose the best path out of this mess and to ensure its success.'

And to keep yourself out of the mire, thought Guy. But he replied, 'How can I be of help?'

'Good chap. I want you to go down to Badminton and give her a personal message. Committing it to paper would be too risky, it has to be verbal.'

Too risky for you, thought Guy. The paper trail would lead straight back to your office if the plan comes unstuck.

'And I'm to say?'

'Stop it. Stop writing to these people. Respect our wishes, don't damage your son's chances of a successful reign. Don't allow people ever to say, in the middle of war, "one rule for the royals, another for us" – that's a sure way to fire up a revolution.'

'Forgive me, sir, but aren't I a bit junior for this?'

'You're young. You're . . . personable. She has a soft spot for chaps like you. She likes paintings. You can talk to her about paintings if you like. Anything to get her to see how stupid this is. I mean . . .'

'Yes, sir?'

'Look, I really shouldn't mention this, but it does illustrate the point. Have you heard of Queen Ena of Spain?'

'Of course.'

'The late king's first cousin. He was very fond of her. He would have been appalled to learn she was literally kicked out of the country at the outbreak of war.'

'I didn't know about that, sir.'

Tommy rattled his teacup. 'She's one of us, really. Only, she's not. Granddaughter of Queen Victoria, of course, born at Balmoral. Made the mistake of marrying the King of Spain, a most undesirable type.'

'How so?'

'A womaniser. A very unsteady figure. And, of course, throneless since the rise of General Franco. Queen Ena and the king parted company some time ago and she came back here to live in London before the war. But booted out, as I say, by the Foreign Office at the outbreak of hostilities. A complete disgrace.'

'Why, if she's a member of our royal family?'

'Forget that. Because of her marriage, she's a Spanish citizen – so she's neutral. But her parents were both Germans – so she's the enemy.'

'Ridiculous.'

'That's war for you. Anyway, she's currently in Rome – enemy territory – and Queen Mary is writing to her. Worse, Queen Ena is short of cash and Queen Mary has arranged for her to be paid money from here in London via Switzerland. That, to forestall your next question, is in flagrant contravention of our currency laws. You can't write to the enemy, Harford, and you sure as hell can't send them money!'

'I really don't see what I can say that will help change her mind.'

'She needs a short sharp shock from someone with the guts to deliver it. Someone she doesn't know. With her, unfortunately, familiarity breeds contempt – or something like it – therefore no courtier she knows would be able to make the slightest impression on her. She's a wonderful woman, make no mistake, but in certain circumstances, a nightmare.'

'I'll need the list of names of people she's written to, and some idea of what she's been saying.'

The old courtier pointed to a file on his desk. 'Read it in the anteroom and memorise. It doesn't leave my office.'

'Very well. When do you want me to go?'

'Tomorrow. They'll be expecting you.'

'Thank you.' Guy rose to leave.

'One other thing,' said Lascelles, motioning him to sit down again. 'This sausages business.'

'Sir?'

'It's got totally out of hand. I've had the Judge Advocate General here warning of the colossal public reaction there'd be if it ever got out – worse than writing to the enemy, worse than illegal money deals. Sausages! He's beside himself with rage.'

'Sausages?' blinked Guy. 'I don't think I . . .'

Lascelles explained.

'Now, when you go down to Badminton and talk to Her Majesty, I want you also to warn her of the dangers arising from members of the royal family breaking food regulations.'

'Food regulations,' said Guy, shaking his head in disbelief. Parrots, laundry, now sausages – what a job.

'There'll be another word for it if Fleet Street gets hold of the story. "Royal family and the black market", they'll say. "Queen uses her position to stock up on sausages".'

'Is she still doing it?'

'No. The RAF officer in question has been exiled to the snowy wastes of the Yukon. If he doesn't freeze to death, he'll die of boredom. I doubt anyone else in his outfit would be foolish enough to follow suit, however much they might love the royals. But you have to din it into Her Majesty's brain that rules are rules, Harford. If our royal family can't behave properly in a crisis, what hope is there for the rest of the country?'

◆ ◆ ◆

'Badminton House, sir?' The immaculately uniformed driver gave Guy a snappy salute and a wink. 'For Her Majesty, is it?'

What *have* I let myself in for, thought Guy, as he slid into the passenger seat of the jeep. He gazed idly as the vast stone mansion gently rolled into view, but its grandeur was lost on him – he could only think that nobody in the whole royal apparatus had the nerve to tell off Queen Mary and neither did he. But while the cowards hid behind the Buckingham Palace railings, here he was.

'Loverly voo, sir,' said the driver as they reached the curve in the drive. He must have said it a hundred times before.

'Yes,' said Guy. Please turn this car around and take me back to the station.

'Been quite busy since 'Er Majesty got 'ere. She loiks gardenin' a lot. If I was you, sir, I wouldn't volunteer for any gardenin' work. You'll come to regret it.'

The jeep drew up by a side entrance and a pretty secretary came out to greet him.

'Mr Harford? I hope you didn't have too bad a journey.'

'No, no.'

'The Palace weren't clear whether you'd be staying, but there's a room made up in the East Wing. It's a bit cramped around here these days.'

'No,' repeated Guy, his eye travelling around the parkland before returning to his host. 'There's a late train. My business won't take long. Queen Mary . . .'

The girl's eyes narrowed. 'Won't you come inside, sir? There's a cup of tea waiting.'

'Please don't "sir" me, nobody else does. It's Guy. Or Mr Harford, if you're on party manners.'

She blushed slightly and smiled.

'Come along in, I'm going to introduce you to Her Majesty's Comptroller, Sir Stretford Mariot. He's waiting for you in the Yellow Drawing Room.'

The figure waiting to greet him looked like a character from P. G. Wodehouse, with a thin, highly coloured face adorned with a minute moustache. He had a nervous sniff and a handkerchief stuck in his cuff.

'Very good of you to come,' he said stiffly. 'There's tea. Or sherry. Sherry's Cyprus.'

'Tea, thank you, Sir Stretford.'

'You're Harford, of course. Tommy told me. I believe you shared an office with Edgar Brampton. I was rather fond of him.'

'Yes. A very sad occurrence.'

'Yes, yes. Yes. I believe there is to be no inquest.'

'I believe not.'

'Quite right, quite right. Least said, soonest mended.'

I wonder what he means by that, thought Guy.

'Let me begin with an apology,' said the old dinosaur, pulling out his handkerchief and fluffing his nose with it.

'Please don't even . . .'

'Her Majesty is not here,' said Mariot. 'She was told you were coming but decided there were more pressing matters.'

Thank heavens, thought Guy. I wasn't able to get a wink of sleep at the prospect of giving her a dressing-down.

However, he replied, 'That's awkward, sir. I've come on the express instructions of the King, with a specific message for Her Majesty to be delivered by word of mouth. When will she be back?'

Mariot shifted in his chair. 'You have to understand Queen Mary is a restless soul. She hasn't taken at all well to country life – she's lived an almost completely urban existence for the past seventy years. Why, when we were driving here on the first day I pointed out the workers in the hayfields to her and she said, "Oh, so *that's* what hay looks like, I've always wondered when people talk about it."'

'Ha ha.'

'It's true. She is slowly bedding herself in but she gets wanderlust . . . Oh,' he said, checking himself, 'mustn't use a German word! She misses her children and grandchildren, and says she feel like an evacuee.' Sir Stretford waved his hand at the silk-lined walls and gilded furniture. 'Though of course all such feelings are relative. When I'm not on duty here, I live in a converted garage.'

And I live in a flat with a leaking gas ring over the top of Victoria bus station, thought Guy.

'But this does put me in a difficult position, sir.'

'Nothing to be done,' said the old boy, shrugging his shoulders. 'You can wait here till she comes back. I gather there's a bed for you.'

'When will she return?'

'Hard to say. She has no engagements till the middle of next week, so it could be then. I imagine she's in London with her nose in some furniture shop today. Always her first point of call. Then there's the bookshops and art dealers and exhibitions. There's no stopping her!'

'Well, Sir Stretford, I've been sent here to speak to her directly.'

'Look,' said the old boy, reaching for the sherry decanter but then deciding against, 'you may just as well face the possibility that Queen Mary has disappeared because she knew you were coming. Is this about Queen Ena?'

'Since you put it that way, yes.'

'I'll have a word. Tommy warned me. Better that you aren't involved.'

'And then there's the matter of the sausages.'

Mariot's eyes crinkled. 'Absolutely delicious!' he chortled. 'You know, the Duchess here does the most amazing job catering for everybody, but there are *never any sausages*. I think Her Grace probably feels they're a bit infra dig, but we in the Household absolutely adore them! Why, only the other night—'

'I hate to put this so crudely, Sir Stretford, but this is no laughing matter. On the information I've been given, it appears the queen has broken the law not once, but twice, on matters which could send others who committed them to jail.

'And even that really isn't the point,' he went on. 'If the British public, fighting for King and country and all that, discover that the royal family is breaking the rules, their attitude may be "if they can break the law, why shouldn't I?"'

'You sound a bit po-faced,' said Mariot with a laugh. 'Around this family, nobody tells tales. And what the eye doesn't see, the heart doesn't grieve over. Queen Mary has given a lifetime of service to this country, and to the Empire, and if in her latter years she finds it difficult to follow every rule and law some idiot has passed, I think the wisest thing to do is look away and forget all about it.'

'*I* don't mind in the slightest,' said Guy. 'That was the speech I was given to deliver by Tommy Lascelles, and I've done it. I'm sorry it had to be you who received it, but I have to confess I'm glad I didn't have to tell the queen to her face.'

'Well, you've said it. I'll pass it on, though perhaps not in words which sound quite so schoolmasterish. Let me find some whisky,' Sir Stretford smiled, and walked over to the mantelpiece and the bell pull. 'And now to Edgar Brampton – what can you tell me about his passing?'

Guy gave an edited version of events.

'It's just that we were in the same regiment – years apart of course – and I rather liked what I saw of him. A kinsman of Sir Topham, of course.'

'Yes.'

'Not a man I care to see a lot of,' said Sir Stretford, sniffing. The way he talked he might almost be royal himself. 'But I did see Brampton at my club just before he died, we had a drink together. He seemed rather anxious.'

'I believe he was disappointed in not getting that job with the Duke of Gloucester.'

'It wasn't that. He was telling me about Lady Easthampton – you know, Gerald FitzMalcolm's daughter-in-law. Gerald is an old friend, and somehow Brampton knew that because he brought it up in conversation.

'We were having a drink in the bar and he asked if I'd gone to the wedding, and I said yes. Absolute corker of a bride, even if she isn't in *Debrett's*. And young Easthampton was lucky to get her – he's pretty useless, you know. Needed someone to give him backbone, and from what I saw, she had plenty of that!'

'What did he want to know, if you don't mind my asking?'

'Come for a walk and I'll tell you. But first, any other business now we've the money-laundering and the black-marketing out of the way?'

'Well, there is one thing . . .' began Guy doubtfully.

'What is it?'

'Do you think life here at Badminton might be enlivened by the presence of a parrot?'

Sir Stretford stood, suddenly and in some agitation. 'You don't mean . . . *Charlotte?*' he breathed.

'Well, yes, as a matter of fact. Of course, you know all about her. But she's currently homeless and I thought it might be a nice gesture to reunite her with the queen.'

'Nothing. Could. Be. Further. From . . .' stuttered the baronet. 'There's absolutely not a single bally snowball's chance in hell of that animal ever coming here – now, or in a century's time, when no doubt it will still be alive, demanding to know where the bally Captain is.'

'I just thought . . .'

'No, no, no! If you can't get rid of it, put it in a sack and drown it – stick it in the oven and roast it! Queen Mary absolutely hates the thing! She was forced to live with it all of her married life – all! – that's forty-three years, for heaven's sake! The blasted animal interrupted every conversation they ever had and would sit on His Majesty's shoulder most of the day when they were at home. Even when he was terribly ill, but the worst had passed, the bally bird was back on his shoulder and the nurses had the devil's own job. No, Mr Harford, that parrot was a jail sentence to Her Majesty – one from which she has finally, mercifully, been released!'

Sir Stretford looked around irritatedly for his whisky – the service at Badminton was devoted, but slow. 'No, Mr Harford, no – it's now your turn for a bit of penal servitude. I hope I make myself perfectly clear.'

CHAPTER TWELVE

The train journey back from Badminton was equally gruelling, the carriages crowded out with servicemen and their kitbags, the air filled with cigarette smoke and frequent off-key bursts of 'Mademoiselle from Armentières'.

'Tickets please.'

Guy fumbled in his pocket for the small piece of pasteboard. He'd been promised a first-class ticket, as befits a palace official, but the train only contained third-class carriages and all were stuffed with soldiery as bored and frustrated as he was by the slow progress. Still, he admired their medal ribbons and their tales of derring-do and wondered how long it would be before the doctors passed him fit enough to don a uniform of his own.

'Excuse me,' said Guy, 'but do you happen to know if this train stops at Slough?'

'Be surprised if it din',' came the guard's reply. 'Stopped every other bleedin' place, ennit? Your ticket says Paddington though.'

'It won't matter if I get off at Slough, will it?'

'*Inky pinky par lay voo . . .*' The raucous chorus drowned out the guard's reply but Guy took his vague nod to be one of assent.

The taxi driver was as disinterested as the train guard, and it was starting to get dark by the time he finally found what Guy was looking for, an ugly mock-Tudor house which backed on to the

River Thames at Bray. The lawn was unmown, the hedge unkempt, and the flower beds a riot of weeds.

The front door was open but Guy knocked anyway.

'Yes?' A man who had clearly only just woken appeared, dressed in a Home Guard tunic, pyjama trousers, and plimsolls.

'My name is Harford,' said Guy, trying to pitch the tone of this first remark somewhere between apology and assertion. 'I work for, er, the government. I wonder if you could spare a minute?'

The man looked at his wrist, but if it was supposed to be wearing a watch it was a disappointment. He turned to look at a clock in the hall.

'If it's about the tax bill I refer you to my accountant. You've no business bothering a serving officer when he's about to go on duty.'

'No, it's not about tax. I wonder, may I come in?' Guy moved quickly forward as the householder opened his mouth to reply. He strode quickly into the sitting room.

'Needs a bit of tidyin' up,' said the man unapologetically, trailing after him. 'The woman stopped coming. Most inconvenient.'

'I take it I *am* speaking to Lord Easthampton? If so, I bring warmest regards from Sir Stretford Mariot.' This was a lie.

'Ah, old Rifle-Sling. I wonder what the devil he's up to these days. He and my pa got up to all sorts of tricks when they were subalterns out in India.'

'He hopes you're doing well and enjoying life.' Another lie – Mariot clearly despaired of his best friend's son.

'Send him my regards,' said the soldier mildly. 'Anyhow, I won't offer you anything. I'm off to do my fire-watchin' stint. Church Tower, eight p.m. sharp. I seem to have lost my uniform trousers.'

'I don't suppose anyone will notice in the dark.'

'Ha ha! That's good! Why aren't *you* in uniform? Are you on leave? Or one of those conshies?'

Why indeed, thought Guy. Aloud he said, quite sternly, 'As an officer, I trust you understand and accept the terms of the Official Secrets Act?'

'What's this about?'

'I want to talk to you about Lady Easthampton.'

'Nothing to say. She's done a bunk. Are you some sort of private detective?'

'I work for . . . the Crown. I've been asked to ask you some questions about your wife.' Another lie – nobody had asked him to ask questions, except perhaps poor Adelaide Brampton. 'Can you tell me when you last saw her and whether you know her whereabouts?'

Lord Easthampton was turning over the cushions on the sofa in a vague attempt to find his trousers, but all he unearthed were a couple of empty bottles. He paused and looked myopically at his interlocutor.

'I have no idea, in answer to both your questions. Lady Easthampton has deserted me and left me to rot in this foul hole. I would divorce her but that costs money. And anyway, as I said, I've no idea where she is.'

'Do you think she's still in this country?'

'Last I heard, Hungary is stiff with Nazi tanks after the invasion, so I doubt she'll have chased off home. I expect she's living it up in London – she always was one for the high life.'

'Look,' said Guy, eyeing his watch, 'we've fifteen minutes before you go on duty. May we sit down? I can make a cup of tea if you like.'

'No tea. We share a tot or two of the good stuff on fire watch, just to keep out the cold. I'm holding on for that.'

'This is a very simple inquiry. Certain people . . . er, in authority, wish to speak to Lady Easthampton.'

'What about?'

'Her friendship with an officer, Major Brampton. I hope you won't mind my saying this, but since you say she's deserted you, perhaps it will come as no surprise that she initiated a close friendship with this Major Brampton, a man who's now dead. So can you understand that it's quite important we find her in order to assist with our inquiries?'

Heavens, thought Guy, I *do* sound official.

'I know almost nothing about her,' said Easthampton. 'We got married in '38 after what the gossip columns called a "whirlwind romance". Come to think of it, that was the last time I saw old Rifle-Sling, at Caxton Hall – the wedding. We couldn't manage a church because she'd been married before.'

'What did you know about her family background?'

The young lord paused in the search for his trousers. 'Came from Budapest in '34 or '35. A wonderful-looking woman, I have to admit, even though I hate her guts. Well, she'd had a few boyfriends but I think she rather hankered after a title. I didn't mind, she was easy on the eye and none of my girlfriends seemed to stick. I like a party, but well-brought-up English gels prefer to go home and get their beauty sleep just about the time I get going.

'Suzy was different. She could match me drink for drink – well, almost – and she made a hit with my pa, which was remarkable. He had some inquiries made about her, silly old fool, but found nothing apart from a few boyfriends after she arrived in London. There wasn't anything unduly scandalous.

'Anyway, after a week I proposed marriage and she accepted. I had to tell her I wasn't much of a catch – I mean, the family goes back to King Malcolm so we've got a thousand years of history, but I'd been made bankrupt, and the pater was making me sit it out rather than paying off the creditors.'

'Did she have any money herself?'

Lord Easthampton sat forward. 'Did she not! Furs and diamonds – everyone said she looked the part – her own car, the works. Anyway, we came to this arrangement. She had a gentleman friend named Zeisloft – a Pole, I think – and he had pots of money. In the arms business, don't you know. She said it would be of assistance to him if he had a friend who was married to a lord, and he was prepared to pay. He gave me five hundred pounds that day, just like that – no strings, in a nice attaché case from Asprey's.'

'How generous.'

'That wasn't the end of it. He then arranged that I be paid a hundred pounds a week for the privilege of being Suzy's husband, and he was as good as his word. Until she did a bunk.' Lord Easthampton gazed around vaguely but seemed to have given up the search for his trousers.

'Look,' he said, 'my lot are pretty lenient if I don't turn up on time. What say we go down the pub?'

'I don't think I need keep you much longer, Lord Easthampton.'

'Ambrose, dear chap, Ambrose. I didn't catch your name.'

'Harford.'

'Knew a chap once who lived in Hertford. Kept chickens in his bedroom.'

'Does Lady Easthampton have a London address?'

'Stays with friends, here and there.'

'Can you give me their names? Some of them? One of them?'

Easthampton dug a cigarette end out from a brass ashtray and straightened it. 'Do you have a light?'

'I don't smoke,' Guy lied. 'The friends?'

'I only know them by their first names.'

'Mr Zeisloft? Where does he live?'

'The Dorchester Hotel, Park Lane. The way he waltzed around it you'd think he owned the place.'

'So she could be there.'

'My dear fellow, she could be *anywhere*. I'm bound to say I'm not much interested in that sort of thing, so I don't mind, but she does have the morals of an alley cat – always off here, there and everywhere with this chap and that.'

'I really do need to find her, Lord Easthampton. A rather distinguished officer has died and she may know something important.'

A vague look crossed the young lord's face. 'Have you any money?' he said.

'Sorry?'

'I said *have you any money?* It's a simple question, isn't it?'

Guy looked at him with pity. 'Will ten pounds do it?' he said, reaching for his wallet.

'Chesterfield House. Chesterfield Gardens, just off Curzon Street. Flat 12A. Send her my regards – I don't think.' The future 9th Earl FitzMalcolm, heir to a tremendous fortune and a thousand years of history, reached out for the banknote, tucked it in his tunic pocket and curled up on the sofa. He was asleep instantly.

Aggie was in her usual acid-drop mood. 'Topsy wants to see you,' she said maliciously, even before Guy had reached his desk. 'In a right old mood, he is.'

'What is it this time? Another parrot? A flock of starlings? Could I have a cup of tea, please?'

'No time for tea – when the Master calls, you go. Quick-smart!' She looked at the expression on his face. 'What's the matter, Mr Harford, aren't you enjoying it here?'

The answer is no but I won't give you the satisfaction, thought Guy. If only the doctors would pass me fit, I'd be off like a shot.

He picked up his notebook and trudged his way over to the Master's office.

'Aha! The Tanja Man!'

'Harford, Sir Topham,' insisted Guy.

'Where on earth have you been? I asked you to come yesterday.'

'Badminton, to talk to Queen Mary.'

'How is Her Majesty?'

'I'm afraid I didn't see her. Mr Lascelles made the appointment but she must have forgotten. I think she's in London.'

'Shopping. Or begging no doubt. Now, pay attention – I asked for a constant stream of information from you on the matter of Major Brampton, but I'm not hearing anything.'

'Nothing more to say, sir. As far as Tommy Lascelles is concerned, the matter's closed. I hope his widow will be receiving a pension?'

'Talk to Privy Purse about that. I'm interested to know what you've discovered.'

'I rather think it's a job for the coroner, sir – they know all the right questions to ask – *if* there's going to be an inquest. I've merely asked around to see whether Major Brampton had been unhappy or depressed before his death. The general impression is he seemed perfectly fine, though of course very disappointed at not getting the appointment with the Duke of Gloucester. Why *was* that, by the way?'

'Not suited.'

'But he'd been more or less told . . .'

'Not by *me!*' roared the Master. His sudden burst of anger filled the high-ceilinged room. Guy glanced away, into the palace courtyard.

'Temperamentally unsuited to such a demanding role. Less than diligent. Eye often off the ball. Shall I go on?'

'That does seem so strange, sir, given that he . . .'

'Gloucester didn't like him,' said Dighton, closing down Guy's probing, though the way he said it didn't sound particularly convincing. 'What else have you in mind with your investigation?'

133

'I'm taking a day off. I'll probably go and stay with Mrs Brampton – so if you have any message for her . . .'

'Talk to Privy Purse, if that's what you mean,' huffed Dighton. 'And be careful what you say to her. At the same time you might get something more out of her, if you're clever.'

'Not quite sure I know what you mean, sir. What am I *supposed* to get out of her?'

'I think she knows a lot more about Brampton's last days than she's let on so far.' It was clear there were unanswered questions in the courtier's mind that he was straining to articulate. 'Give her a good grilling, don't pull your punches.'

This is no family matter, thought Guy, it's a crude attempt to discover what's known about Ed's last days, and their link to Sir Topham himself. The mysterious errands Ed had been sent on, the missing notebook, the sinister connection with Suzy Easthampton – the Master of the Household clearly knew much more than he was letting on.

Aggie had the kettle on when he got back. She seemed in a sweeter frame of mind.

'How was Badminton? Her Majesty?'

'I didn't see her.'

The clerk's gaze flickered. It said, in a momentary flash: Couldn't you even do a simple job like deliver a message? I arranged the travel warrants, telephoned ahead to the queen's secretary to alert her of your arrival, fixed up the transport, sorted out the train ticket – and then you couldn't even manage to do what you'd been sent to do?

'I don't think Mr Lascelles will be thrilled to hear that.'

'Dammit, Aggie, the woman ran out on me!'

'We don't use language like that, Mr Harford. Nor do we refer to majesties as "the woman". Remember the words of her old friend Lady Pembroke: 'We never speak ill of a crowned head in this house.' It's time you learned to bite your tongue, otherwise it'll get you a reputation. Some people round here' – she gestured with a backward movement of her head – 'get very *bitter* working in the Palace, but really it's all a question of mind over matter. Don't let anybody else hear you talk like that.'

Guy sat down moodily at his desk.

'Speaking of Pembrokes,' went on Aggie, 'the King and Queen are down at Wilton now, having a couple of days' rest with Lord and Lady P. Pressure's off.'

'Really? The royal standard's still flapping away on the roof. I always look to see whether they're in – along with the rest of London.'

'Yes, they've started doing that,' confided Aggie, who loved to show her superior knowledge. 'A bit of a white lie, of course, since everyone believes if the royal standard flies over the Palace, the King must be in residence.'

'Yes.'

'It's to fool the Germans – a good thing.'

'I wonder if the Germans can see all the way from Berlin. It fools the British public, too – not so good.'

'It keeps up morale, Mr Harford. I see,' she said, picking her moment, 'you haven't had any more floral tributes.'

'What?'

'I just wonder how it got in here, that rose. And the chalk cross on your desk. I locked up the office that night, good and proper.'

'I have no idea, I told you. It's really of no importance.' He paused. 'You didn't throw it away, did you?'

'I pressed it in our copy of *Burke's Peerage* – nice and heavy. On the shelf behind you. It'll have dried out in a fortnight or so.'

Guy suddenly awoke to the realisation Rodie's rose had turned into a guilty secret, a weapon Aggie could use against him at some future date. Now, even talking to Rodie – as he had in Claridge's the other day – could be grounds for instant dismissal, particularly if Topham Dighton got to hear of it.

But was Aggie, too, now spying on him – or was he imagining things? Was the pressure of work at the Palace getting on his nerves?

'Thank you. Do you happen to know if there are any empty rooms in the Mews that I might use as a studio? I'm thinking of doing some painting again.'

'That'll be nice,' said Aggie. 'Will you be painting the rose?'

Guy suppressed his irritation. 'No, I've been asked to paint a portrait or two. I don't know how successful an experiment it'll be – I've only ever done one before – so I thought it would be wasteful to take on a studio with all the cost involved.'

'Who are you going to do,' asked Aggie, suddenly interested. 'Man or woman? Is it a nudie you'll be doing? I like a nice nude.'

'Not at all. I may be going to paint someone quite famous, but I'm going to have to experiment on someone else first. Perhaps you'd like to volunteer.'

'Never volunteer!' Aggie rapped out the age-old service motto.

'Well, I might do one of the kitchen maids then.' Guy could tell what a mistake he'd made, equating Aggie with the lowliest of palace servants, and quickly changed the subject.

'I've decided to go down and see Mrs Brampton. Do you think you could get me a petrol chit?'

'I don't know. Are you going back to see Queen Mary again, make it a round trip? That would make the requisition easier.'

'Not necessary, I think she's got the message – I had a long talk with Sir Stretford. But seeing Mrs Brampton is business, too.'

'Mm.'

Aggie had her nose in a book. Guy had been dismissed.

CHAPTER THIRTEEN

It was at night, in summer, that London really came alive. No matter the deadly danger from above, nothing could rob the young of their high spirits and their headlong rush into love.

As dusk fell, Guy walked along the long tree-lined avenue in Hyde Park, the metalled path echoing with the sounds of soldiers' boots and the squeals of their newly acquired girlfriends. At the park gates, military police in their red-topped caps stood moodily about, waiting for trouble, longing to throw their weight about.

'Feeling lonely, dearie?' said a voice out of the shadows, and though in truth Guy was, he waved and smiled without looking at the painfully thin blonde a step or two away. Reaching the gates he halted and lingered, waiting for a bus to take him down to Chelsea.

About Ed Brampton's death, he realised, he felt entirely neutral. They'd shared an office, but Ed had been distant, polite, at no stage offering friendship to Guy. Maybe that was because Guy had known Adelaide since childhood – and probably knew more about her than Ed did.

In addition, Ed may have suspected – as people engaged in subterfuge often do – that Guy was watching him, ready to report back to Adelaide in the country. It would help explain why he kept their conversations so short, so distant.

The traffic on Park Lane was busy, but the buses were few and the queue was getting longer. Guy was sunk deep in thought – why, he asked himself, was he pursuing this? Was it to appease Adelaide? To right a wrong? To prove that despite the Master of the Household's cynicism he was perfectly capable of solving a mystery?

Am I convinced that Ed was murdered? If not, why carry on this fruitless task?

If he was murdered, who pulled the trigger, and was Lady Easthampton involved? If her plan all along was to get close to the Duke of Gloucester, did she kill Ed out of frustration that he didn't get that private secretary job? It didn't make sense – there had to be something more to it than that.

Since he was no longer in residence at his Chelsea home – that much Guy had established – could it be that by this time Ed had been *living* with Suzy Easthampton? Guy had got from her pathetic husband that she'd packed her bags about the time Adelaide moved to the country and Ed locked up his Markham Street house for the last time. Where did they both disappear to?

'Got a light, mate?'

'So sorry, I don't smoke.' That bus was never going to come.

'That don't matter, neither do I.' The young man edged closer, smiling up at Guy, raising his eyebrows.

'Not tonight,' said Guy, smiling back.

Abandoning his previous plan, he stepped off the pavement and was nearly run down by two cyclists, panting as they made the lengthy climb up to Marble Arch. Crossing the road, he strode past the Dorchester Hotel – where, he reflected without malice, people carried on as though war had never been declared – and plunged forward into the streets of Mayfair.

A few minutes' easy walking brought him to Chesterfield Gardens and the orderly if anonymous block of service flats he was seeking. The doorman was burly and bored.

'Good evening. I've come to see Lady Easthampton.'

'No you 'aven't.'

'Er . . . yes . . . Viscountess Easthampton,' Guy insisted.

'Nobody 'ere of that name,' said the man gruffly.

'Flat 12A,' insisted Guy.

'I *told* you, mate. You must ha' got the wrong block.'

Knowing my luck I probably have, thought Guy, but I do hate people being rude.

'No, no. Lady Easthampton sometimes stays here, even if it isn't her flat.'

'Look, mate,' said the man. 'There's enough goes on 'ere without my letting disappointed boyfriends in to cause trouble with those as has other fish to fry.'

'No, no,' said Guy, shaking his head. 'It's not like that at all. I've come with a message from Lord Easthampton.'

'How many more times? Nobody 'ere of that name.'

Guy reached for his notecase.

'Don't bother,' said the man witheringly, looking him up and down. 'You can't afford what I cost, mate.'

'May I leave a written message, then?'

'I tole you,' said the man, squaring his shoulders. 'Nobody 'ere of that name. Now shove off or I'll call the law.'

'Well, thank you, and sorry for troubling you.' Guy turned on his heel and retraced his steps back to Park Lane. While waiting in the bus queue he'd almost decided to let the Ed Brampton business go – so what had made him suddenly change his mind and trail all the way over here? Was it a sense of duty, or more a deep-seated curiosity to see what a real-life Mata Hari looked like in the flesh?

And then he realised it – he'd never seen her photograph, never heard her voice, but her story, her reputation, told him that he had to paint her.

The bus, when it finally came, took him south to a hidden-away pub called The Surprise, lost in the jumble of tiny streets crowding the bottom end of Chelsea. It was untidy, not particularly clean, awash with beer and fogged with cigarette smoke, but it offered succour of a kind no smart West End establishment ever could.

''Ello, lovely!' said the barmaid with a bright smile. ''Aven't seen you before.'

'Looking for Mr Amberley. Painter.'

'Over there in the corner. Big red beard.'

Guy tossed a half-crown on to the bar. 'What's he having?'

'Nelson's Blood, dear. "Pour the brandy in first," he says, "then slow with the red stuff."'

'Make it quick with the red stuff,' laughed Guy. 'He'll never know the difference.'

He walked round the bar to where the old fellow was sitting. 'Guy Harford,' he said. 'Am I addressing Adrian Amberley?'

'Was it poured slowly?' The words escaped from the beard in a whisper.

'Took an age,' lied Guy with a wink. He liked the man already. 'I think you know Nina Hamnett,' he went on. 'We worked together in Paris in '31.'

'The Queen of Bohemia!' rasped Amberley, his voice as colourful as the blotches on his cheeks. 'I fancy she found Paris a little too fast for her taste. But perhaps it's more your speed?'

'Tangier,' said Guy. 'That's my speed – when there isn't a wretched war going on. I heard you had a spare room in your studio.'

'Do you drink here often? I haven't seen you before,' came the cautious response. Amberley, for all Guy could tell, was thinking he might be opening his door to a Nazi spy.

'Not recently. I haven't lived in Britain for nearly ten years.'

'And what do you do now?' asked Amberley, looking askance at Guy's appearance. 'Looks like you have an office job.'

'I work for the government.'

'As an artist?'

'Not exactly. I have the chance to do an exhibition but I need to do some more portraits to fill out the portfolio. In Tangier I was concentrating mostly on land and seascapes.'

'A pretty rough lot in Tangier as I recall,' said Amberley, balancing the two glasses of port and brandy in his hands, the old and the new, as if weighing one against the other. 'They're a pretty rough lot down here as well.'

'Home from home then, you might say.'

Amberley gave a wheezy laugh. He looked at Guy, sizing him up.

'Ten bob a week,' he said suddenly. 'I'm not supposed to sublet, so you'll pay me in cash and say you're just there for the day if anyone asks. A week's trial and if we get on then you can stay. A contribution to the gas and light can be paid in here any time after six p.m. And if you need a bed,' he added, nodding his head firmly, 'there's a small room at the back. Don't make too much noise.'

'No, no, I . . .' said Guy. 'There's someone I'm hoping to . . . I don't think she . . .'

'Dear fellow,' said Amberley, 'I can tell you haven't done much portraiture. They get cold sitting about, poor lambs, and need a little warming up from time to time.'

◆ ◆ ◆

Adelaide lay quite still in the hammock, a book in her lap. Bees buzzed, the air was still; across the other side of the meadow a small herd of deer chewed lazily at the hot grass.

'I wonder if you've ever noticed,' she said.

'Mm?' Guy was sketching her face, half-hidden by a straw hat.

'We were talking earlier about Ed and the Queen. You're drawing my face, but I wonder how you'd cope with hers – she has two, you know. The lower half is all smiles and compliments, sweet words and what-have-you. But the upper half, with those hard, calculating eyes which miss nothing – I've never seen another face like it.'

'I rarely see her,' said Guy. 'What are you saying?'

'That smile moves strong men to tears – no, really, Guy, it does! It wasn't just Ed – the charm she has, she uses it like a lethal weapon, but behind it the steel. And the ruthlessness. Without her the King wouldn't last a day.'

'Oh?'

'He's brittle, bad-tempered, always seeking to find a way to belittle people. Ed told me he was inspecting the Coats Mission people up at Sandringham – you know, his little private army – and for want of something better to say he complained about the state of their cap badges.' She laughed sardonically. 'Trivial, petty, just trying to score a point, while there they are, ready to die for him!'

'Maybe it's her they're ready to die for. Like poor old Ed.'

'Poor chap. Poor chap.'

Guy was thinking about the discarded portrait on the floor of Adelaide's Chelsea house.

'Did you love him?'

'I may have done. But in the end, no, I came too late to do him any good.'

'You did a rather fine picture of him, I seem to remember.'

'Oh, that! I hated it. I did it to please him and he liked to see it hanging on the wall, but it's going on the bonfire.'

'Never do that with a painting. Stick it in the attic.'

'The flames might do me good.' She turned over a page of her book.

'I'm going to tell you something about him which you might find painful. Do you mind?'

'That he was a secret pansy?'

'I think, far from it. Have you ever heard the name Suzy Easthampton?'

She put her book down and looked at him. 'You know, Guy, that's exactly how one's best friend starts a conversation when she's about to tell you your husband is in love with another woman.'

Guy looked at her with a steady gaze.

'Oh,' said Adelaide. 'Oh!'

'The moment you left Markham Street with the children to come here,' said Guy, 'he disappeared. That's to say, he locked up the house and wasn't seen there up until the time he died, three months later. There are letters – I won't say how I know – letters and cards showing that he and Lady Easthampton were meeting. The easiest conclusion to draw is, with nowhere else to live, he moved in with her. He turned up at the office every day looking immaculate and as though everything was right in his world. But where did he spend his evenings and nights?'

'Well, nothing you could say would surprise me more,' said Adelaide. 'We'd talk on the telephone most days but that would be at drinks time, when he'd still be in the office. He always used to call me. And he sent the children letters and cards but he'd put them in the palace postbox – so how would I ever know where he was? But how bizarre – did he set up home with this woman? That seems so unlike him!'

'Do you know her?'

'I know the name. Her husband's a pretty useless sort, I gather. But I think his father is Lord FitzMalcolm – we can ask Pa at dinner, he's off doing his ARP at the moment, digging trenches nobody will shelter in. Well, *he's* not digging at his age, but he likes to advise others on their spade technique. How long are you staying?'

'Just the night. I'm on palace standby. If the balloon goes up, back I go.'

'Are you enjoying it?'

'Partly. The royals themselves are fine; it's the others I find hard to get along with.'

'I don't suppose you'll stay there very long, you're hardly my idea of a devoted courtier.'

'Maybe not – nothing's certain these days. I was being sounded out about the Gloucester job that Ed didn't get, but it's not really my cup of tea.' He finished his sketch and put down the pad. 'Did you ever think any more about how things went wrong for Ed?'

'It was strange. All the time he was working for his real boss – Tommy Lascelles – everything was fine. But remember it was Topsy Dighton who got Ed the job, and he used to get called into his office all the time. It was a bore for Ed, but it was also a worry.'

'How so?'

'Dighton is a very strange man,' said Adelaide. She thought for a moment. 'Because he's held a senior position longer than anyone else at the Palace, he's more or less untouchable. He feels he can reach out and meddle in other people's lives. He did that with Ed. Ed was constantly being called in to run what he called "extracurricular errands" for Topsy. It worried him, I could tell. I used to ask him what it was all about but he kept it to himself. Then one day I came home late – I'd been to the theatre – and he was sitting in the drawing room, dead drunk.

'That wasn't like him at all. I got a cold flannel and sloshed it round his face to wake him up, then I made him a big cup of coffee. While he was drinking it, I told him it was agony for me, his wife, to see him in such a state – him being so upright generally – and that he had to tell me what was wrong.'

'Did he?'

'Oh yes, it all came tumbling out in the end. Though to start with I couldn't work out what he was saying. He kept on talking about "the Misters" and I thought he must be having hallucinations.

I was worried because the children were upstairs asleep and he was making a hell of a racket.

'Anyway, after a bit he calmed down and I began to understand. The Misters, he told me, are members of a secret group called the English Mistery. I'd never heard of them, have you?'

'No. Are they a bunch of schoolteachers? A folklore group?'

'No, they're all old-school aristocrats – diehards from the Edwardian days – who passionately believe the country's gone to the dogs, and to save it, we must turn back the clock.'

'Surely . . .'

'They believe in a nation of racially pure Englishmen led by a monarch who's supported by strong leaders like themselves. They hate the emergence of the Labour Party, they fear the rise of communism, and they're scared this war will smash the class barriers and we'll all emerge at the other end as equals.'

'A good thing, surely?'

'You'd think so, wouldn't you, Guy? Pour me some lemonade and give this old hammock a push.'

He obliged. 'So how was Ed involved in all this?'

'Well, of course he wasn't. He was a pretty old-school sort of chap but believed in democracy – these people don't.'

'Who are they, these Misters?'

'I hadn't heard of half of them, obscure names mostly, but there are a few Members of Parliament involved. Ed didn't exactly say this, but I got the impression that Dighton was a founding member of the Mistery and was struggling to keep it going. Ed's errands were all to do with that.'

'Why was he so upset – it's not illegal, is it?'

'According to Ed, it could be. They're always talking about bringing a vote of no confidence in Churchill – even though he's doing a good job – and they see their way to exercising influence on a weakened government. The problem was that there are now other, more extreme groups which the Misters have defected to, and Dighton was struggling to keep the remainder of the membership together.'

'What groups?'

'Honestly, Guy, you'd think grown men had better things to do. There's the Paladin League, the Henchmen of England, the Nordic League, the Right Club.'

'The Henchman . . . ?'

'All wooden-headed types from a certain background who think they can do better than the present government. But from what Ed said, these people present a huge danger in wartime – subversive at the least, actively pro-Nazi in some cases.'

Guy shook his head. 'I find this so hard to understand. The war isn't going well, surely this is the moment when the whole nation pulls together?'

Adelaide smiled. 'You've been abroad too long, Guy. Over the last ten years there's been a rise in what I suppose you might call extremism – Oswald Mosley and his Blackshirts, for example – and they all think they know a better way of running the country than the old traditional method of one man, one vote.'

'True what you say,' agreed Guy, 'about being away too long. Very easy, when you're in Paris or Tangier, to ignore what's going on back home and just think that dear old England is sailing along, full steam ahead.'

Clutching her skirt, Adelaide struggled out of the hammock – 'No ladylike way of escaping this!' – and picked up the tea tray. 'Let's go in. There's more to say about Topsy but there's supper to think about, too.'

They walked back across the lawns to the big rambling house, passing the folly with its battlements and flagpole atop the tower. Inside, the big rooms full of chintz-covered sofas and gilt-framed pictures seemed as though war had never touched them, but overhead they could hear the heavy thunder of RAF bombers returning from a raid.

Guy sat at the kitchen table peeling potatoes. 'I don't understand why Ed put up with this errand-boy business.'

'He felt compromised. Topsy had the hold over him – "I got you this job, if you don't cooperate I can always kick you out, send you to the Tower."'

'He threatened me with that, too.'

'I don't think in your case, Guy, you'd mind in the slightest if you were fired. For Ed, the job was his life – and of course, a golden opportunity to spend time with Her Majesty.'

'Was he really in love with her?'

'Besotted.'

'Makes it all the more strange that he should . . .'

'Get off with this Lady Easthampton? Gosh, Guy, you don't know much about affairs of the heart, do you?'

'I wouldn't say that.'

'Others might, dear man,' smiled Adelaide. 'Ed loved the Queen but nothing was ever going to come of it. But, left alone in that house in Markham Street, with me and the children in the country . . . I suppose I mustn't be surprised he found himself a popsy. It's not as if we were that close any more, if you understand my meaning.'

'So these people Ed was ordered to deal with . . . they sound a pretty ruthless lot,' he said.

'Desperadoes, some of them. Feeling they're protected by the stone walls of their estates, or their titles, or their family connections to people of power. Isolated and angry, Ed said.'

'Do you think one of them could have killed him?'

'Why? Why shoot the messenger? Dighton was desperately trying to save his crumbling organisation, this English Mistery – he'd be begging people, not threatening them or harming them. It was Ed's job to seek them out in their clubs and be nice to them. He hated it, despised them. But he felt he had to do it. The Palace was his dream job.'

'Look,' said Guy, 'I'll be frank. You asked me to look into Ed's death and I've looked. But there's no answer to it – just a lot of questions, and now you've made things more complicated.'

'Have I?' Adelaide smiled indulgently. 'Try that.'

She handed him a morsel of food.

'Mm,' said Guy non-committally. 'What is it?'

'Nut rissole. It's that or roast squirrel this evening. Choices!'

'Lovely,' said Guy, his face puckering. 'As I was saying, I want to help but I don't think I can. On the one hand there's Ed's association with Suzy Easthampton. Her backer is a Polish arms dealer, currently in France and therefore, if he's got his head screwed on right, working for the Nazis. His prize asset is this woman who's slept her way to the top. Her target, quite clearly, is – or was – the Duke of Gloucester, in the belief that one day he may take the throne. Dangerous company, Adelaide, perhaps lethal.

'Then, on the other hand, we now find Ed deep in the mire with a bunch of extremists who, for all we know, are on the point of being arrested. I've learned enough since I've been back here' – mostly from my flatmate, he thought – 'to know that people are being interned if they hold right-wing views or sympathies. Would one of them shoot Ed rather than go to jail? By the sound of it, they would.'

'Two things against that,' said Adelaide. 'One, he wasn't blackmailing them, he was cajoling them. Second, which of them would be able to get into the Palace and shoot him there?'

Guy immediately thought of Rodie.

'It may be the most famous palace in the world, guarded by the world's finest soldiers,' he said, 'but to some it's an open door.'

CHAPTER FOURTEEN

'Stalin,' said Ted Rochester conspiratorially, 'takes a great interest in the Windsor-Simpson story.'

'Really?' said Guy.

They were sitting in the window of Rochester's club, a diamond-paned Elizabethan house near Temple Bar, where Fleet Street meets the Strand.

'Yes indeed. He can't understand why Mrs Simpson wasn't liquidated.'

'Ha ha.'

'Don't laugh – our man in Moscow says it, therefore it must be true. Anyway, Uncle Joe's not the only one fascinated by it all. Me too – I was hoping your friend Foxy had a few gems to share on how things are going with the lovebirds over in Nassau.'

'If I knew, Ted, I wouldn't tell you. And neither would she.'

'Just doing my job,' said the journalist comfortably. 'How's the business going with old Ed Brampton?'

'There is no business, Ted,' said Guy irritably. 'I thought you'd invited me here so I could help you with a nice article on the war work of the dukes of Gloucester and Kent – the royal supporters. Brothers in arms. All that guff.'

'We'll get to that,' replied Rochester, signalling to the waiter. 'I'm just intrigued by the whole Brampton thing – a gallant officer lost, as my headline-writer might put it. Shooting *accidents* don't happen – shooting accidents are what we in the scribbling business call an oxymoron.'

'Nonsense, they happen all the time.'

'Not like that. I wonder whether he discovered too much about Harry Gloucester and his habits, realised he couldn't cope with it all, didn't know how to get out of it and, well . . .' Rochester put two fingers to his temple and made a puffing sound.

'The general consensus,' replied Guy, shaking his head, 'is the Duke's not the sharpest man in the world, but he's loyal and dedicated. He's been in the thick of it – bombed and all that – and emerged with honour. What more do you want, Ted?'

The reporter sniffed. 'He's not what he seems. There's a young child toddling around whose bills are being paid by him. When he was in Africa with the Prince of Wales, he fell for this adventuress called Beryl Markham. They were in Kenya big-game hunting, and both princes, believe it or not, were bedding her. Not,' he added quickly, 'at the same time, you understand. But she became pregnant and turned up here in London.'

'This is just gossip, Ted. I don't think we should . . .'

'Gossip, dear boy, is what I deal in, and gossip has a habit of turning out to be true.' Rochester smiled. 'Anyway, Harry Gloucester set her up in a suite in an hotel at the back door of the Palace and they lived there happily till she had the baby. Queen Mary was appalled when Mrs Markham's brother came a-knocking asking for support for the child, but the royal family was forced to cough up and Harry was in disgrace. That's when they sent him off to Japan – to get him away from her. A most undesirable woman, Guy – except, of course, in that one sense.'

'I'd like to see you write that into your article,' came the crisp reply. 'Anyway, what's this got to do with Ed Brampton?'

'Just saying . . .' said Rochester with a grin. 'Just saying that there's a lot more to Gloucester than meets the eye, and maybe Ed couldn't face the immense burden. There are quite a few tales about him. Now, I gather, he's rattling round the Palace with nothing much to do and getting very frustrated. Altogether a bit of a nuisance.'

'I wouldn't know,' said Guy firmly. 'Is this the sort of article you want to write?'

'No, no,' said the reporter smoothly, 'this is just a chat between friends. Off the record.'

'*Are* we off the record?'

'At the moment.'

'Well,' said Guy, 'off the *record*, Ted, poor Ed didn't get the job. Everyone thought he would but he didn't. He was a bit depressed about it all. Draw your own conclusions.'

'Oh!' said Rochester, deflated. 'Then no story there, after all! I just was convinced – the urgent arrangements, that overblown service at the Guards Chapel, getting me to write something about him in the paper – I'll be frank and say I smelt a rat.'

'Let's talk about something else.'

'Foxy told me you're doing an exhibition of your paintings.'

'I might, if I can get a gallery and enough pictures together. Most of my work's still in Tangier – I don't think it'll be finding its way here any time soon.'

'Don't forget I offered my help,' said Rochester. 'If you need a gallery, if you need to find some people to paint, the resources of a great national newspaper are at your disposal.'

'That's kind of you.'

'But one good turn deserves another – I need something on the Windsors, Guy. The Windsors! There are all sorts of stories circulating about them – I need to know what's going on down their end of things.'

'Nothing doing, old chap. There are plenty of other people to write about.'

'Nothing catches the public imagination like a paragraph or two on our runaway king and his moll. Have you seen my column today?'

Does he really think I have time to read the *News Chronicle*? thought Guy. Always the same with journalists – they're convinced theirs are the first words you read on waking each morning. 'Was there something special?'

'I've never really cared for The Dorchester, have you? They let in all sorts these days. Thought I'd better give them a warning they're letting standards drop.' He handed over a copy of the *News Chronicle*, conveniently open at the page bearing his name. Guy read:

```
In The Dorchester the sweepings of the
Riviera have been washed up - pot-
bellied, sallow, sleek-haired nervous
gentlemen with loose mouths and wobbly
chins, wearing suede shoes and check
suits, and thin painted women with fox
capes and long silk legs and small
artificial curls clustering round their
bony, sheep-like heads.
```

'Sounds like it's goodbye to all those free drinks you've taken off the management all these years,' said Guy.

'Oh,' said Ted lazily. 'They switched off the tap last week, old boy. Told me the party's over, I was a bit too thirsty for the jolly old Pol Roger apparently. QED.'

They got up to leave. 'By the way,' drawled the journalist, 'the brat I was telling you about – Harry Gloucester's . . .'

'Yes?'

'It isn't his.'

'How do you know?'

'Did the arithmetic, old boy. When they first met, when the child was delivered. Not possible. The trouble with Harry is he can't count.'

Guy wandered out into Fleet Street, down the ancient alleyways through the Temple and on towards the river. Even here in this, the citadel of law, there was no escape from the conflict. There was glass all over the pavements, gaps between buildings, piles of rubble. Police signs warning 'Danger – UXB' were planted here and there, and everywhere there were the strained expressions and signs of fatigue that were a daily spectacle, even on the faces of the well-fed barristers and judges.

From Hyde Park, Guy could hear the orchestra of guns start up, though he'd heard no air-raid siren and people weren't making their usual rush to the nearest shelter. Must be a false alarm, he thought, wandering down the Embankment towards the House of Commons. A false alarm.

Or maybe, like that night in The Berkeley with Foxy, we just don't care any more – let it all come down . . .

◆ ◆ ◆

Leaning over the rail by Westminster Bridge, waiting for him, Rupert Hardacre presented a passable imitation of a Post Office worker whose labours were done for the day, gazing south across the River Thames, maybe dreaming of his holidays.

Guy approached his flatmate with caution. He'd grown to like Rupert, but the idea that he'd been planted in the flat to spy on him – or, at the very least, to watch him – rankled. True, when he arrived back in Britain he possessed secrets from his activities with the Count of Paris and the genial Teddy Dunlop, but did they, now the skies were full of planes, amount to anything much? Why had he been gifted this cuckoo in the nest?

'Dancing tonight?' said Rupe, nodding a welcome.

'What?'

'The Palais. Rodie sent you the tickets, remember?'

'Damn! I'd forgotten all about it. Probably not. Look, if . . .'

'If I were you, I *would* – she's a tremendously valuable asset.'

'She steals the possessions of dead people,' said Guy crossly. 'In Tangier they'd cut your hand off for that.'

Rupe lit a cigarette and let the match flutter into the Thames. 'Be nice to her,' he said in a low voice. 'We need her.'

'I'm not "we". I don't have much idea of what you're up to, but whatever it is it's not my game, Rupe. I have a palace job, not some cloak-and-dagger role with a nameless government agency. My days are filled coping with the weird errands I'm given without having to consort with criminals who, incidentally, could cost me my job if I was ever found in their company.'

'That won't happen,' said Rupe with conviction. 'So no need to worry about that. She wants to dance – take her.'

'*You* take her if it's that important.'

'I'm not her type.'

'So her *type* is a washed-up artist with a dicky heart and a sinecure of a job at the Palace? Not too many of those around – maybe she should cast her net a bit wider.'

'Go on, Guy – she's lovely. And a wonderful dancer, according to Lem.'

Guy tried his best to mask his irritation. 'No,' he said finally, 'no. No dancing tonight. I want you to come and see my new studio – we can catch a bus or walk, your choice.'

'Let's walk. I've been sitting all day.'

The pair set off at a brisk pace across Parliament Square and along the Victoria Embankment, both glad of the exercise.

'Making any progress with Suzy Easthampton?' asked Rupe.

'I'd love to know what *your* interest is in her. Is it the same as mine? That she may've had a hand in Ed Brampton's murder?'

'Not exactly. She comes under the heading of "foreign", so "no" is the answer to your question. I'm more of a homebody myself.'

'So you're MI5, not MI6.'

'Some might put it that way. I'm not one for labels personally.'

'And you were put in our flat to watch me?'

'It's not quite like that. More a sort of protection.'

'Am I in danger, then?'

'I was asking you about the elusive Lady Easthampton.' Rupe could deflect a question so easily. 'But yes, you could be.'

Am I truly in danger, thought Guy, or is he just saying that? And if so – who exactly is the enemy? Do they think I know something I don't? Are they fearful I might spill the beans about the cock-up in Tangier? Or is it closer to home – the Ed Brampton business? Are they coming after me like they went after him? Are they going to leave me on the floor of my office with a gun by my side that doesn't belong to me?

Whoever 'they' may be?

Guy bit his lip, then reluctantly replied, 'I went round to her flat.'

'How on earth did you find *that*?'

'First I dug out her husband, Lord Easthampton. He sang like the proverbial.'

'Good Lord, you *are* catching on fast!'

'A ten-pound note always helps. He gave me her address in Mayfair.' He told the story of the doorman. 'But I couldn't get past the brute to knock on her door. And since I don't have her telephone number, I've hit a bit of a brick wall. I don't really know what to do next.'

'There's a way around that,' said Rupe. They were marching past the brick colossus of Battersea Power Station, the clouds of smoke belching from the twin chimneys casting their shadows across the river.

'There is?'

'Your dance partner. Whisper sweetly in her ear at the Palais tonight and – open sesame! Although since it's such a heavily guarded block I wouldn't suggest going in yourself, just in case things go wrong. Best leave it to the professionals.'

'*Rodie?* For heaven's sake, Rupe, I'm doing my best to put as much distance between myself and that woman as I can – and here you are, dragging her back. I really can't . . .'

'Look,' said Rupert, coming to a halt and turning to face Guy, 'if I understand you correctly, you want to meet this Easthampton woman and grill her about Ed Brampton. Do you?'

'Well, yes. But . . .'

'There's a war on. We're all incredibly busy. If you feel the job's important, get it done. I say again, Guy, it's wartime. Certain rules have been suspended.'

'No.'

They walked on. Soon they turned up from the river into the narrow intimacy of Tite Street.

'Just up here,' said Guy, pointing to a row of red-brick studio houses, their tall upper windows blinking at the sky. 'I heard about this place from a friend.' He let them both in. 'I have the studio from lunchtime on – my landlord, Adrian Amberley, only paints in the morning.'

'Very impressive,' said Rupert impatiently, looking around and then at his watch. 'Hadn't you better be getting a move on? Don't want to keep Rodie waiting.'

'A pint in The Surprise first.'

An hour later the taxi dropped him at the roundabout and he joined the throng heading up Hammersmith Road to the Palais. Standing opposite the entrance was a barely recognisable Rodie, dressed far too extravagantly for a wartime hop. She was tapping her foot.

'Did I keep you waiting? I'm sorry. I had to have a quick drink with Rupe.'

'*You – are – very – late,*' she said, not looking at him. '*I – don't – like – to – be – kept – waiting.*'

'Well, there was a bit of confusion. I thought we might . . .'

'Come on!' ordered Rodie, stepping into the traffic. 'Got the tickets?'

'Oh! I . . .'

'Thought not. Come this way.' Grabbing his wrist, she pulled him through the crowds and around a corner to the stage door. With a bright 'Thanks, Nancy!' she sailed through, Guy following like a dog on a lead. Behind them, the queue trailed back around the block. It would take an hour for them all to get in.

'You seem to know all the right people,' said Guy, cloaking his guilt with a compliment. 'Can I get you a drink?'

'We're here to dance, sunshine. Let's dance!'

The band was playing 'Begin the Beguine'. Rusty from years without practice, Guy was forced to work hard to keep up with his partner, but he finally found the rhythm.

'This is nice. Haven't danced for years. You're good. So am I, apparently.' He swirled her round.

'Wait till we get to the tango, mate, then we'll see how nifty you are.'

'Tango? I'll be watching, not joining. My skills don't go that far.'

'Don't sell yourself short. You're doing all right.'

This is ridiculous, thought Guy. I'm not sure I should be here, and I certainly don't want to be seen with this woman. How soon can we go?

The great barn-like room echoed with raucous shouts from the crowd, which seemed to be growing bigger by the minute. The band played 'In the Mood' twice in a row and still they yelled for more.

'Never seen anything like this,' Guy shouted breathlessly. 'There must be a couple of thousand people here.'

'Every night is their last,' replied Rodie, gripping him tighter. 'They all want one more dance before the ship sinks.'

Guy glanced over her shoulder at the pink faces and elaborate hairstyles. The crush of dancers, the heat, the noise heightened the atmosphere. It made it hard to focus his thoughts.

'Look, Rodie, there's something I want to discuss . . .'

'Discuss as much as you like – over dinner. Where are you taking me?'

'Anywhere apart from The Dorchester. Apparently there are too many men there with loose mouths and wobbly chins – might put you off.'

'You can take me to the fish-and-chip shop in Lisson Grove.'

They found a table near the bar and sat the next one out.

'You know that job you did so brilliantly in Markham Street?'

'I put everything back,' she said defiantly, leaning back and looking at him.

'No, it was a great job.'

'I thought it was a waste of time.'

'Something came out of it. In the end. I was very grateful for what you did.'

'That's a change of tune, Mr High-and-Mighty. Every time I see you, you're giving me a lecture about what's right and what's wrong, and somehow it's always me what's wrong.'

'Sorry, I can be a little hasty sometimes. Britain was a very different place when I left eight years ago. Times have changed – I must learn to change with them.'

'That's a bit more like it. Oh – listen, they're playing "Jealousy". Come on!'

'Is that a tango? I've got a sore foot.'

'Don't be such a coward – come on!'

'No, really I won't. What I'm trying to do is get you to concentrate. I need you to do another Markham Street job. Did Rupe pay you?'

'He told me to help myself. But *because of you* I had to put 'em back. Come on!'

'No – sit, sit!' He had to shout as the band ripped through the chorus of the song and the crowd started to shout of their jealousy in unison. 'Another job. Will you?'

Rodie stuck her face in his.

'Depends. Do you love me yet?'

CHAPTER FIFTEEN

'What's the point in training you up to be a courtier if you can't make a bit more of an effort?' said Aggie next morning. There was a crunch of Glasgow granite in her voice. 'Most people in your position would give their eye teeth to be in Buckingham Palace.'

'Mm,' said Guy.

'Mr Lascelles will be wanting to see you. Not happy with the way things turned out with Queen Mary.'

'Ah well.'

'And what have you done about the parrot?'

'A plan of action is under way,' said Guy vaguely.

'And another thing. Topsy wants a . . .'

Guy got up. 'Just before I go upstairs for a carpeting – *two* carpetings – may I just ask you some questions about Ed Brampton? Our masters can wait.'

'Ask away,' replied Aggie, looking at him sideways. 'I've told you all I know.'

'What was Ed's relationship really like with Sir Topham?'

'Unhappy.'

'Like me, he was employed to work for Lascelles, but he was doing jobs for Topsy as well.'

'Yes.'

'Many jobs? What did they entail?'

'He was kept busy taking people out for drinks. And . . . other things. Occasionally bringing them to the Palace when there weren't too many people about, showing them round. You know – like everybody does.'

'Oh?' said Guy. 'I didn't realise Buckingham Palace was now open to tourists to come and poke their noses around. Did he bring Lady Easthampton here?'

'How do you know about *her*?' Aggie's expression had frozen.

'Did he bring her into the Palace?'

'Look,' said Aggie, 'you're still new here. Sooner or later you'll get the picture – when the cat's away, the mice will play. Virtually everyone who works here brings in their friends to take a look around. I don't know how many backsides have sat on the thrones in the Throne Room or picked up a stick and knighted somebody. Or helped themselves to a nip of something from a decanter. This palace doesn't exist just for the people at the top, Mr Harford – we all have to get something extra from working here because the conditions are poor, the wages are low, people look down their noses at you, and there's precious little thanks.'

'Don't think I hadn't noticed.'

'So people wander in and out – as *guests*, you understand – and Major Brampton could have brought anyone in. I wouldn't know.'

'You know about Lady Easthampton, though.'

'Let's change the subject,' said Aggie, shaking her head as if to clear it. 'Not only does the Master want to see you, but that man from the Coats Mission has been in, asking questions.'

'Captain Broadbent? What about?'

'He asked me what I know about someone called Ruby Carr.'

'Rodie . . .' corrected Guy automatically, before stopping himself. Well, the cat's out of the bag now, they all know about her, why did I think it wouldn't come out? 'A friend of a friend,' he said, trying not to think about their night in the heat and crush of the Hammersmith Palais. 'Not directly connected with me, you understand.'

'The captain said you were supposed to be helping him with Ed Brampton's death. But that you were being . . . awkward. He said she had something to do with it, this Ruby. Who is she, exactly?'

'Look,' said Guy, running his hand through his hair, 'this is getting completely out of hand. As far as Mr Lascelles is concerned, Ed's death is past history. A sad loss and all that. But meantime this Broadbent, and old man Dighton, seem intent on keeping it alive. What's it all about?'

'Mr Harford!' said Aggie, suddenly aggressive. 'Why shouldn't people ask questions when it looks like nobody's trying very hard to clear up the mess. No questions being asked,' said Aggie, shaking her head, 'no questions being answered. And him such a fine fellow.'

'I never asked,' said Guy quietly. 'Did you like him?' It didn't seem possible this angular spinster could like anybody.

'He was . . . difficult,' said Aggie slowly. 'That old war wound didn't improve his temper, and I think all the time he was here he felt he was on borrowed time – Topsy never allowed him to feel at home. Major Ed was never settled and that made him – irascible, is that the word? But underneath he had a heart of gold. More than can be said for that wife of his, I can tell you.'

'Adelaide? What do you mean? I've known her a very long time, you know, and I wouldn't have said . . .'

Aggie looked at him coldly. 'Oh, you lot!' she said contemptuously. 'You all stick together, you toffs. You'll never hear a word said against one of your own.'

'Really, I don't think . . .'

'I can tell you this, Mr Harford, she was cold. Cold towards him. I think he only got that silly pash on the Queen because Mrs

Brampton shut him out. It wouldn't surprise me if she didn't have something to do with his death.'

'*What?* What on earth do you mean?'

'She was on the shelf, you know. Mrs Brampton. Nobody wanted her till Major Brampton did the decent thing and proposed. If it wasn't for him she'd be a spinster still – no children, no family, a Miss Whatsername doing good deeds and getting in everybody's way like they all do.'

'I don't know what you're talking about, Aggie. She's a very practical woman – and doing her bit for the war effort.' He wasn't sure about this last bit – he hadn't asked her. 'True, I hadn't seen her for a long time, but I can honestly say that she is one of the best . . .'

'She had the children by him then shut him out. She'd got what she wanted. She hated the fact he only had one leg – *he* told me that. So I ask you this – if she hated his disability, why marry him?'

'I think because she felt sorry for him,' replied Guy quietly.

'Far from it! She got her society wedding, she had her children, then she left him to go and live in the country. Leaving him to stew on his own in Chelsea. She had a boyfriend, you know – no names, no pack drill – and he got to hear about it.'

'Adelaide? I don't think so!' protested Guy.

'What would *you* know, Mr Harford? You've only been here five minutes! You have no real idea what goes on inside these palace railings. It wouldn't surprise me if that didn't have something directly to do with his death.'

'She's not the type to . . .' he responded weakly. 'And anyway, anyone with children who's got any sense would get out of London before they found themselves under a pile of bricks – that's why she left, not to have some hole-in-the-corner affair. No, you've got it all wrong!'

'Have I, Mr Harford?'

'For heaven's sake, I've known her nearly all my life – I feel certain she could never be unfaithful.'

Did he? How well, actually, did he know the woman who'd been his childhood playmate? He turned to face Aggie, shocked by what she'd implied.

'This is serious. Are you saying Adelaide Brampton caused her husband to kill himself? If so, you'd better speak up – there are people round here' – he waved his hand vaguely – 'who think it's more complicated than that.'

'I'll say this. Everything seemed to be going along on an even keel until she suddenly left for the country. Major Ed said he didn't know how she could suddenly up sticks without warning. After that, he was a very different man. A tragedy really. A tragedy.'

'Do I get the feeling that you . . . *admired* Major Brampton?'

'None of your business, Mr Harford. I don't even know why we're talking like this.'

'Let me ask you something else then. I've been looking for Ed's diary. I think – since people seem so determined to keep the investigation into his death alive – it may well contain the answer to the mystery. It wasn't *you* who took it, was it?'

Aggie reddened. 'Somebody came into this office without permission. *Somebody!* When the door was locked! They left . . . *evidence.*' Aggie waved her finger at Guy's desk. 'All I'll say is that Major Brampton's diary was there before that somebody appeared, and it wasn't there afterwards.'

What on earth could Rodie want with a diary? And why didn't she tell me when we were spinning round to 'In the Mood' or afterwards in that fish-and-chip shop – why didn't she say she'd pinched it? But rather than pursue this thought, Guy decided to switch tack.

'Help me with this, from what you know. I'm talking about Lady Easthampton. My feeling is that, whatever it was between them, it wasn't romantic. Am I wrong in that assumption?'

'I have no idea, Mr Harford.'

'Yes you do. That she was using him to get to something far bigger. Am I wrong?'

'I couldn't possibly say.'

'But now you're suggesting that Ed's death could be due to no more than the breakdown of his marriage, caused by Mrs Brampton having an . . . affair . . . with someone else.'

'He felt betrayed when she took the children to the country.'

'Nonsense. It was the proper thing for her to do.'

'She did have somebody.'

'How do you know?'

Aggie looked at him but didn't answer.

'Whatever the answer, it's probably in Ed's diary, I assume. Which is why you've hidden it.'

He said this more as a smokescreen, to get the thought out of Aggie's mind – if it had ever entered – that it was Rodie who'd burgled the office. But her face said nothing.

A sudden thought struck him. 'Is it the case that you and Major Ed were having an affair? And that actually you know a great deal more about his death than you've let on? Is that what it is?'

Aggie burst into tears. Just then the telephone rang.

'Mr Harford?' inquired a woman's imperious voice. 'I wonder if you didn't get the message from Mr Lascelles? He will see you now.'

'Ah, yes,' said Guy, wrestling with the handset while offering Aggie his handkerchief.

'That means *now*, Mr Harford!'

◆ ◆ ◆

'Go easy, I've only got one can of this stuff, I don't know if it'll get round the room.'

'Where did you get it from? There's a war on, you know.'

'Oh, really, is there? There's a wonderful man called Digger, he's the porter on the Tradesmen's Gate at the Palace. Possibly the nicest chap in the whole place. Even the King says good morning to him – that's rare for below-stairs. Knows everybody, can get anything.'

'Black-market, then, is it?' Rupert sniffed as he ladled out the battleship-grey paint into a tray.

'Certainly not. It's what's left over from painting the guard-room. Going begging. I had to cover these walls before I could get started. Too confusing to work in.'

They were in the smaller room of the Tite Street studio, a space covered from top to bottom in the previous tenant's daubs and experimental sketches and patches of colour. It took an hour or two to finish the job and the paint did not quite go round.

'It'll do,' Guy said. 'I've got some bottles of Mackeson, or we could go to The Surprise for a pint.'

'Both,' said Rupe.

'Good. I want to talk to you about Ed Brampton. And Topham Dighton. And Suzy Easthampton – the works, really. It may take some time.' He levered open two bottles of stout.

'If I could, I'd drop this investigation,' he continued. 'I've done all I've been asked, and achieved the required result – that's to say, nothing. My boss Tommy Lascelles is quite content – he wants to forget Ed Brampton ever existed. But I'm being pushed around by Dighton, and to a lesser extent by the man from the Coats Mission. They're both egging me on to find out things they can't find out themselves. I explained to you about Dighton's part in the English Mistery. He's prodding me, I think, because he wants to know if Ed ever blabbed about the Mistery. If it got out, he'd be arrested and a lifetime of devoted royal service would end in disgrace.'

'We've got our eye on the Misters,' said Rupe. 'Collectively they're a dangerous force, but as the war wears on, they seem to be retreating into the backwoods. Less of a threat.'

'Even so, one of the King's most senior and trusted courtiers meddling in political plots . . .'

'Agreed.'

'Against the Prime Minister.'

'Yes.'

'Who he welcomes with a glass of brandy when he pops into the Palace for his weekly chat with the King.'

'Mm.'

'I can't help wondering,' Guy went on, 'whether there's something more – that Dighton, having got Brampton to do his dirty work, wanted to shut him up.'

'You mean, have him killed?'

'Stranger things have happened. The trouble is, we don't know how Ed died, apart from a gunshot wound. Was he murdered, did he commit suicide, or was it truly an accident? Without a post-mortem, without an inquest, we're completely in the dark.'

He poured more beer before continuing. 'So that's Dighton as a suspect – murder. Against that, the clerk in my office, Aggie, thinks Ed killed himself because his wife was having an affair – so it's suicide. Beyond that is the vaguest possibility that she herself did it, because Ed was devoting himself to Suzy Easthampton. And then there's Lady Easthampton – an enemy agent, I think we can take it, though hardly a dangerous one. Probably the most lethal thing she's come up against are the cocktails in The Savoy. So you see, it's a maze.'

'Why go on, then?' asked Rupert. 'Now we've painted this place out, won't you be spending your spare time preparing for that exhibition?'

Guy unrolled a brown paper parcel and took out a handful of brand-new paintbrushes. Then he reached behind his chair and lifted out a blank canvas, turning it one way and then the other, inspecting the way the late-afternoon light bounced off its surface.

'Between you and me, Rupe, I believe I have my first commission – Pamela Churchill, the Prime Minister's daughter-in-law.'

'That's a catch. How did you manage that?'

'A friend of Foxy's – a rich American called Betsey Cody.'

Hardacre's eyes flicked momentarily. 'Have you met her?'

'Not yet. I'm going to dinner with her tomorrow night. She's a great patron of the arts, I'm told.'

'Well done. But extraordinary that she should pick you out to shower with her patronage.'

'Isn't it? I'm so delighted, I can't tell you. She has a great deal of money and likes to make as many people happy as she can. But of course, no doubt part of that is what the other hostesses are doing – Emerald Cunard, Sybil Colefax, Mrs Greville – all busy making names for themselves by being agreeable to the right people.'

'And you're the right person, Guy? Don't get me wrong, but there are dozens of portrait artists out there – why you? To paint Winston Churchill's daughter-in-law?'

Guy was opening a box filled with tubes of paint, breathing in their heady aroma. 'Mm? Oh, she saw my portrait of Foxy on the wall and said she liked it.'

'Have some more beer and come and sit down,' said Rupert.

'Yes?'

'I want you to forget I told you this, but we're not sure about Mrs Cody.'

'Not sure – what do you mean?'

'Just – not sure. Listen carefully, if you will, to what's going on when you go to dinner. It could be a great help.'

Guy plonked down his beer glass. 'What's this? After Dighton and Lascelles and the Coats Mission, I'm being sent off on another wild goose chase? And by my own flatmate?'

168

'I see you're getting the hang of this work,' answered Rupert smoothly. 'Nobody's asking you to do anything special, just keep your ears and eyes open. You're good at that.'

'And what about Lady Easthampton, what am I supposed to do about her?'

'Did you go dancing with Rodie?'

'Yes. Much against my . . .'

'And?'

'She agreed.'

'Agreed what?'

'To sit. I need to get my hand in again before I have a go at Mrs Churchill. She has a . . . marvellous face. Problem is I can never exhibit the finished picture – if it's discovered I'm associating with her, I'm for the high jump.'

'How high can you jump, Guy?'

'What do you mean?'

'She's up in court tomorrow morning. Bow Street. Burglary, use of explosives – she could be going away for a very long time.'

'*What?*'

'I need you there at ten o'clock.'

CHAPTER SIXTEEN

'The plan, Your Worship, was to break into the Toller and Maschler warehouse at Elephant and Castle, drag out the safe from the warehouse office and drive it away. The means of execution had been arranged some time beforehand, it was just a case of waiting for a particularly heavy air raid to cover their movements.'

The magistrate looked down without surprise at the bewigged lawyer in the well of the court.

'Yes?'

The prosecutor adjusted his glasses and carried on. 'You will recall we had that lengthy air attack the other night, Your Worship. Thompson, Bates and Murphy were sitting in the lorry waiting for the fourth member, the woman Carrigan . . .'

Guy, wedged anonymously in a corner of the public gallery, looked down at the diminutive figure standing in the dock. Her face was white, her Eton crop dishevelled. Completely absent was her customary fighting spirit.

The light in the old courtroom somehow diminished all four accused, looking worn and fragile as they did in their cheap clothes. Who would imagine that only two nights before they'd been pumped up with adventure and bravado, poised on the brink of a successful blag?

'Thompson was recently dismissed from his Air Raid Precautions post but retained his uniform and tin helmet, so that his presence on the street would go unremarked,' the prosecution lawyer went on. 'He had learned from a factory hand that the security guards changed their shift at two in the morning, making this the best time to break in.

'Carrigan, who was to do the breaking and entering, had had a key made from a wax mould which would open the gates. They waited until the air raid was at its height – and the street empty – before they made their move.

'You will hear, Your Worship, that when the time came, Thompson drove forward. Carrigan, who, as we shall learn, is not inexperienced in these matters . . .'

A small man sitting alongside the prosecutor rose to his feet, saying, 'Your Worship . . . I really don't think . . . er, prejudicial . . .' before sinking ineffectually down again. The magistrate ignored him.

'Continue, Mr Simkins.'

'Sir, Carrigan who has, er, some expertise, forced a window, then jemmied the main warehouse door open from the inside. Within moments they were all inside the office, manhandling a huge safe out to their lorry.

'But, Your Honour, we have Herr Hitler to thank for their apprehension. As they emerged from the warehouse, a high-explosive bomb dropped in the yard and they were blown off their feet. When they picked themselves up and dusted themselves down, they discovered the bomb had destroyed the gates and turned the lorry upside down.'

Two of the three men accused looked on with boredom, their countenances indicating this was a hole they'd found themselves in many times before. The third, Bates, had become engrossed in the activities of a shorthand writer wearing a tight-waisted dress and was paying no attention. Only Rodie appeared to have the slightest interest in the proceedings.

'The three men had their safe, but no means of transporting it away. They attempted to escape. The fourth accused, Carrigan – looking up – saw that the nightwatchman had been caught in the blast, which had, quite extraordinarily, thrown him up on to a high ledge. Somehow she managed to get to the injured man and prevented him from falling to an almost-certain death, given his other injuries, and stayed with him until the fire brigade arrived.'

Just for a moment the magistrate looked down with interest into the dock. Rodie gave him a wink, and he glared at her before looking away.

'That act of selflessness, I am obliged to call it, Your Honour, will no doubt have cost this woman her liberty and she must have known it would. The police arrived at the same time as the fire brigade and she was handed over. The other three were apprehended a few hundred yards away trying to steal a van to make their getaway.'

After this opening statement, the proceedings rumbled on in the usual torpid manner of magistrates' courts. At the lunch break, Guy waited outside in Bow Street until the lawyer, Simkins, emerged.

'Might I have a word?'

'Who are you?' said the barrister aggressively. Prosecutors are rarely accustomed to a friendly face in or near their place of work.

'Guy Harford, Buckingham Palace,' said Guy, who had never introduced himself that way before. He handed the man his palace entry pass, surprised at the impact it made.

'Good Lord,' said Simkins, stuttering slightly. 'How unusual. How . . . how . . . can I be of assistance?'

'May we walk? Do you have a couple of minutes?'

'But of course, of course!'

Gas masks over their shoulders, the two men strolled past the Opera House into the Covent Garden piazza, a few flower stalls still dotted about the place but with the vegetable stalls cleared away for the day.

'Miss Carrigan,' said Guy. 'A most impressive piece of heroism.'

'In other circumstances, she might find herself receiving a medal,' agreed the lawyer. 'How she got up on that ledge I do not know, she'd had to have been very courageous as well as agile.'

'May I take you into my confidence?'

'Of course, of course.'

'Strange as it may seem, and it will seem strange, Miss Carrigan is undertaking work on behalf of the Crown.'

'Yes, I *do* find that strange, Mr Harford. She's a burglar.'

'That is undeniable.'

'The men she was working with are called the Jellied Eel Brigade. I learned that this is a joke,' the lawyer went on, 'which indicates they may have some acquaintance with gelignite, while also paying tribute to their favourite supper. Had not Mr Hitler beaten them to it, no doubt they'd have created a bang or two themselves the other night. I really can't picture that sort of behaviour being condoned by His Majesty.'

'I think you'll find King George is a most enlightened man,' said Guy smoothly. 'In these unusual times, and especially since the Palace was bombed, he has come to realise it takes many different types to weave together the fabric of the nation.'

'How can I be of assistance, Mr Harford?'

'It's really more of an inquiry than any kind of request, you understand. As you yourself have outlined, Miss Carrigan has exceptional skills – rare skills. She had been given the task of utilising those skills on behalf of the Crown.'

'The King wants her to go and burgle someone?'

Well, yes, thought Guy – in a manner of speaking, he does.

'Nothing like that,' he reassured Simkins. 'But there's nobody else who can manage the task she's been given. You might say she's unique.'

Simkins looked down at his well-polished shoes. 'And what, ah, advice is it you are seeking?'

'Have you ever been to the Palace?'

'No.'

'You should, you should! Quite a remarkable place. Lots to see. And a chance, sometimes, to sit on the throne.'

'Good Lord!'

'Unofficially, of course.'

'Of course, of course!'

'I'll arrange it. His Majesty will be away for a few days – can't say where! – but I can telephone to see if you're free.'

'How can I help in the matter of Miss Carrigan?' The lawyer looked at Guy in an old-fashioned way; it was not the first time he'd been bribed.

'From this morning's evidence, indeed in your own words, she's something of a heroine for saving that chap's life.'

'Agreed.'

'The attempt to rob the warehouse was foiled. No harm was done to the building that wasn't multiplied many times over by Herr Hitler.'

'Yes.'

'One might argue, therefore, that since no money was taken, no offence had occurred.'

'Sorry. Leave to one side the safe with the wages, they were caught trying to steal a getaway van.'

'Not Rodie – er, Miss Carrigan.'

'True.'

'Her work for us at the Palace is of . . .' – Guy paused – 'an unconventional nature. But vital to the war effort. I was wondering whether you couldn't have a word with the Chief Magistrate and separate out the charges – burglary, conspiracy to burgle, attempted robbery of a motor vehicle for those three old lags. And separate charges for Miss Carrigan. To be answered at a later date.'

'What later date?'

'When this bleedin' war is over,' Guy said, quoting the old First War song.

It took quite some time for his wish to be granted. Having persuaded Simkins of the importance of Rodie's freedom, he had to wait while the lawyer chewed it over, consulted various books for legal precedent, and considered which of his wife's hats she should wear when they nipped into the Throne Room. Finally, Simkins decided on the rabbit-with-pheasant's-feather and went back to make the case to the Chief Magistrate. His task was not helped by the defence counsel, who suddenly glimpsed an opportunity to get the charges against the other ruffians in his care dropped.

The magistrate – short-tempered, high-handed, and bloody-minded – was in no mood to preside over an afternoon of fruitless argument. But as with every other corner of British public life, the magic words 'Buckingham Palace' had a curiously disorienting effect on his judgement, and before the end of the afternoon Rodie was free.

She came down the court steps into Bow Street to find Guy waiting for her.

'What on earth do you think you were doing? Burgling a warehouse? In Elephant and Castle? I thought you were a bit more stylish than that!'

'Needs must,' replied Rodie with a toss of her head. 'Bills to pay.'

'You know, I doubt you bother about life's little conventions like bill-paying. You were doing it for the hell of it.'

'What if I was?'

'You could have gone to jail, you idiot!'

'Where are you taking me, sweetie? Are we going to celebrate?'

'Let me explain something,' he said curtly. 'You are, in many ways, a most remarkable person. That much I grant you. Courageous, resourceful, quick-thinking and . . .'

'Adorable,' finished Rodie, looking up at him, eyes sparkling.

'. . . and as dangerous as a rattlesnake. What's more, you drag others around you into your danger zone. And I will *not* be dragged!'

'No need for the lecture, you love me really.'

'If you weren't such a complete idiot,' persisted Guy, 'you'd probably be in for a medal. You saved a man's life – it could be a whole new beginning for you. Instead you winked at the magistrate. You nearly ended up back in the dock.'

''E's an old sweetie. I'll send 'im some flowers.'

'You'll do no such thing.'

'Where are we celebrating?'

The answer was not what she was expecting. Guy steered her by the elbow down to the Strand and into Trafalgar Square, where the black-and-white-uniformed Nippies of Lyon's Corner House waited at the door to greet them.

'A pot of tea and whatever sandwiches there are,' ordered Guy.

'No champagne? I'm a free woman!'

'You're free for one very good reason. There's a job for you to do.'

Rodie looked at him suspiciously. 'What sort of job?'

'What you do best, Rodie. Climbing into somebody's window.'

'Are you mad?' Rodie shouted so loud the customers at the next table looked around. 'I've just escaped by the skin of my teeth from the hands of the law and now you're suggesting I do a job?'

'It'll be a piece of cake.'

'Look,' said Rodie, shoving her face across the table. In this light it's a remarkable face, thought Guy. 'You're a lovely man, but you have no *idea*! Three hours ago I was looking at a year inside Holloway. OK, you rescued me, but if they collar me again it'll be two years – three! Do you honestly think I'm going to chance that?'

Guy looked at her. 'What else are you going to do, Rodie? Join the Salvation Army?'

'Very funny.'

'It's a simple job. Just get inside a mansion block in Mayfair and find the whereabouts of the woman who lives there.'

'No.'

'Chesterfield House. There's a grumpy man on the door so you'll have to find a way of bypassing him, but otherwise I can't see it'll be a very great test of your considerable skills.'

'I'm going straight. I value my freedom.'

'Nonsense. When you wake up tomorrow you'll be back to your old ways. But what on earth were you doing risking your liberty with those three no-hopers? You're smarter than that!'

The Nippy brought the tea.

'In Tangier,' said Guy, 'I learned from the natives that you repay kindness with kindness, courtesy with courtesy. Forgive me for saying this, Rodie, but you owe me.'

'Huh!' she spluttered, heaping sugar into her cup. 'This time last week you were Mr High-and-Mighty, Mr Butter-Wouldn't-Melt, looking down your nose at people like me and Batesy and Murphy. Now look at you!'

'There's a war on. Let me tell you . . .'

'Are you joking? You've turned into one of us, Guy!'

Maybe I have, he thought. But why? Nobody really cares about poor old Ed Brampton's death – Adelaide had gone off him and is happy with her new life, Tommy Lascelles got the closure he wanted, the police aren't interested, and Topsy Dighton only wants to find out what I know, not what happened to Ed.

The only person left who cares is me.

'There's a woman called Lady Easthampton. She's probably working for the enemy; we don't know, but it looks like that. What she's doing is more complicated than just spying – that's all I can tell you. She's gone missing and we need to find her. She's been staying in a flat in Mayfair but it doesn't look like she's there any more.'

Rodie looked at him shrewdly. 'This is to do with that chap – Brampton is his name? – isn't it?'

'Not really.'

'I'll take that as a yes, then. Was he Lady Easthampton's fancy man?'

Am I that transparent? thought Guy.

'I couldn't say.'

'He was then. The trouble with you, Guy, is you're no good at hiding a secret. Your eyes give you away. But they're very nice eyes, has anyone ever told you that?' She leaned across the table.

'Number 12A, Chesterfield House,' he said firmly. 'It's on the second floor, but after you shinned up the wall to save that man at the warehouse, I don't suppose it'll present too much of a problem. Plus, I imagine there's a service entrance if you can't get past the doorman. Get in there and see if you can find where this woman has got to – any addresses, letters, notes that might give a clue. And please understand, Rodie, this is very important.'

'Are you going to be telling me to put things back, like you did last time?'

Guy pondered this for a minute.

'You didn't ask me that question and I didn't answer,' he said. 'Now get going!'

CHAPTER SEVENTEEN

To look at the way Mrs Granville Cody treated her guests, you'd never know there was a war on. As the double doors to her apartment overlooking Grosvenor Square swung open, a discreetly suited young man bowed gently and took coats. Another stood ready with a shimmering drinks tray. Beyond, a pair of sensibly coiffed women circulated with silver dishes and starched linen napkins.

'We meet at last!' said Betsey, when Guy finally made his appearance. 'The famous young artist! Come in, come in!'

The party was for a dozen, but such was the crush there must have been as many servants as guests. Glimpsing Guy's look of surprise, Betsey waved her hand. 'Borrowed from the Embassy, my dear. Darling people doing that little bit more for the war effort. Amazing what an extra few dollars can do to help the world seem a better place. Now, who do you know?'

Over by a window criss-crossed with anti-shatter tape, Guy could see Ted Rochester talking to a man in US Army uniform next to the wife of a prominent Member of Parliament. Nearby were people whose faces seemed familiar, maybe from the newspapers, together with an actress or two – but there was nobody else he knew.

'You're my guest of honour,' purred Betsey, touching his arm. 'I feel so very lucky to have found you!' She looked remarkable – as extravagant and expensive as her apartment, as warm and as welcoming. He breathed in as he was handed a glass of champagne – she was wearing a satin dress and diamonds, with a brooch at her shoulder which could have come from the Crown Jewels. She *smelt* rich.

'This is delightful,' he murmured. 'So kind. Is Foxy . . . ?'

'Not tonight, darling, she's off with her intended. Such a handsome man – they say the handsomest in the entire House of Lords! But it means I get the chance to get to know you without her grabbing your attention every other second. I saw that portrait you did,' she teased, 'a labour of love, I'd call it!'

Steady on, thought Guy, you've already promised me a gallery for my exhibition *and* my first celebrity to paint – no need to heap on the flattery as well. Or is that what you do to all your guests – is that why you're such a celebrated hostess?

'Come along now, meet some people – I'll have you to myself later. This is Lord Waterhead.' She put her head to one side to say, *I can be satirical about my guests because I am rich.* 'He once drove a taxi at dawn from Paris to Rome, wearing pyjamas and a gardenia – but he forgot his *toothbrush*, can you imagine?

'This is Lady Culpeper, whose family owns the entire state of Virginia – have you ever been? And George St John August, who – can you see? – looks just like Shelley. His mother makes bird's nests and every Thursday she . . .'

On prattled Mrs Cody, making it up as she went along, until Guy had been presented to everyone. It was made clear to them all that he was the star of the show tonight, but as he listened to his hostess's facile chatter, he could quite easily detect a sharper brain at work within. There was a vitality to her, and the way her eyes constantly scoured the room for lost sheep needing to be drawn into the fold showed how deft an operator she was.

Ted Rochester sidled over as people were being ushered to the dining table. 'You're a lucky boy,' he said out of the side of his mouth. 'You don't have a title, you're not rich, you haven't been in the newspapers and you haven't won the Victoria Cross. Those are the people who sit next to Betsey Cody – why you?'

'She wants me to paint her portrait but she can't ask. She's waiting for me to mention it first.'

'Are you going to?'

'I might.'

'She's very rich.'

'That may come into my deliberations.'

'Ha ha! You're a cool one, Guy – all this, and then she tells me she's getting Pamela Churchill to sit for you as well. That's an introduction most young artists would kill for.'

'Let's see if it comes off. I've got a new studio down in Chelsea – I need to put some work in if there's to be an exhibition in the autumn.'

'Can I write that in my column?'

'Pamela Churchill? They don't like personal publicity at the Palace.'

'Ah well. But since you mention it, how's the Ed Brampton business going?'

'It's over, Ted.'

'No inquest?'

'There's no time these days. Don't you read your own newspaper? People dying all over the place – sometimes hundreds in a night – what's an accident with a revolver among all that? The poor chap's gone, pretty soon he'll be forgotten, and we'll be wondering why there was such a fuss.'

'Come along,' said Ted, taking his elbow. 'Time for you to sing for your supper.'

Dinner was startling – turtle soup, lobster, lamb cutlets en gelée, ice, cheese. Guy's good manners prevented him from asking where it all came from, but he recoiled as he saw some guests pushing their plates away half-finished. For these people, he thought, there's no such thing as rationing.

Betsey Cody lavished her attention upon him as course followed course, but as she pressed closer he began to find her possessiveness slightly alarming.

'We ladies will leave you now,' she said at a lull in the conversation. 'No more than fifteen minutes, gentlemen. Brandy and cigars will circulate. The port, I'm sorry to say, is rather regrettable, according to the butler.'

A red-nosed pixie standing by the door nodded conspiratorially at Guy, and for a moment he wondered whether the port was off because the man with the nose had swallowed most of it.

'Sit over by the window, Guy, when you come – I want to talk to you.'

You've done nothing else all evening, he thought, but when the men rose from the table and joined the women in the drawing room, she was already sitting waiting for him.

'Foxy tells me you're limbering up to paint Pam Churchill – you've got yourself a studio and you've found an early volunteer to practise on.'

'I'll be frank, Betsey, I haven't done many portraits recently, apart from the native women in Tangier. And since their faces are always veiled, it's quite an easy job, as you can imagine.'

'Ha ha! Pam is young and very beautiful – as you'll see when you come round to tea next week. She's going to be something special, and from what I've seen of your work you are the perfect artist to paint her. I love the one you did of Foxy, and of course that one of Suzy Solidor in Paris – perfection!'

'It was a great feather in my cap, Betsey, and so is this. I'll never be able to thank you enough – especially your getting me the Gulbenkian gallery as well.'

'He'll be glad to have you there. But there is something you can do for me in return, Guy.'

'It'll be my pleasure.'

'It's my dear Granville. He works so hard for the Aircraft Exchange Commission – he's here, there and everywhere. I'd like him to take things more easily, but he won't.'

'I've heard he's doing wonders. Was it he who got Averell Harriman to come over here from Washington?'

'They're old friends. Averell wants to help Britain – he's a great fan of Winston.'

And an even greater fan of Winston's daughter-in-law, thought Guy – she's twenty-one with a baby and he must be fifty.

'I know what you're thinking, you naughty man! But your portrait will be his present to Pamela. A token of undying affection, let's say.'

'So how can I help, Betsey?'

'Granville needs some country air. We know the Windsors of course, and we know the Kents, and naturally we've met the King and Queen, though we don't know them well. Harry Gloucester is doing his bit by inviting all sorts of people up to his place, Barnwell Manor, and I thought it would be a treat for Granville to get away for a weekend. He's a pretty good shot, and he appreciates a nice garden. And, of course, we and the Gloucesters have a lot of people in common, so conversation wouldn't be a problem.'

'Well, I . . .'

'Foxy tells me Tommy Lascelles wants you to become Harry's private secretary, otherwise I wouldn't have asked.'

'I think that probably won't happen. I may not be at the Palace for too much longer.'

'But you're there now! Won't you have a word with Lascelles? I just think it would be a nice thank you to Granville for all that selfless work he's putting in. All those hours, all those dangerous flights!'

Guy looked at the large brandy balloon in his hand and put it down. 'Of course I will, Betsey, though I must say it's an unusual request. Most people would rather *not* stay with the Duke – he's a bit of a handful.'

'Well,' replied Betsey, 'I gather he has time on his hands at the moment – nothing much to do. It seems like an ideal opportunity to get to know them both better.'

Some people, thought Guy, like to collect royals like others collect court cards when playing bridge. No matter how rich, how worldly, they want to be able to say they have stayed under a royal roof.

'I'm certain there'll be something we can do in return,' said his hostess with a sparkling smile. 'And, of course – you, Guy! We mustn't forget you! Tell me what your fee will be for painting Pamela, and don't be shy about it!'

◆ ◆ ◆

Later that night, Ted Rochester sat at a table in his small service flat high above St James's Street, turned back his cuffs, flexed his fingers, and thought for a moment about how he would describe an evening in London.

Writing for New York's *Boulevardier* was so much easier than writing for the British prints. Here he could express his true feelings – his contempt for the world he moved in, his dislike of virtually everybody, his suspicion and anger and disappointment at the hand life had dealt him. Readers of his *News Chronicle* column would quite soon be reading an oily account of a lively evening at Mrs Granville Cody's, where Vivien Leigh gave an impromptu song-and-dance act and guests, including the valiant Viscount Waterhead, whispered about the latest fashionable artist (no name, he'd promised) who'd soon be portraying a member of Mr Churchill's family. There'd be a list of the guests (minus Guy) and a hint of the splendour of Betsey's hospitality – without enough description to make the reader feel that this woman must be breaking rationing regulations.

No, his true feelings about the beau monde in which he moved only came out when he wrote under his pseudonym Caliban for *Boulevardier*. Here, describing his night's perambulation, he could express just what he felt about the world without fear of Britain's draconian libel laws. It was liberating.

```
In the expensive restaurants of Mayfair
and Knightsbridge, pink well-scrubbed
schoolboys masquerading in Guards uni-
forms are drinking bad martinis with
girlfriends in short fur capes and
Fortnum and Mason shoes.

Grass widows in black, with diamond clips
and pearls, are finding the conversation
of Polish officers difficult to follow.
Ugly but vivacious ATS girls are order-
ing vin rosé at the Coquille. A famous
film actress goes through the swinging
door of The Aperitif with David Niven at
```

```
her derrière. This is a world of hotels
and bars, and the little pubs that have
become the fashion overnight - small
drinking clubs run by gangsters who make
a nice profit out of the prostitutes and
the dope racket - while everywhere is
packed with RAF pilots, Canadian offi-
cers, blondes, and slot machines.
```

He paused and lit a cigarette. The extravagance of Betsey Cody's hospitality had left a sour taste in his mouth, though in truth most of his meals were at somebody else's expense and he hardly had the right to complain.

```
Along Piccadilly from the Circus to
Hyde Park Corner is an incessant parade
of prostitutes. In Berkeley Square,
the railings are down. The royal
family . . .
```

And so he rattled on into his portable Remington. The words came easily but as he typed he found himself distracted by the thought of Guy and his sudden celebrity at one of the most exclusive tables in London.

He formed in his mind a suitable paragraph which one day he might use, depending on how far the whippersnapper climbed up the slippery pole – Rochester was notorious for crushing people when their star started to fall.

```
His arrival in London and his sudden
social success caught many by surprise.
After studying in Paris, he took his
```

palette and easel to Tangier, where
there are few European painters to
present any competition. This period,
mostly spent in and around the Grand
Socco, produced a large number of canvases whose merits few will be able to
judge, since he left them all behind on
his flight to London after a diplomatic
incident which he prefers to forget.

A short period in the Foreign Office
allowed him to prise open the doors
of Buckingham Palace, where, despite
a moderate success completing a dismal
series of errands, he found sufficient
favour to be put forward as private
secretary to the King's brother, the
Duke of Gloucester. However, Harford
believed his superior talents were in
painting people's faces and in this
he was lucky to be taken up by Betsey
Cody, impossibly rich wife of Granville
Cody, the . . .

To say he was jealous of Guy would be an over-simplification –
Rochester was jealous of everybody – but the secret of Ed Brampton
irked him. He hated to miss a story, and now he was so celebrated
a columnist he believed it was others' bounden duty to tell him
everything about their lives, leaving nothing out.

Furthermore, the way Betsey Cody, his prize possession as a gossip columnist, had bypassed him to get to Guy was vexing. He clung

to his stories, trifling though they were, as if they were the Crown Jewels. Every famous-name person met, every private telephone number acquired, every crumb and morsel of information – these were his children whom he ferociously guarded.

Just then the telephone rang. He glanced at the clock – 1.30 a.m.

'Toby Broadbent here. Not too late for you, old chap?'

'They'll be serving the first drinks in El Morocco around now. And anyway, I never sleep. How goes the guard duty?'

'Mm? To be frank, old chap, I think the days of the Coats Mission are numbered. Nobody's invading Britain, the King and Queen are safe as houses, and everyone's getting just a wee bit bored.'

'I heard you had a bit of a mishap the other day. Shame I can't write about it.'

'Look,' said Broadbent, his words weighed down by what had clearly been a heavy night in the officers' mess, 'not our fault it all went haywire.'

'The Coats Mission ambushed a general. One of our own side!'

'In our game, you've got to set yourself realistic targets.'

'He was going out to lunch!'

'Makes no difference.'

'You nearly killed him with all the smoke bombs you chucked into his car.'

'Look!' shouted Broadbent. 'The chaps are keen as mustard. They keep on their toes!'

'Then you kidnapped Merle Oberon.'

'None of your business.'

'She's a Hollywood actress, Toby – a woman. What on earth were you targeting her for?'

'All good clean fun,' chuckled Broadbent down the telephone. 'Had a few drinks with her in the mess afterwards. She was very sweet. I got her autograph.'

'You know, if I were His Majesty I'd be worrying about my personal safety. You lot are a bunch of comedians.'

'Don't be fooled. To the last man, to the last bullet. We will never let him be captured.'

'Hmph. Anyway, why the call, Toby?'

'This man Guy Harford. You and I discussed him at Edgar Brampton's funeral. I have something which may be of interest to you.'

Rochester sat forward in his chair and picked up a pencil. 'Yes?' He was suddenly wide awake.

'You can never be too sure these days. People get knocked over in the street, attacked in broad daylight, fall under a bus. Harford's a valuable asset at the Palace, I'm told, so I gave him a spare chap as a bodyguard. Just to be on the safe side.'

'Does he know?'

'Where would the fun be if we told him? No, of course he doesn't know!'

'And your purpose in this cloak-and-dagger caper?'

'Well, good training for the man involved and, actually, he's turned out to be a bright star.'

'How so?'

'He popped into Bow Street Magistrates' Court yesterday, and who should he find there . . .'

'Let me guess. Did they have Harford up before the beak for cycling without lights? Dropping litter? Whistling in the street? I can't imagine what else – he's a pretty innocent sort of chap.'

'You won't think so when I tell you what my man discovered.'

'Yes?'

'Harford's involved with a gang of criminals who launched an armed raid on a warehouse in south London then got themselves arrested.'

Rochester stood up. 'Impossible!' he squeaked.

'Don't take my word for it. My chap followed him into the courthouse. He went into Number 1 court, where committal proceedings had started against three men and a woman. I'll spare you the details, all I'll say is that at the lunch break Harford approached the prosecuting lawyer and they had a long chat in the street. When the lawyer went back into court, the case was adjourned while both sides consulted the Chief Magistrate. When his nibs came back in, he announced that the case had been deferred, and Harford walked off with the woman. Looks like he used his palace appointment to get her off.'

'I don't believe it.'

'I'll show you a photo of them having tea in Lyons Corner House if you like.'

'Who is this person?'

'She's a common thief, goes by the name of Rodie Carr. Irish, possibly. Wonderful-looking woman.'

'This is extraordinary,' said Rochester. 'A senior – well, semi-senior – palace official not only consorting with a common criminal, but actually going into court for her. Is she his mistress?'

'Doesn't look like it. They didn't hold hands or anything.'

'For heaven's sake, Toby! You don't have to hold hands when you're . . . Do you know anything more?'

There was a muffled belch at the other end of the line. 'Are you going to write something in your paper?'

Rochester gave it a moment's thought.

'Probably not in the national interest just now, what with the King and everything.' The information he'd just received was far too valuable to share with his readers – it would go in his private files for use at precisely the right moment.

'Well, I wouldn't have bothered you if I'd known,' replied the soldier, clearly put out. 'I should have thought it would make a damn fine story. For any newspaper.'

'Come and have a drink at the club tomorrow,' said Ted. 'Bring that photo and I'll explain everything.'

CHAPTER EIGHTEEN

They were back at The Berkeley; it was as safe a place as any.

'Tell me about Betsey,' said Guy. 'She seems too good to be true.'

'How do you mean?' The sunlight caught Foxy's profile, etching for a moment her fine nose, lighting up her green eyes. Guy realised he would have to paint her again.

'It's baffling. One mention from you to this woman and suddenly I've got a gallery, an exhibition and Pamela Churchill waiting in the wings.'

'Stop complaining.'

'No, I'm serious. And I'm curious – I can't believe one person can be that generous to someone she doesn't even know.'

'She knows you now. And likes you very much. She said you were quite the star of the show at dinner.'

'I'd say that she's the star – no wonder her husband stays away from those dinners! But there's a quid pro quo – I have to get Granville and Betsey invited up to Barnwell by the Duke and Duchess of Gloucester.'

'Well, there you are then, one good turn deserves another. Give me a cigarette.'

Guy lit up for them both.

'I don't really understand it. She's already on friendly terms with the Duke and Duchess of Windsor and the Duke and Duchess of Kent. Why now the Gloucesters?'

'That's the way it affects some people around the royal family,' said Foxy. 'Especially the rich ones – they want to become part of the family themselves, like to think of them as relatives. You know, Betsey came from nowhere – she was a secretary in a bank in Wisconsin and yearned to get out and up. She married her boss, moved to Chicago, married again, and eventually snapped up Granville, who'd recently been widowed. That was a big leap for her. As you know, Granville's got more money than you can shake a stick at, and she had to find something to give back in return for his providing her with colossal wealth – so when they came to London she made it her job to get him known by becoming a society hostess. Because she was American, nobody cared where she came from, they all came rushing to her table because of the riches on display.'

'Well, she's charming, I must say, though in what you might call a professional way.'

'You've got her spot on – but she's generous with it too. She used to leave the most ridiculous presents on her guests' dinner plates – Cartier, Van Cleef and Arpels, Asprey – though she's had to tone it down a bit since the war began. But she achieved what she set out to do – Granville's now highly regarded socially, and you could say that he has been given this important war work because of the people she introduced him to at their dinner table.'

'She bought her way into society, then.'

'That's a coarse way of putting it, Guy, I'm surprised at you.'

'Would you sit for me again?'

She looked at him with hooded eyes. 'Not a chance, Hugh absolutely would not like it. He's suspicious of you. He thinks "artists and their models".'

'So does my new landlord Adrian Amberley. Expects it, in fact. Pointed me to the back bedroom.'

'Amberley? That old goat?'

'He's an astonishing painter. As good as Augustus John – who, by the way, is just down the street if and when you come to call.'

'I won't be doing that, Guy.'

Guy smiled. An old waiter finally limped over with their cocktails.

'Back to Betsey. What more do you know about her, if I'm to effect an introduction to the Gloucesters?'

'Very little. When I came here from Paris she took me up – rather like you just now – and because I knew Wallis and David, and so did she, and the fact we're both Americans in London, we became quite close. She throws her money around a bit, and she can take a joke against herself. That doesn't make for bad company.'

'I just find it all a bit strange. The way she's pounced on me.'

'She wants you to paint her. Didn't you get that?'

'And I daresay I'll oblige. I imagine the portrait would have to have pride of place in the exhibition.'

'*Now* you're getting the idea, Guy! And it's sure to guarantee a royal presence at the opening party – the Duke of Kent's like a puppy with her. If she calls, he'll come wagging. Duties permitting, of course.'

'This isn't quite how I envisaged my painting career going.'

'*Carpe diem*, Guy. If Prince George likes what you do with Betsey, he'll probably ask you to paint Princess Marina, who everybody describes as the most beautiful royal in the world, though I can't say I agree – you'll have to do something about her nose. But then – away you go, *everybody* will want you!'

Guy looked around. It was still early, and the room was only slowly filling up. They sat surrounded by a sea of empty chairs.

'What's the news from across the water? I keep being nudged by Ted Rochester for tidbits about the Windsors.'

'Not good, so I don't expect you to pass this on. Do you remember that little man who performed the marriage ceremony in the Château de Candé four years ago?'

'I don't think I do.'

'A reverend fellow called Jardine, came from a mining town in the north of England. The only person in the whole Church of England prepared to marry David and Wallis. Drummed out of holy orders as a result, so off he went to California.'

'To do what?'

'Heaven knows. But he's been saying in the American press he believes David is ready to regain the throne if anything happens to the King. He's talking about him making what he calls "a strong bid" to become king again.'

'Does this come from the Duke, or is he making it up?'

'Couldn't say. He *is* a man of the cloth, so surely he can't be.'

'Well,' said Guy, 'that's pretty astonishing. Just as well the Duke's far away in the Bahamas, out of trouble.'

'Not at the moment. He and Wallis landed in New York a few days ago. Nothing in the press here, of course, but I had a letter from my sister this morning – she said they're staying at the Waldorf Astoria and brought over a hundred pieces of luggage with them. All the way from Nassau!'

'How Ted would love to write that.'

'Well, don't tell him, and especially don't tell him that Wallis has gone shopping-mad. Buying up Fifth Avenue, my dear. My sister said she'd heard Wallis had bought thirty hats – and they've only been there a couple of days!'

'Well, if she's going to come back here to be queen, she'll need them.'

'Ha ha. But I must say, if this man Jardine is saying to the American press we have a weak king, an ailing king, and that we have his older brother planning to steal the crown back – it doesn't look good, does it?'

'No newspaper here would publish that sort of thing. Even Ted Rochester couldn't get that in his column, however hard he tried.'

'Same sort of self-censorship by Fleet Street, as during the Abdication?'

'Worse.'

Their eyes travelled round the room as they chatted.

'Anything else I should know?' asked Guy. 'One learns so little at the Palace.'

'Well,' said Foxy, 'I worry about Georgie Kent. Like you, he's fed up with the footling jobs he's being given. He's sent here and he's sent there, they salute him and he salutes them back, and that's about the measure of it. He's an adorable man, worthy of so much more.'

'Curiously I've never met him,' replied Guy. 'The staff at the Palace absolutely dote on him but he's been away a lot and so I've never been introduced. I've often wondered why he wears a Royal Air Force uniform when he served his time as an officer in the Royal Navy.'

'I'll tell you the story one day. You know, of course, he longs to go and work for the Americans – or with them at least – he wants to get away from the royal pressure-cooker, he hates things the way they are these days. And of course Marina . . . very disillusioned all round, I've heard.'

'No! I didn't know that.'

'Seems to me you don't have an ear for gossip, Guy. Everyone knows it – well, within our circle, anyway.'

'But, Foxy, I'm not in your circle. You seem to have forgotten that, till recently, I was living a blameless life, oblivious to the affairs of royalty, sitting on a mountainside in Tangier.'

'You're still pretty well-connected. I should have thought the jungle drums would have thundered the news out to you.'

'They didn't – not a single thud.'

But by now Guy had lost interest in the machinations of court life – he got it every day at work.

'Look,' he said, 'I don't suppose you and Hugh would like a parrot as a wedding present? Very conversible, one previous owner, comes from a loving home?'

'For heaven's sake, Guy, haven't you got rid of it yet?'

Later – much later – he stood tieless by the tea bar on Chelsea Bridge, watching the snakelike swirl of the river and listening to the chatter of the night owls with their mugs of coffee standing in the near-dark.

She was taking her time, probably paying him back for keeping her waiting when they went dancing.

'There you are. I thought you said eleven o'clock?' He had new shoes on and his feet were hurting.

'Lawks, is that the time?' laughed Rodie. 'Black, no sugar, thanks!'

'There isn't any sugar.'

They took their mugs and sat on a nearby bench. She seemed to be shivering, though the night was warm.

'Would you like my jacket?'

'What? Oh, no, I'm always a bit trembly after a job. It was lovely of you to ask, though – what a gentleman you are.' She pronounced it 'jennelmin'.

'Are you OK?'

''Course I am!'

'Did it go off all right?'

Rodie turned and smiled at him in the half-dark. 'A cakewalk, my darling.'

'Tell me.'

The front entrance of Chesterfield House had, as usual, been guarded by the grizzly bear. A walk around its perimeter suggested a number of ways of gaining entry but, as Rodie pointed out to Guy, you never ignore the bleedin' obvious, so she went away and found a telephone box. Twenty minutes later her friend Lem appeared.

'Dressed up to the nines she was – not like me in my work clothes,' said Rodie. 'She had that doorman round her little finger in no time, and while he was in his cubby-hole finding the glue pot for her broken heel, I just sailed through. Straight up to 12A and through the door like a hot knife through butter.'

'And?'

'Let me tell it my way, mister. First off, it's a very large apartment and I hadn't a clue what I was looking for. Lem came up quite soon after me and I got her to take a look around an' all, but she was useless. So she just spent her time trying on all the clothes in the wardrobe.

'While she was having fun I tried all the usual – going through the desk drawers, kitchen, bedroom and all that. There was a load of papers but I was getting nowhere. Then Lem come out in the hall wearing a fox-fur coat and bingo! She'd got the answer!'

'Which was?'

'A piece of paper in the coat pocket. Whadja call it – a clue!'

'How d'you know it's the answer?'

'*Because*,' said Rodie, as if talking to the village idiot, 'of what went with the address.' She produced a postcard whose printed inscription said:

Underneath, in pencil, ran the message 'No door number for 11c. When you get to 11b go through the service entrance gate and follow the passage round to the back of the building. There's a black-painted door – that's it.'

'Oh,' said Guy in confusion. 'Oh!'

'What?' said Rodie, irritated her discovery wasn't being greeted with a round of applause.

'We'll have to go round there. Now!'

'Well, that's a disappointment,' came the sarcastic response. 'The only clue I find in two hours of searching – I was hoping for a bunch of flowers, not an order to do overtime!'

'Come on!'

Guy marched speedily up Sloane Street with Rodie struggling to keep up. 'What's the bleedin' hurry?' she asked several times, but got no reply. Only when they reached Knightsbridge did he deign to answer.

'I've been wondering what to say. How to tell you this with-out telling you. I can't do the next bit without you, but I simply don't know if I can trust you to keep your mouth shut,' he said grimly. 'But I don't have any choice. All I can say is, if you ever breathe a word of what I'm going to tell you to anyone else, I'll probably be arrested. I will probably go to jail, and it'll put paid to my reputation as an artist for the rest of my life. Do you understand?'

Halting at the kerbstone, Rodie stood up on tiptoe. 'What a dreadful person you must be – not bein' able to trust people who try to help you out!' she replied. 'You have no faith. That's depressin'.'

'Who got you released from that court case?' asked Guy, rising to the bait.

The row that followed looked, to the occasional late-night passer-by, like an ongoing lovers' tiff. Maybe the man had looked at another woman, maybe the woman was saying she was off to pastures new. The words were angry and plentiful, if lost in the night.

By the time they reached Hyde Park Corner the worst was over, and Guy had made up his mind.

'You're not to breathe a word of this to anybody.'

'You already said that.'

'Because it's top secret! There are various contingency plans if the royals are bombed out, or we're invaded or . . . well, there's a number of other scenarios. The first thing, obviously, is to get them away from the Palace as quick as possible. There are a handful of safe houses prepared for them dotted around the country and a group of dedicated men' – he thought briefly of the tiresome Toby Broadbent – 'who'll protect them and make sure they end up where nobody can find them. Do you understand?'

'Pretty obvious plan,' said Rodie, unimpressed.

'The first stopping-off point is a large flat in walking distance of the Palace.'

'Yes?'

'In Curzon Street. In Harbledown House.'

'Oh,' said Rodie, not entirely comprehending. 'So your Lady Easthampton . . . ?'

'I don't know *what* she's doing there, if she's there at all,' said Guy in exasperation. 'But she shouldn't even know about the place. She could pose a very severe threat to the family's safety – the very fact she even knows the existence of this place busts our plan A. She's probably working for the Germans, Rodie – and she knows where the King will go in an emergency!'

They reached the corner of Curzon Street. The red-brick block of flats was set back, unnoticeable behind a large shopfront.

'Number 11 is His Majesty's bolthole,' said Guy, whispering even though the street was almost empty. 'Flat 11B is where the equerry and lady-in-waiting sleep. 11C is for the servants. I just don't get it – what on earth is she doing there?'

'*If* she's there,' repeated Rodie. 'Let's just take a look.'

For a royal residence, however secret, there was a worrying lack of security. The building itself – empty, anonymous – gave the feeling of being abandoned, while the front door sprang open the moment Rodie worked her magic on it. Inside, a wide entrance hall gave no indication as to the number or quality of residents – it looked like a place where retired civil servants might live.

Despite the fact he'd brought her here to burgle the place, Guy was amazed by the speed with which the tiny figure had completed her business. In less than a minute she'd located the right floor and pushed through the service entrance like a Sherman tank. Two seconds later they were round at the back of the building where the promised black door awaited them.

'Just a jiffy, darling.' She pulled something which rattled out of her pocket, and within five seconds they were inside the flat's hallway.

'Nobody 'ere,' said Rodie with a practised air. She spoke softly but with authority. 'I'll put the kettle on – one lump or two?'

'Don't be so silly!' hissed Guy. 'They could be back at any minute.'

'Who's they?' replied Rodie in a normal voice. 'Nobody's been here for days.'

'How do you know?'

'I can tell, mate. Years of practice.'

Emboldened by her confidence, Guy switched on a few lights. A quick walk round established it was a flat with three bedrooms, a kitchen, bathroom, sitting room and dining room.

'We could be very comfortable here, darling, you an' me,' said Rodie, with a laugh. 'And safe – what with His Majesty next door. No chance of burglars!' She dissolved in fits of giggles.

'Come on,' said Guy anxiously, wanting to get away. 'Let's get this over and done. I need your intuition – if Lady Easthampton isn't here and she isn't over the road in the other flat, where the hell is she?'

Rodie gave no answer – instead she sized up the sitting room, furnished in precisely the same old-fashioned, down-at-heel style as the rooms at Buckingham Palace which housed the worker bees. Dull, plodding pieces were augmented by prints of sailing ships on the walls, drab curtains, and listless antimacassars on the lumpy sofas.

'Call this royal?' she said, looking at Guy. 'It's a bit of a dump, ain't it!'

'We courtiers like to live simply.' He smiled, lightening up. It was extraordinary how her presence, her confidence, filled the room.

'Let's have a look-see,' she said, disappearing through a doorway. 'You help yourself to a whisky.'

'Certainly not!'

Five minutes later she was back. 'Your friend's been living here, *and* a man. Clothes are the same size and style as in the flat across the road – she's not short of a bob or two, is she? Bond Street, this lot.'

'Any indication where we might find her?'

'Not yet. Come into the big bedroom.'

Guy followed behind her into a large room whose closet doors were flung open. 'Here's the man's stuff,' said Rodie, pointing. 'You know about men. Regimental ties, that sort of thing – you should be able to work out who her partner in crime is.'

It took less than a minute. There on the dressing table were two silver-backed hairbrushes bearing a monogram and the initials 'EVMB'.

Guy picked them up, turned them over, put them down again.

'So this is where Ed Brampton went into hiding,' he said slowly. Turning to Rodie, he asked, 'You're sure that the clothes in the closet belong to Lady Easthampton?'

'If the woman living in the other flat was Lady Easthampton, yes.'

'In your opinion, were they living here together as . . . man and wife?'

'Hard to say. Her clothes are in here but they're also in the room next door. He might have had this room and she moved her clothes in after he died.'

'Well,' said Guy briskly, 'we have to find her. Any clues?'

'I'm looking, I'm looking!'

Rodie was right; the atmosphere here was the same as in Ed Brampton's Chelsea house – a suspended animation. Furthermore, the sounds a residential building usually gives out – distant doors closing, the sound of a lift, the occasional clanking of water pipes – were all absent. The place was empty.

He wandered back into the sitting room, opening drawers and feeling under sofas and chairs. In a cupboard he discovered a dusty telephone, disconnected, its wire wrapped around the handset. In its base was the slim drawer reserved for emergency numbers. He pulled it open to discover a written sheet bearing the switch-board details of Buckingham Palace and St James's Palace, Windsor Castle, Sandringham and Balmoral. Further up the list was a listing for 'Fort Belvedere'. All were written in a cramped but scholarly style, but at the bottom one new number had been added in an altogether different hand.

D.
PADdington 6971

'Gotcha!' said Guy triumphantly.

CHAPTER NINETEEN

'I don't suppose, in that strange dark world you inhabit,' said Guy, pouring tea, 'you'd be able, if I gave you the number, to find the name of a person who owns a telephone?'

'Might do,' said Rupe, stretching his legs and accepting the cup like a pasha in repose. Once again they'd run out of whisky.

'It's quite important.'

'There's a thing called the GPO back-to-front directory, if that would be a help. What's the number?'

Guy told him.

'Leave it with me. How's everything going, generally?'

'I know what you really mean by that – have I been able to get rid of the parrot yet. Well, the answer is no. I've tried Queen Mary, I've tried Lord Sefton's future wife. I even tried Aggie, my clerk. Nobody wants her.'

'Have you thought of just leaving the door to her cage open, window ajar? Maybe an irresistible treat on the windowsill outside?'

Guy looked shocked. 'Let the king's parrot out into the street? Look at her, Rupe!'

His friend refused to turn his head, even though Charlotte was a mere three feet away, having a contented conversation with herself.

'She was one of the old king's most treasured possessions – let her out and she'll certainly die. Run over by a bus, caught in an air raid or something equally gruesome.'

'Do I hear the sound of a man talking himself into owning a lead weight that'll be with him for the rest of his days?'

'I'm doing my best, Rupe, I'm doing my best!'

Rupert got up and pointedly put the embroidered cover over Charlotte's cage. 'Don't want her hearing anything untoward,' he said with a wink. 'Tell me about Suzy Easthampton.'

Guy brought his flatmate up to date. They discussed Rodie's unparalleled skill at getting through a door – 'You see how vital she is to the war effort, Guy' – and how Guy had used his influence as a Buckingham Palace courtier to pervert the course of justice with the help of a biddable Bow Street brief.

'Rupe, what on *earth* was she doing taking part in a wages snatch? She seems to have enough money to live on, why risk a jail sentence?'

'Let me explain something. You think she's just a gifted criminal, no more than that. In fact, she's far more, and if she weren't quite so ill-disciplined she could be playing a significant part in the war effort. She's exceptionally bright, though I doubt she's ever read a book to the last page, and there's something extraordinarily intuitive about her which sets her apart.'

'But turning over a warehouse with that bunch of no-hopers! You should have seen them standing in the dock – jailbirds, now and for the rest of their days. And then Rodie, alongside them, chalk and cheese!'

'That's her crazy nature. She loves adventure, she's as brave as any man I know, and she gets bored easily.'

'For heaven's sake, why doesn't she get a job?'

'She wouldn't last an hour, that's why not. Listen, before I recruited her we had several lengthy chats, and to put it in a nutshell, her activities are an expression of frustration.'

'What d'you mean by that?'

'She grew up one of six children in Elephant and Castle – not exactly Belgravia, you know. Her mother died when she was two, and her father spent his time in the pub – I guess to get away from his children, who were a rowdy lot. There were two sisters who ran the show, then two brothers who were the naughty boys, then Rodie, and finally a baby boy who everyone doted on.

'In that rabble, she got talked down to, pushed around, and bullied by the two older brothers. What she's doing now – what she's doing so spectacularly well – is getting her revenge. The burglary is just a way of expressing her power, showing she couldn't care less about life's rules. She escaped her childhood and decided she'd live life for her – nobody was going to tell her what to do.'

'Poor girl.'

'Far from it. She lives life on the crest of a wave. Her childhood made her what she is – and just at the moment, in this war, she's a useful cog in the machine. Plus, as I'm sure your artist's eye has not been slow to gather, she is a quite remarkable-looking woman.'

'Are you . . . ?'

Rupe shook his head vigorously. 'Not my type.'

Guy wondered briefly who was Rupe's type; he never seemed to express any special interest. 'What you say does sort of make sense – I've been struggling to understand her. She's been so useful in this search for Suzy Easthampton – though why I go on with it, I really don't know. Out of some sort of sense of duty, I suppose. To Ed Brampton, or Adelaide, I'm not really sure.'

Rupert opened up a notebook and riffled through its pages. 'Don't be so despondent,' he said. 'Believe it or not you're being of tremendous help to us. The newspapers are always saying no spy has escaped the attentions of the security services, but that's not true. We think we know where everyone is, and what they're doing, but that's not really the case. If I can put it this way – we've got a load of suspects locked up in a room, but outside it's dark and how many more of them are surrounding the house? We simply don't know.'

'And Suzy Easthampton is in or out of the room?'

'I'll be frank. We just don't know what's in her mind, what she's trying to achieve. She arrived here to win friends and influence people, that much we know – passing back whatever gossip she heard to this man Zeisloft. She could be part of a plan by the enemy to win over key members of the royal family – Gloucester, possibly Kent – but we're not sure. That's why you're being such a help in trying to track her down – we're overstretched, Guy, and things are getting worse by the day.'

'London is crawling with enemy agents, are you saying? But you don't know who they are or where they are?'

'You said that, Guy, not me.'

'Do you think she killed Ed Brampton?'

'I've no idea.'

'I ask because, if you can get me a name and address for that telephone number I gave you, I may have found out where she's hiding. And I'd just like to know what the chances are of another funeral being booked for the Guards Chapel sometime soon.'

'I'll let you know in the morning. What's the latest on Topsy Dighton?'

'He's at Windsor, I haven't seen him.'

'Does he go there often?'

'Not since I've been at the Palace. He was up at Balmoral for a time when I arrived. Why do you ask?'

'He could be a person of interest, Guy. If you know what I mean.'

'Ah,' he replied. 'Could that be something to do with the English Mistery?'

'Anything's possible – they could be a threat. It's not what's happening now, but what might happen in the future. The war isn't going well, Guy. We all put a brave face on it but Dunkirk, the Blitz, Dakar, Crete – the list of defeats goes on and on. If Churchill's seen to be losing the war, you can bet your life the Misters will suddenly rear their ugly heads – plotting and planning to preserve their way of life no matter what happens to the rest of us.'

'They'll become collaborators?'

'Some of them, yes. Look at those aristocrats who flocked to Berlin in 1936 – building bridges, establishing contacts, taking out their insurance policies.'

'Treason, then.'

'Depends what you're talking about. If we're invaded, if the King goes, if some puppet is put in his place, it's likely these vested interests will rally to the new king's side. They've had it their way since the Norman Conquest, they're not going to give it all away now just because Hitler parks his boots in 10 Downing Street.'

'And you think Topsy Dighton would have a part in that?'

'I don't think, Guy, I *know*.'

Despite all that had happened in recent days, the Catholic Church of Our Lady of Sorrows still heroically advertised a Lotto afternoon every Friday at 3 p.m. It was the one building in the street the conflict had left untouched, all the others mangled by the Luftwaffe or left for dead by their neglectful landlords.

The terrace of houses opposite the church once had aspirations to grandeur, with pedimented windows on the first floor and solid-looking front doors. But the street lamp outside number 47 leaned at a crazy angle, pointing to an array of broken windows and, in the early-evening light, a disorderly pile of rubble.

Somewhere inside, lost in the chaos, was a telephone bearing the number PADdington 6971 – Rupe had confirmed the address with his back-to-front directory.

Guy had no idea who lived here, or what their connection to Suzy Easthampton was, but it was his only lead.

He rang the bell.

No response. He waited and tried again.

Still nothing. He looked up and down the deserted street and wondered whether everyone had left ahead of the bulldozers' arrival. While in Mayfair there was undeniably a war going on, out here near Paddington station things looked very different. The houses had long ago descended into slums and, really, wasn't Hitler doing everybody a favour by finishing them off?

But then Guy spotted an abandoned pram, one wheel missing, and in an instant the tragedy of Bellure Street came home to him.

'Was you knocking?' A head was poking out of the first-floor window of the next-door house.

'I'm looking for Suzy.'

'Right-o. 'Old on a minute.'

The head withdrew and a moment later stuck itself out of the front door.

Guy nodded but offered no form of identification. 'Lady . . . er . . . Mrs Easthampton?'

'Oh,' said the woman, whose body seemed bowed down by a heavy weight. 'No, sir, you've got the wrong place. I thought you was looking for someone else.'

'Suzy.'

'Well, yes, there *is* a Suzy. But not that other name.'

'Well, I think it must be her. There's no reply here. Do you happen to know where she might be?' His voice trailed off. 'I've got a message from her husband.'

The woman looked him up and down, weighing up the lie she'd just been told. After a pause she said, 'Over there', nodding towards the church. 'She does the cleaning.'

'Thank you.'

'We had a direct hit,' she said.

'I can see. I'm so sorry.'

'My Freddy had just gone down the corner shop to get a scrap o' something to eat. He never come back.' She was looking at Guy but her eyes, he could tell, did not see him.

'I'm very sorry – is there anything I can . . . ?'

'Go in there an' say a prayer,' said the woman bleakly as she shut her door. 'For us, for everybody.'

He walked across the street and pushed his way into the church. Though the exterior had survived the direct hit, part of the wall behind the altar had collapsed. A woman was attempting to cover the worst of it with a bedsheet, as if somehow her actions might hide the enormity of what had occurred not a week ago.

She was on her knees with her back to Guy but she stiffened when he spoke.

'Lady Easthampton. My name's Guy Harford. Might you spare me a minute?'

The woman did not turn.

'Lady Easthampton.'

Looking towards the altar she said slowly, 'That's not my name. I am Mrs Gertler.'

'I'm a friend of Edgar Brampton.'

She got up slowly and turned around. 'How do you know this is me? How do you find me?' Her enunciation was clear but coated with the patina of another tongue.

'With great difficulty. Can we sit and talk?'

'Put some money in the offertory box, then you speak to me.'

He walked back to the door and emptied some small change into the box with a series of thuds.

'Come and sit here. But not too close.'

She wore no make-up and the housecoat loosely hanging around her body made it look as though there was nothing more than a skeleton inside. But her face was still beautiful, with its broad cheekbones and sharply defined chin, her eyes a misty grey-green.

'You prefer your maiden name these days?'

'My married name.'

'I'd have thought your married name was Lady Easthampton.'

'My first husband. Gertler.'

'Ah. Are you all right? I mean . . .' What he wanted to say was, how can you be all right, living here in this bombed-out slum when only weeks ago you were living in Mayfair, drinking champagne, cuddling up to the great and good and maybe murdering my friend?

'I really just want to be left alone,' she said. 'This a terrible place, a terrible time, but with faith, things will get better.'

It's a horrifying thing, thought Guy. I'm sitting next to this tragic beauty who could hold the key to a man's murder and all I'm thinking is, if only I could get out my sketch pad, what I could achieve. Didn't Betsey's friend Gulbenkian say that he wanted the faces of war in his exhibition? What better image could there be than the layers of sorrow in this beautiful but broken face?

'I came to visit you at Chesterfield House but you'd already gone,' he said by way of explanation. 'I needed to talk to you – Ed, you know. If I'm right, you were the closest to him when he died.'

She looked away. 'I live a simple life now,' she said. 'No more tricks.'

'I came to visit you in Curzon Street too.'

There was a sharp intake of breath. 'How do you know about that place?'

'I have a very clever friend.'

She looked ahead to the altar. 'Edgar,' she said, emphasising the whole of his name, 'gave me shelter. He was good to me when there was nothing in it for him.'

'They think you killed him.'

'In a way I did.'

'But not actually?'

'Not actually, no.'

Guy looked down at her hands – refined but strong, perfectly capable of pulling a trigger. Did it make her face more intriguing because she might be a killer? He certainly wasn't convinced by her too-easy denial.

He shifted slightly. The pews were hard and unyielding.

'Why are you here in Paddington – what happened? Three months ago you were living in the lap of luxury and now you're here – why?'

'Someone very close to me. He would . . . take care of me. The Nazis took him away.'

'Stani Zeisloft?'

The name triggered a shocked response from the woman. She jerked back, pulling her housecoat tight against her pitifully thin body. 'You're not from Buckingham Palace, are you? It's a joke! You're a . . . *spy!*' she hissed. 'What did you say your name was?'

'Guy Harford. Look, here's my palace pass.'

She took it but didn't look. 'Proves nothing,' she said angrily. 'I know your name because Edgar told me about you. But he was suspicious right from the start – he thought you might have been put in his office to spy on him.'

Let me savour this irony, thought Guy, when I've got a flatmate who's spying on *me*.

'Far from it. But I've been given the job of finding out what happened to him. Which is why I'm here.'

'Did *you* kill him?'

This is ridiculous, thought Guy – I think she may have killed him; she thinks I may have killed him.

'Look,' he said, 'you have to try to trust me. I actually quite liked Ed, though now you've told me what he thought I can see why he was rather distant. But Mrs Gertler – may I call you that? – what did he have to hide, why was he suspicious? Had he done something terribly wrong?'

'*I* was the thing he did wrong,' said the woman. 'He died because of me.'

Guy looked at her.

'What happened? How did you become involved with him?'

She looked at him warily. 'Are you going to arrest me? *Shoot* me?'

'Of course not. Look, I'm just a pen-pusher at the Palace. I have absolutely no authority, and pretty soon I won't be working there any more.'

'You don't look dangerous,' she conceded. 'I know dangerous men – you lack the devil inside.'

A woman came into the church, the door shutting behind her with a slam. 'Mrs Harnett,' said Suzy, a movement of her head saying it was nothing to worry about. 'She comes to do the flowers.'

They both watched as the newcomer nodded then walked up to the altar. She had brought with her sprigs of buddleia, no doubt plucked from the bomb sites outside, which she arranged in a pair of stone vases. Once, they may have seemed like a pathetic offering to the Almighty, but in the present circumstances they looked bountiful. She topped up the vases with water and was gone.

Guy looked at Suzy Easthampton – or Gertler, as she now called herself. If there was to be any point to all the trouble he and

215

Rodie had gone to, he had to find out what she knew in order to help find Ed's murderer – unless she herself was the culprit. He'd get nowhere by a full-on interrogation; he would have to take a gamble.

He hesitated before plunging in.

'I'll tell you what I know about you. Then, if you want, you can tell me what you know about Ed. Is that OK?'

'I have nothing else to do.'

'I doubt it'll come as a surprise to learn that you've been watched, more or less since the moment you arrived here from Paris in 1935.'

'Yes, of course. In every country I have lived, people watch. They spy, they snoop, they tell.'

'It's not really like that here. But you're, well, you're a most unusual person. You came here with this man Stani Zeisloft but after six months he disappeared, apparently back to Paris. To those watching you, it looked as though he'd set you a number of tasks, most of them to do with getting close to men in powerful positions. Zeisloft's obviously a very wealthy man, since he kept a suite at the Dorchester Hotel and he found you that flat in Mayfair. Am I right so far?'

'Your spies don't impress me much. What more have they got?'

'Your name is Zsuzanna. You were used to get information out of these men which you then passed back to Zeisloft. He's an arms dealer, and he used what you told him to help build up his empire. Or maybe he just sold the information on to the highest bidder. Either way, and put simply, a rich and crooked man uses a beautiful woman as a front to get information he couldn't gain access to himself.'

'It's not against the law.'

'I didn't say it was,' said Guy, smiling. 'I lived for many years in Tangier and, out there, you'd be granted honorary citizenship for your enterprise. But back here it's a dangerous game. Do you have a gun?'

'Everybody has a gun.'

He wondered if it was nearby, maybe in her bucket of cleaning materials.

'For a time you were very rich. Don't you find this . . . these circumstances you're in . . . rather difficult?'

'It was never my money. I worked for Stani, it was a job. I didn't like it much but he'd rescued me from a difficult situation in Budapest. My husband was murdered, I had no money and nowhere to go. He took me to Poland, and we had what you might call an affair, but mainly it was business. He was a kind man, Mr Harford.'

'He was an arms dealer. Anyway, he provided you with enough money to play the role of socialite. Eventually you found your way to Ambrose Easthampton and married him. He sends his regards, by the way.'

'You've seen him?' She didn't seem particularly surprised, but then long ago she'd come to terms with the fact that in a police state there's no such thing as privacy.

'Yes. He told me you paid him to marry you.'

'Yes.'

'And gave him pocket money to stay married to you.'

'Ambrose is a child. He's a drunk, he's bankrupt, he's fat and he's lazy. But like all you Englishmen, he thinks he's better than everyone else.'

'Not me,' said Guy, shaking his head. 'I work for a living.'

'What do you do, then, when you're not bobbing and bowing to the King and Queen?'

'I'm a painter. But let me finish this – you used your new-found status as a future peeress of the realm to get to know the people surrounding the royal family. You went with your father-in-law Lord FitzMalcolm to a ball at Balmoral Castle, and that's where you met Ed Brampton.'

'Yes.'

'But how on earth did you end up sharing a flat with him in Curzon Street, for heaven's sake? When he had a home, a wife and family, and you had your, er, protector Zeisloft?'

She looked at him coldly with her grey-green eyes. 'You are going to kill me,' she said with an emotionless voice.

'Don't be ridiculous! I've told you, I'm a low-paid assistant private secretary working for the King and Queen, I don't kill people.'

She sighed. 'I don't mean you, personally,' she said. 'But if I tell you this, I will die. I'll die anyway, one way or the other. Maybe another *direct hit*' – she spat out the words, waving her hand to embrace the broken street outside – 'maybe another *bullet* like Ed's . . .'

Guy shook his head.

'Well, I'll tell you. My husband – my real husband – was a doctor in Budapest. He had a brilliant start and a dazzling career ahead. But he was a Jew and he spoke his mind. In Hungary we had a man called Gömbös who did not like Jews – need I say more? It wasn't safe for me to stay in Budapest after my husband died, and Stani Zeisloft took me away. We lived in Warsaw, then Paris, until we came here. He is a very clever man.'

'And an arms dealer.'

'No longer an arms dealer, Mr Courtier. He was arrested by the Nazis five months ago. I don't know where he is or what's happened to him.'

'Arrested? By the Nazis? I thought he was their man? Working for them?'

'He, too, is a Jew. Jews don't help Nazis, except in one way.'

Guy ran his hand through his hair. Rupert's briefing on Suzy Easthampton – Gertler now – seemed to have been pinpoint-accurate. But suddenly the picture had turned hazy.

'I'm sorry, I'm confused. I had a very clear picture in my mind as to what you were doing, cosying up to the royal family. But now I'm getting the feeling it can't be right. Tell me, please, what you were paid to do by your Mr Zeisloft. And why.'

'It can't hurt now. It was his idea to engineer me a place at the centre of London society so that I could eavesdrop conversation and pass it back. To someone in Stani's position, every last morsel of information has a value – and to him, the further you rise up, the more value it has. People's attitude here to the war was very important to him. Not everybody is one hundred per cent behind a continuation of the war – many are not, for a whole raft of reasons. What they want is an honourable settlement.'

'I don't think, where Hitler's concerned, there's such a word as "honourable".'

'Your opinion's not worth very much though, is it? It's what *those* people think and, as you've said yourself, you're just a poorly paid pen-pusher at the Palace. These are people with power!'

'So – you and Ed?'

'I met him in the ballroom at Balmoral. My father-in-law – Lord FitzMalcolm – was talking to the King and Queen, and Edgar was standing around with nothing much to do. I could see he was in a bit of pain and went to talk to him. He told me about losing his leg in the last war, and we had a nice little talk. He told me he was disappointed that his wife and children had left London for the country and that, as far as he could tell, he'd be working every day until the war was over with no chance to see them. Duty, duty, duty, he said. So I told him his first duty was to take me out to tea when he was back in London and he was so delighted. I think everybody took that poor man for granted, including his precious wife.'

'So what happened next?'

'We saw quite a bit of each other – it was always very proper but I could tell he had a soft spot for me. And that was it, really – I thought we'd probably go out to dinner a few times and I'd get some gossip and pass it back to Stani, and that would be it.'

'You weren't trying to get close to the Duke of Gloucester?'

'Who? Oh, the man who Edgar was going to work for? No, why would I? He would hardly be likely to start selling me royal secrets, now, would he?'

'You didn't have instructions from Zeisloft to get close to the Duke? To seduce him? To get him to think differently about, how shall I put it, his loyalties to the country?'

Suzy Gertler looked at him oddly. 'I don't know where you get that from, Mr Harford. My job was to get gossip, and plenty of it. Not to hang around some useless royal duke and listen to him hee-hawing his way through life. I don't think he would know anything that'd be of use to Stani.'

Guy paused. 'So let me get this straight. You were never asked by Zeisloft to ingratiate yourself with the Duke? To win him round? To encourage him to think that the throne might be his in the event of a German invasion? That his position as Regent meant that when the King was removed, he would become, overnight, both king and emperor under the German flag?'

The wasted beauty looked at him in astonishment.

'What on earth are you talking about?' she said.

CHAPTER TWENTY

Ted Rochester looked with pride at the typed sheets of paper in front of him. Thank heavens the libel laws, which High Court judges used to club poor journalists to death in England, did not extend to America and the New York *Boulevardier*!

> People can be so unkind in wartime. When the bombs are falling and our youth are dying, why do they spend time talking about the Marquess of Carisbrooke?
>
> Maybe it's because, as the grandson of Queen Victoria, he made a fuss when forced to give up his German title of Prince Alexander of Battenberg during the last war.
>
> Drino, as he's known, thought he'd be made a Duke - but when old King George got wind of this, he marked him down to Marquess.

People call him a snob, but now they call him worse. Word has got out that in Madrid, just before the war, Drino was arrested in a public lavatory. The details do not bear repetition in a newspaper of repute but he made the cardinal error of calling upon his sister, Queen Victoria Eugenie, to make bail. People in London say that if you're lucky enough to have a sister who is a queen, you should not embarrass her. Drino, 55, has been married to saintly Irene, only daughter of the Earl of Londesborough, since 1917.

Such a shame his British readers would never get to savour this delicious morsel! Nor this:

What is it about Sir Oswald Mosley's moustache that entrances them so? Currently languishing behind bars in London's Holloway Prison – Fascists are *so* out of fashion these days! – Sir Oswald still has a string of admirers who come to visit on an almost daily basis. A recent arrival was the Hon Sonia Cubitt, daughter of the garrulous Mrs Alice Keppel (and, it's said, of her paramour King Edward VII). Few women can resist the baronet – for example, while married to Lord Curzon's daughter

Lady Cynthia, he became ascloseast-
his to Cynthia's younger sister Lady
Alexandra. *And* to her stepmother Grace,
Lady Curzon. Mercifully, locked away in
jail for the duration, he will have to
pay more attention to his second wife
Diana, who deserted her first husband to
be with the Fascist leader. Let's hope
the warders at Holloway keep a copy of
Debrett's handy to check how to address
their top-drawer visitors!

The typescript had a final paragraph and it was to this he paid closest attention. Dare he do it? Would he get away with it?

As the saying goes, you can't get the
staff these days. Even Buckingham
Palace is having problems filling the
gaps made by old retainers dropping
off the perch. Once upon a time, blue-
blooded devotees of royalty would queue
up at the Palace gates eager to serve
their Sovereign. Nowadays it's Tom,
Dick, and Harry who clock in - chaps
who spend all their spare time in the
pub with a lady of easy virtue, and
worse. Time for His Majesty to get a
grip on his staffing!

Ted Rochester knew not the meaning of loyalty. Though he'd done well out of Guy since his arrival at Buckingham Palace, with the occasional story about the King or Queen dropping like rare crumbs from the table, he continued to resent the fact that Guy knew about the Windsors and he didn't. But he wondered whether this paragraph – if it ever got back across the Atlantic – would cut off his one and only royal contact.

He decided to drop it.

Instead there was a piece of candy-floss nonsense about the Princesses Elizabeth and Margaret Rose.

> The younger princess is a bit of a miracle - she is, after all, not quite eleven years old. Word reaches me that recently she hurled all her German textbooks to the floor and announced she would never study the language again.
>
> And here (pictured) she is with her big sister, both in their kilt skirts and woolly jackets, at Windsor. They lean on their garden hoes enjoying a well-earned break, for in their personal garden every particle of the work has been done by their own hands. They made the paths and rolled them; they found, carried, and placed the bricks and white ornamental stones. It is a bold weed which attempts to flourish here!

Rochester lit a cigarette and, with the match still alight, contemplated setting fire to this last piece of unctuous drivel. He hated himself when he had to write something uplifting.

The telephone rang.

'Come to dinner. I have Edwina Mountbatten and Noël Coward,' commanded Betsey Cody from her Grosvenor Square eyrie. 'I expect there'll be something for you to write.'

Such invitations were manna from heaven.

'Now, Ted,' she went on without waiting for a response, 'I want to talk to you about the Duke of Gloucester.'

'No, Betsey! It's impossible to find anything interesting to say about him. He's . . .'

'He's doing nothing, Ted. He's the Regent of this country, for pity's sake, and he's doing nothing.'

'Well, I couldn't possibly write that in my column for *News Chronicle*.'

'He's barely done a stroke of work this past year.'

'It would never get in.'

'Well then, how about a piece for the *Boulevardier*? Don't you have space in your next column?'

'As a matter of fact I do. Until now I'd contemplated telling your great nation how wonderful our two little princesses are, digging for victory in their kitchen garden at Windsor.'

'Sweet. They *are* doing well. But seriously, one or two people I've spoken to recently are deeply disappointed by Harry Gloucester's performance. When you compare him to his big brother the King and his younger brother . . .'

'Your dear friend the Duke of Kent.'

'Ha ha. But honestly . . .'

'What's he been up to?'

'Nothing at all. Hanging about the Palace, getting in everybody's way. Complaining. He occasionally goes off and shakes a few hands but he's not pulling his weight.'

'You'd like to see that in print?' Ted Rochester didn't always feel the need to ask further when his great benefactor suggested a paragraph or two. She was so well-connected her stories were never wrong and usually her tales turned out to have some purpose, even if Rochester couldn't always see what it was. Betsey was a bit of a mystery, but only in a good way.

'I'll give you some details,' she replied briskly. 'Have you got a pencil?'

◆ ◆ ◆

They'd returned to her flat across the street. Because of the direct hit, virtually every ceiling in the street was fractured or had come down, windows were cracked and shattered, and every door lintel had shifted. Guy had to put his shoulder to the front door with some force to gain entry.

'Leave it,' said Suzy as he tried to shut it again. 'Frankie downstairs usually sees to it.'

Nothing could prepare Guy for the shock as he followed Suzy into her tiny first-floor sitting room. He'd seen the opulent place in Chesterfield Street which had been her home, he'd spent time in the Curzon Street flat. Each was crowded with closet upon closet of expensive couture clothes, while in the bedrooms every available surface was littered with discarded jewellery.

Here, in Bellure Street, there was nothing. The room was tidy but lacking every comfort, the bedroom beyond was furnished with a single iron bed and a washstand.

Two shabby chairs were placed by the window and Suzy motioned to Guy to sit. She went to stand by the fireplace.

'It always ends like this,' she said.

'Sorry?'

'You drown yourself in furs, you weigh yourself down with diamonds, you are chauffeur-driven from The Ritz to The Dorchester and back again, but it always ends like this. For everyone. In the end, there are no possessions except life, and even that can be taken away like *that*.' She swivelled her marvellous eyes to left and right.

'Tell me about your second husband. Lord Easthampton.'

'They are a very ancient family but terribly flawed.' She managed a light laugh. 'Queen Victoria once said, "There are men, there are women, and then there are the FitzMalcolms" – meaning not quite human. Even back then it was recognised there was something wrong with them. Somehow, with Ambrose's father, it skipped a generation – he's sane and charming, got his head screwed on, as you English say. But Ambrose inherited the lot – the madness, the profligacy. He's handsome enough, I grant you, and I thought when I married him I could possibly make a go of it.

'Stani taught me that in life, if you want something you have to work for it. He said, "There is a castle, a vast estate in Scotland, as much money as you will ever need, a tiara and, when the time comes, a Coronation robe. One day you will be Countess and all the hurt and disappointment, all the things you have had to do all your life, will melt away."

'But, like he said, you have to work for it, and Ambrose Easthampton was the job I had to do. So I agreed, and we married, and I found him tolerable enough. But Stani paid him pocket money and he used it to go back to his drinking. It would have been better if we'd left him poor. After a few weeks Lord FitzMalcolm realised what was going on and offered me a room in his house in Cadogan Square. I told Ambrose it was me or the bottle, you can guess which one he chose, so I moved in with my father-in-law.'

Guy raised his eyebrows in an unspoken question. 'No,' she said. 'Nothing like that. Though I did sometimes share a bed with him when he was cold – he's eighty-seven, you know. Then Stani got me the flat in Chesterfield House.'

'What happened to your real job,' asked Guy. 'Getting information to pass on to Zeisloft?'

'That's the ironic thing. I'd gone through with this absurd marriage so I could swing around town on the arm of a titled husband, using his family connections to open doors. Instead, every night he was drunk under the table and my new escort, my father-in-law, almost never left the house.'

'But he took you to a party at Balmoral.'

'That was different. He came to life at Castle Malcolm – and, of course, nobody turns down an invitation to Balmoral. And there I met poor Edgar.'

'Go on.'

'I saw Edgar as my Ambrose-substitute. He was to all intents living a bachelor existence, he was well-connected, a lovely man, and in need of company.'

'So . . . ?'

Suzy came to sit next to him on the hard chair. 'There was a knock on my door at Chesterfield House. That was pretty unusual – it's almost impossible to get past the doorman.'

'I know that,' said Guy with feeling.

'Two men, very menacing. They said they were coming in to empty the safe and if I valued my life, I'd disappear. They told me Stani had been arrested in a raid in Paris. If he was tortured he'd reveal where his secret papers were, and someone or other would be around soon to collect them. I've seen too much in my life not to know when there's real danger, so I just walked past them out of the door and kept walking. I'd got my day-clothes on but no coat, no purse – I had to borrow some pennies from the doorman to telephone Edgar, and he came and rescued me.'

'And took you to Curzon Street?'

'You know, of course, that it's the King's safe house, with extra flats for the courtiers. The Duke and Duchess of Gloucester stayed there a few times after they got out of York House, and Edgar had a hand in getting it ready for them. They were in the big flat, and he was given the key to the staff flat. He knew that the building was almost never used, and when I said I had nowhere to go, and that my life was in danger, he suddenly became very heroic.'

'So you stayed there together? I found out that he locked up his Chelsea house and walked away. Nobody at the Palace knew he'd switched addresses, they all assumed he was still going home every night.'

Suzy fiddled with the gas ring by the fireplace. 'We can have some tea,' she said. 'I feel comfortable with you now. It was a shock your coming up behind me, like those men at the flat.' She knelt with a match and started back as the ring ignited with a loud pop.

As she got up, Guy said, 'Please look at me.'

'Yes?'

'Did you kill Ed? Did you shoot him?'

'No.'

'Look at me when you say that.'

She stood perfectly still. 'No,' she said very slowly, 'I didn't kill him. How could I? Why *should* I? He was like a knight in shining armour to me! He was protective, he was kind, he was understanding. He thought my life had been terrible and that now everything would be all right.'

'But how?' asked Guy. 'Did he mean that he was going to leave his wife for you?'

'It wasn't like that between us! He was comforted by my company. He was terribly upset when – is her name Adelaide? – left for the country without consulting him. I think he felt he'd somehow failed her, that she didn't love him any more. Poor Edgar!'

'So you both lived there for – what? – two, three months?'

'Until he died. When I heard the news, I thought the people who were coming after me had decided to – how do you say it – pick him off as a warning, as a threat? They didn't know where I was, because all those months I rarely left the building in daylight.

But Edgar was always out and about – much easier to track him down and' – she caught her breath – 'put a bullet in his poor head.'

'Why would they want to get you?'

'If they had got . . . certain facts out of Stani . . . they would know I had a lot of information that would be useful to the Axis war effort.'

'What sort of information?'

'Mr Harford, you really don't want to know.' The way she looked at him told Guy he'd get no more from her on that. 'So then I came here – left everything in Curzon Street just as I had at Chesterfield House. Came here with the clothes I stood up in – no money, no anything. I knew the priest here from the Anglo-Hungarian Society, and he found me this place. He is a saintly man.'

Guy had finished his tea. He lit two cigarettes and gave one to Suzy.

'So the Germans killed Ed,' he suggested.

'I didn't say that.'

'Someone working for the Germans.'

'I didn't say that either.'

'Who then?' asked Guy in exasperation. 'I'll be frank, I started out trying to find out who shot Ed because I thought it was the right thing to do – the high-ups too ashamed by an apparent suicide on royal premises to want to do anything about it. The police kept well back. A vaguely raised eyebrow here, a shrug of the shoulders there. Apart from one madman in the King's personal bodyguard, nobody seems to care any more. I've chased lead after lead to track you down, and all for nothing. I believe you when you say you didn't kill Ed – but if you don't know who did it, how will I ever find out?'

'I didn't say that,' said Suzy. 'I'd be very surprised if the security at the Palace was so lax that someone could walk in without having the first clue where Edgar's office was, locate it, shoot him, tidy things up to make it look like suicide, and make his escape without anyone being the wiser.'

Guy got up in impatience. 'So it had to be someone inside the Palace.'

'You're not much of a detective, are you?'

Guy screwed up his face. 'You never spoke a truer word! I am *not* a detective – never was, never wanted to be, never can be, never will be!'

'I have some plum brandy – Pálinka – on that shelf. Pour us both a thimbleful.'

Guy obeyed. The sweet, sharp spirit caught his breath and calmed him. He walked over to the window, eyeing the street beneath and a woman scrubbing her front doorstep in defiance of the devastation which surrounded her.

'I just have to go over all this again. Maybe you can help. If it's someone in the Palace, who? Could it be the clerk, Aggie? She's tough. She's from Glasgow, she could do it. Maybe she was sweet on him – she certainly knew about you, and might have been jealous.

'Could it have been Adelaide? She's been very cool about the whole death business – effectively told me her marriage was over, that she'd stopped loving Ed. But I've known her all her life, she wouldn't – she couldn't – do a thing like that.

'Could it have been the Master of the Household? Ed was running all sorts of dangerous errands for him – if Topham Dighton was going to be found out, it would ruin him – he very well could turn to murder. Except that the old boy's nearly eighty, and I can't see him being spry enough to stick a gun against poor old Ed's temple.

'Beyond that it becomes unfathomable. There are many, many people behind those palace railings who are handy with a firearm and have access to one. If one single person was persuaded by an outside force that Ed had to go – for whatever reason – it could easily be done. It's a huge place, like a small town, people buzzing about all over the place.'

Suzy looked at him for a long moment. 'I know nothing about detection,' she said, 'but in my life I've seen many strange things. Danger makes you cautious, but it makes you curious too. You constantly ask questions when you find yourself threatened – "Should I do this? What if they do that?" – and I've been doing that about Edgar, of course I have.

'So I say this to you, Mr Courtier – stop looking for who killed Edgar and concentrate on who *wanted* him killed. And why!'

As he walked home through the blackout, it slowly came to Guy that his life could be in as great a danger as Suzy's. She, at least, knew her enemy – those Nazi agents who wanted the information she carried in her head, the information she'd gleaned from her high-rolling life, from the society people who'd so briefly been her friends.

But Guy?

I've done nothing wrong, he said to himself, yet somehow I've landed in a bear pit and I don't know who's coming to tear me apart. I'm occupying Ed Brampton's office, searching for answers to his death, dabbling in things I don't understand – am I next on the list for a bullet? And if so, who's going to pull the trigger?

His footsteps took him past the shambles which had been the driveway up to Paddington station. Much of the debris had been cleared away, but the smell from the landmine that had decimated the flank of the ornate building still hung sharp in the air. Behind the broken facade, life went on, the steam trains huffing and clanking and shrieking – a reassuring sound in normal times, but in this half-light sounding more like echoes from a cosmic torture chamber.

Who is it, thought Guy – is it Rupe, whose movements are so secretive he could easily be working for the other side?

Is it Topsy Dighton, the colonel-in-chief of a bunch of dangerous plotters against the state? Or Toby Broadbent, a trained killer, a bully and a man so patently without a conscience?

Or is it someone else? And do I even know them?

CHAPTER
TWENTY-ONE

As usual, it was Aggie who gave Guy his marching orders for the day. Since it was the first time he'd attended the weekly Investiture, his role would be no more than that given to groomsmen at a wedding: stand at the door, bow slightly, hand out a printed sheet, and show the sometimes-bewildered guests to their seats. Repeat as required.

The atmosphere in the Grand Hall was stuffy – the low ceiling and cramped seating took care of that – but the more usual venue upstairs had been declared out of bounds for the duration by Topsy Dighton. Frighteningly efficient at his job, the Master of the Household had timed the walk down the Grand Staircase with his gold half-hunter before declaring it would take an extra four minutes to get to the air-raid shelters if they continued to hold Investitures upstairs. 'They'd all be dead,' he judged, and the King, recalling the air attack which had done such damage to his beloved London residence, agreed.

The room filled quickly with men and women, many still recovering from their wounds, some with their eyes bandaged and guided by loved ones, several in wheelchairs. The air smelt vaguely of medicament. Guy helped place the queue of recipients in order of precedence – 'the bravest first,' ordered Aggie – and soon their citations were being read out by the ancient Lord Chamberlain.

At times the old boy's voice wavered as he related in brief each act of heroism, and as Guy stood at the back of the scarlet and gilt room, he suddenly saw the point of it all. Like many who toiled within the royal compound he'd quickly acquired a jaded view of the whole royal apparatus, with its pyramid of courtiers intent upon self-aggrandisement and the raft of below-stairs servants all with an axe to grind; the internal politics of the Palace were easily a match for anything in Tudor times.

But here in this ornate room the nation gave thanks to those who'd risked their lives and survived – the struggle, the pain, the suffering were now to be publicly acknowledged. And, thought Guy, there's nobody else who can do this – when the King thanks you and bows his head to your sacrifice, it's as if the entire British people are, in that same moment, right there in the room. Millions of them, all silently applauding.

The ceremony lasted ninety minutes, and after seeing the guests out Guy walked back to his office, where Aggie, queen of all she surveyed, sat in waiting.

'Did it go well?'

'Astonishingly well. The King was superb, the arrangements went off like clockwork, those decorated were suitably impressed and flattered. All those heroes! It was extraordinarily moving – even old Topsy had his handkerchief out, dabbing at his nose.'

'When you're that old you get sentimental,' said Aggie coldly. 'You had a telephone call from Major Ed's wife. Widow.'

'Any message?'

'She's coming up to London and would like to see you.'

'Thank you.' Guy settled at his desk and looked over the daily briefing. Yet to come was the pleasure of handing over King Haakon's laundry, sorting out the various bills coming in for Ed

Brampton's funeral, and a moment with the head chef, Ronnie Aubrey, to arrange a small party for Mrs Ferguson, the Palace's housekeeper, whose birthday it was. Later he would look in at the King's air-raid shelter and make sure everything was shipshape.

His eye strayed across the room to where Aggie sat, with her no-nonsense spectacles, her subfusc dress and her greying hair. He'd seen her like this most days since joining the Palace staff, but for the first time he looked at her with the question in his mind: Is she a killer? And did she get someone to do the killing for her?

Or was he just clutching at straws? After the briefest of moments he realised the idea was ridiculous – why would she *kill* this innocent, upright, well-meaning chap just because she was in love with him?

Aggie took herself off to the Stewards' Room and Guy asked the switchboard operator for a number in the country.

'Adelaide, it's Guy.'

'Hello. I'm just leaving, catching the 3.30. Are you free this evening? There's something I want to discuss.'

'Where will you be?'

'I'm not going to open up the house, I'm staying at the Lansdowne Club – come and see me there.'

'Tell me this, are you an animal lover?'

'What?'

'An animal lover?'

'Well, you saw for yourself when you came down here, Guy. The place is overrun. Horses, dogs, cats, hens, ducks, more foxes than you can count . . .'

'Have you ever considered having a parrot?'

Foxy Gwynne and her friend were looking over premises near Trafalgar Square.

'Granville thinks the President is ready to come into the war, but his hands are tied till after the elections in November,' said Betsey. 'I'd like to have a club and headquarters for the American Red Cross up and running once he's made his declaration. The more we do now, the easier it'll be later.'

Foxy opened the door into an abandoned billiard room. 'What'll we do with this?'

'Leave it as it is, we can put the bar in the corner. The curtains will do, and nobody will notice the state of the carpet once the place is filled with people.'

'I do admire you,' said Foxy. 'Your vision. And all the money you're putting into this.'

'Something had to be done. If our boys decide to fight, there'll be a hell of a job to do. I'm happy to pay whatever it takes – well, Granville is – but I can't do it alone,' replied Betsey. 'There'll have to be a fundraising committee. Do you think Lord Sefton will agree to join?'

'I can certainly ask.'

The two women wandered out to the kitchen area. 'Well,' said Betsey, wrinkling her nose at the dusty, cramped quarters, 'it'll just have to be sandwiches! Now tell me about your friend Guy.'

'What's there to say? He's bumbling along at the Palace and getting in some paintbrush practice before he does Pam Churchill. Doesn't leave much time for anything else – and, in case you're asking, no, he hasn't got a girlfriend.'

'Really? You do surprise me, Foxy, a handsome man like that. Anyway, what I wanted to ask is, how's he getting on with taking up that job with Harry Gloucester?'

'Oh, I don't think he's that keen. You know, he got dumped in the Palace because the Foreign Office didn't know what else to do with him, and certainly he seems to have impressed Tommy Lascelles sufficiently for the job to be mentioned. But there's nothing definite so far – I think they're still in a bit of turmoil after Ed Brampton's death.'

'*Not* a very efficient organisation, then!' said Betsey dismissively. 'In Granville's outfit, the Aircraft Exchange Commission, they'd have had a replacement in within twenty-four hours.'

'I don't think things work like that at the Palace. And anyway, I'm not sure that Guy sees his future there – you know he's had this heart problem and is waiting for the all-clear from the doctors, then he'll join up.'

'He won't, if the Palace want him.'

'As I say, I don't think he's particularly enamoured of the Duke.'

'Well, he *should* be!' hissed Betsey, turning suddenly to face her friend. 'He's supposed to be helping me with the Gloucesters, and in return I've got him that art gallery exhibition he so hankers after. One good turn deserves another!'

Foxy stepped back, astonished at the sudden change in her friend. Betsey, normally so relaxed and laissez-faire, appeared to be extremely angry – and over something of such little consequence.

'I don't think you can expect him to shackle himself to Harry Gloucester just because you found him a place for his exhibition, Betsey. Be reasonable! And anyway, why do you care?'

The society hostess clapped her hands together. 'If I take someone under my wing,' she said grimly, 'it is for a purpose.'

'Does that go for me too?'

Betsey ignored this. 'I've asked Guy to arrange for Granville and I to go stay with the Gloucesters in the country. The invitation hasn't arrive,' she snapped imperiously. 'He hasn't kept to his side of the bargain.'

'Well, you know, Betsey, it doesn't quite work like that over here. The Gloucesters are free to choose who they have as house guests. I know they're doing their best to invite as many people as they can.'

'But has Guy actually put our names forward?'

Foxy looked at her friend and suddenly saw her afresh. Gone was the polish and the charm – in its place a dogmatic urgency, anger and frustration. Mrs Cody expected to get what she asked for – no matter whether people were royal or not. It seemed mildly grotesque that she should feel her husband's money could buy anything, even in wartime.

'I'm sure he's doing what he can.'

'He'd better try harder, tell him, or he can forget the gallery!'

'I'll do no such thing!' said Foxy. 'Tell him yourself, Betsey. I don't pass on messages of that nature.'

The other woman's anger subsided. 'Let me tell you something, Fox. I want Granville to get on in this war. He's doing a wonderful job – do you know how many airplanes he's managed to export from the US, through Canada, for the war effort? That goes against public opinion in the States, you know that!'

'If the extent of his role becomes known, and we *don't* come into the war, that could seriously damage his public standing back home. Being close to the royal family gives him a real boost – you just know how us Yanks love the royals!' she added in a jokey voice.

'Well, Bets, you've done your bit with the Duke of Kent following you round like a lost sheep. And David and Wallis – they're your chums, too.'

'But don't you see,' replied Betsey in exasperation, 'the only two who matter now are the King and Harry Gloucester, the top man and the Regent Designate, as it's so fancifully called. We'd just call it the Number Two. We feel – *I* feel – we should know Harry and Alice Gloucester socially. We have many things in common and, I happen to know, Harry's not doing very much at the moment. So what's the harm in having a nice old American couple to stay for the weekend?'

The harder you push at that door, thought Foxy, the more firmly it's likely to stay shut. 'And eventually you hope for an invitation to Windsor or Sandringham?'

'That would naturally follow,' said Betsey in lordly fashion. 'We see no reason why, with all that we're doing for this country, we shouldn't be befriended by the King and Queen. So you see, Guy needs to get his skates on – we have an election in November. If it goes the wrong way, you people in Britain are going to have to wage this war all by yourselves.'

'Don't forget I'm a Virginia girl.'

'When you marry your lord you'll go native,' said Betsey with a slight sneer. 'You're already losing your accent.'

Was she jealous – or was it something more?

'So you're not really interested in the *Gloucesters*,' said Foxy, nettled. 'You're just using them as a stepping stone to pal up with the King and Queen.'

'That's where you're wrong. Harry Gloucester is a vital part of the war effort.'

'Wait a minute – you just told me he wasn't doing anything much. Hanging round the Palace, making a nuisance of himself.'

Betsey looked at her as a teacher might look at an amiable but stupid pupil.

'The two things do not necessarily cancel each other out,' she purred. 'Now – are we or are we not going to take the lease on this dump?'

There was always a bit of a business as to where you put your gas mask when you came indoors. In the sitting room of the Lansdowne

Club some had plonked them on their knees, or a side table, others underneath their chairs, others on a hook nearby.

'I'll hang them up,' said Guy. 'I've got some things to tell you.'

She looks much better, he thought; it didn't take long to get over her husband's death – is that because war forces you to recover from bereavement that much quicker? Or is it something else?

'How are things?'

'The children are with Ed's sister so I thought I'd take the opportunity to come up to town. Makes a refreshing change,' Adelaide said.

'How are they? Have they been badly affected by Ed's death?'

'You know, they didn't see that much of him. Once he went to work at the Palace, it was always the job. They're all right.'

'Will you be coming back here permanently?'

'I'm going to let the house till the war's over. Would you like it? I'd prefer it to go to a friend and my first thought was you. Peppercorn rent, as they say. You can paint my picture in lieu, if you like.'

Guy was taken aback. 'I don't know,' he said. 'I'm waiting for the all-clear from the doctor, then I hope to join up.'

'What if there's no all-clear?'

Guy was jolted by the implication in her question – you're not getting better, you might get worse.

'I hadn't thought of that. Thanks for asking and I'll let you know,' he said stiffly.

'Don't leave it too long. Any news about Ed?'

'What do you want to know?'

'What d'you mean, Guy, what do I want to *know*? He was my husband, he died in questionable circumstances, I thought you were investigating! Haven't you heard anything?'

'Let me ask you something first. When I came down to St Walke, you told me your marriage with Ed was over.'

'Yes.'

'That you had never really loved him.'

'I was sorry for him always. He was a good man.'

'May I ask . . . have you found someone else?'

'Very definitely no. I can't see myself marrying again. I've got the children to look after, and my father – he's not getting any younger.'

'Boyfriends?'

She smiled slowly. 'Jealous, Guy?'

'I think we're more like brother and sister after all these years, aren't we?'

'Not quite . . . but in answer to your question, yes, there've been a couple.'

'Before you moved from London? That's to say, when you and Ed were still living together in Markham Street?'

'Good Lord, Guy! You sound like some tuppenny-ha'penny gumshoe, working up evidence for a divorce!'

'There's a point to all this, Adelaide. Will you answer the question?'

'Then – yes. Yes. I did something I regretted, I had an affair with one of Ed's colleagues.'

'Who, if I may ask? It's quite important.'

'A Guards officer.'

'If it's over you may as well tell me – we've known each other long enough.'

'He's in the King's private bodyguard – you know, the Coats Mission. Toby Broadbent, d'you know him?'

'I do. Perhaps too well.'

'Of course you do. I saw you both chatting after Ed's funeral at the Guards Chapel. He turned out to be a rotten idea. Another of Topsy Dighton's errand boys, just like Ed.'

Guy shook his head.

'It was a mistake. He's handsome enough – and knows what's what, which is more than I can say for old Ed – but in the end he was just another toady in thrall to Topsy Dighton. I don't know what it is about that man which makes grown men topple over backwards to do his bidding; he's more regal than the King himself. I hated the way he blackmailed Ed into running his errands.'

'And Toby Broadbent too?'

'Yes. But it was more than that. He's a good-enough sort, I suppose, but a bit of a rough diamond.'

'All part of his appeal, I expect.'

'I couldn't possibly say,' said Adelaide, looking away. 'But yes, he had to go.'

'How did he and Ed get on?'

'Pretty OK, I think. They had drinks a few times in Ed's club.'

'And your affair, how long did it last?'

'Four months. That's usually how long they go on, isn't it?'

I wouldn't know, thought Guy. But I do have in the back of my mind something Aggie told me.

'I'm going to ask you something you may never forgive me for.'

'Try me.'

'Did you get Toby Broadbent to kill your husband?'

Adelaide went white, and for a moment Guy thought she might faint. '*What?*' she whispered at last.

'Did you hope,' he went on, 'that by asking me to investigate his death, that I'd be so incompetent that I would muck up any proper inquiry that was going on?'

'No, of course not! What are you saying?'

'Did Toby ask you to marry him? And you said, because you're a Roman Catholic, you could only do it if Ed was dead?'

'No . . . really . . . no! I can't believe you're saying this! You've known me nearly all my life, you must know I couldn't do anything like that!'

He recalled Suzy Easthampton's instruction to look, not for the killer, but for who *wanted* him killed.

'Broadbent had the opportunity, the motive, and the means. Most people, if they wanted to kill someone in these circumstances, would have to wait till they emerged on the street – it would be too difficult for them to get past the gate or over the wall.'

Unless your name was Rodie Carr, he thought.

'But Broadbent could go over any time to Ed's office without anybody even noticing. Ed was working late the night he died – Broadbent could have seen a light on and wandered in. You said yourself Ed didn't have a gun, but the gallant captain had access to a whole arsenal of firearms. He joined a unit that's pledged to fight to the last bullet and the last man to defend the King – those men, Adelaide, are trained killers. And Ed, at his desk, hampered by his wooden leg, would present no challenge at all – a sitting target!'

Adelaide struggled to light a cigarette but Guy did not lean forward to help.

'You're so wrong,' she said, tears starting in her eyes. 'Except, dear boy, the bit about you not being terribly good at solving a mystery. You *are* pretty hopeless, aren't you? I see that now. By the time Ed was killed, Toby and I had split up. It was the reason I moved to the country. Yes, the children would be much safer there, but I'd stayed on in town while Toby and I were an item. In the end, I saw through him – all that Guards officer swagger is very attractive, you know, but at heart he was just a caveman – and yes, he did want to marry me. But when he saw there was no hope, he walked away.

'*And,*' she added with a spurt of anger, 'the very next week he had another girlfriend! Some woman I've never heard of – her name's on the tip of my tongue but I just can't . . .'

'So he had no motive to kill Ed any more.'

'No.'

'And you didn't want him dead.'

'Of course not! He was lovely with the children and always very polite to my father. He *did* have that thing about the Queen, which, frankly, was a bit spooky and difficult to live with. And she did like him a lot in return – he was always such a gentleman . . . but no, I never hated him.'

'Did he know about you and Broadbent?'

'I've no idea.'

'Aggie seems to think he did.'

'Oh,' she said, suddenly ashen-faced again. 'I wouldn't have wanted that for anything. Poor Ed! Poor man!'

'Let's go and sit in the bar. I'll bring the gas masks.'

They walked through the Lansdowne Club's pillared hall, filling up with the pre-theatre crowd, and into the bar where Guy ordered dry martinis. 'I'm going to tell you now about Ed's disappearance – but on your honour, Adelaide, not a word to anyone, not even your father.'

'Do I really want to hear this?'

'You will. We both know Ed's death is weird. Weird because we still don't know whether it was suicide or murder, weird because everybody wanted it hushed up – on the most ridiculous grounds possible. Weird because if it *was* a murder, there seems to be no motive for it. And a whole lot more weirds as well. And I couldn't be certain until just now you hadn't ordered him to be killed.'

Adelaide put down her glass with a clatter. 'For God's sake, Guy – "ordering" a killing! This is *me* we're talking about! Adelaide Brampton, well-brought-up gel from Oxfordshire!'

'Anything's possible, my dear, especially in war. Anyway, I hope you'll revise your opinion of my detective skills when I tell you this . . .'

And he told Adelaide about Ed and Suzy Easthampton living in the Curzon Street royal residence, undetected, for three months.

'Then *she* must have killed him!'

'I don't think so, Adelaide,' said Guy, shaking his head. 'But the number of suspects is slowly dwindling . . .'

CHAPTER
TWENTY-TWO

'Aha, the Tanja Man! Walk this way, if you please!'

Guy cursed his luck in meeting Topsy Dighton on the Ministers' Stairs. Together they progressed at Dighton's parade-ground quick march through the White Drawing Room and the bow-windowed Music Room, with its colossal dome and chandeliers twice the height of a man, into the Blue Drawing Room. The place was deserted.

'The most heavenly creation in this whole palace,' breathed the old man as they entered. 'The wonderful legacy of George IV – such taste, such distinction!'

Guy, who rarely found himself in the state apartments, looked around with curiosity. As with other rooms in the Palace, it was created in order to impress, to awe and to diminish any guest who entered its portals. Gilt and onyx and faded blue – with oil portraits twice life-size, and massive mirrors stretching to the richly worked ceiling – completed the picture.

'I've been meaning to have a word,' said the Master, 'but business has kept me at Windsor.'

This was palace-speak for 'the King has been entertaining me and Lady Dighton at the Castle and I daresay you'd like to know what we had for dinner, and what we talked about, but it's a secret'. Guy had come across this sort of talk before, the dropping of deliberate hints that the speaker was far closer to the monarch than other courtiers, that they were the preferred one, the one upon whom Their Majesties most relied. It was one of the more tiresome aspects of court snobbery, but since it had prevailed unchecked for centuries, it wasn't likely to change any time soon.

Dighton ran a practised eye around the room – more like a barn, certainly large enough to play cricket in – and gave out an approving wheeze. Clearly, from his perspective, all was well.

'How did you get on with the Investiture?' he asked, striding over to the window.

'Very well, thank you, sir. I found it rather moving. The best—'

'Good,' broke in the old man, brushing aside the rest of Guy's reply. With thumbs jammed into his waistcoat pockets and forefingers drumming his irritation at the need to converse with lesser mortals, he added, 'I'll put you on the rota. Gather you did a good job.'

'Thank you, sir.'

'Now, I want to talk to you about the Duke of Gloucester. Word reaches me you've been offered the position.'

Well, that's news to me, thought Guy, unless it was handed to me in coded language – in which case could I have the code book? Everyone seems to think I've been offered the job, so obviously that's the way it works around here, but nobody's actually said.

'Gloucester's a bit of a handful,' the Master went on, 'and it will take time for you to bed in, get used to his ways. Being Regent Designate is a thankless task – on the one hand you're on permanent standby in case something disastrous occurs to His Majesty, on the other your job is to keep in the background and allow the spotlight to fall on Their Majesties and the two princesses. It's frustrating for HRH, and since his return from France last year he's been kicking his heels. Your job will be to keep him sweet and at all costs *to keep all avenues open* so that he's informed, not just through official channels, but unofficial ones too. Do you get me, Tanja Man?'

'Yes, I think I . . .'

'You know that Queen Mary refuses to speak to Tommy Lascelles because he wouldn't tell her what's going on? We can't have that sort of situation with HRH, understand? Tommy will be feeding Harry Gloucester the same guff Queen Mary gets until something happens, then he'll get the lot – Cabinet papers, military briefings, the whole bang-shoot.'

Dighton turned to Guy but, instead of meeting his eye, he rested his gaze on the ornate plaster reliefs above his head. 'It's far better that *other* avenues of opinion are left open to him – now and in the future – and I want to be sure you understand what I mean by that.'

'You'd like to brief him yourself,' said Guy. 'Separately, privately.'

'Good man, just the ticket. Say no more, just bear it in mind. Now, back to work!'

As Guy wandered away, his shoes cutting their way through the thick pile of the carpet, his mind worked furiously. What was meant by the orders he'd just been given? Was Dighton hoping to seize power in the event of Gloucester landing the top job? Was he ordering Guy to become part of a palace revolution? In the middle of a *war*?

He retraced his steps back towards the Ministers' Stairs, but as he reached them Toby Broadbent appeared out of nowhere. Guy nodded, his body language rejecting any prospect of conversation.

'Don't see you round these parts much,' said Toby.

'I prefer the Mews,' replied Guy tersely. 'Less ornate.'

This went over Broadbent's head. 'You know, old chap, every time I see you there seems to be only one topic of conversation – what's happening with your inquiry? The other chaps in the Coats Mission are just keen as I am to hear the news. A good soldier like that!'

And one whose wife you were keeping warm at night, thought Guy.

'All over, no further action. I'm busy with other things now, as I expect you are. Will you give a loving home to a parrot? One caring owner.'

'Ha ha! Seriously, though . . .'

'I *am* being serious. It's not generally the sort of thing I'm expected to do, looking into the odd unexplained death. I'm more of a parrot-minder.'

Broadbent took the hint and dropped it. 'Did I see you chatting to the Master upstairs?'

'Did you?' Are you *tailing* me?

'He's very keen on your taking the Gloucester job, I hear,' went on Broadbent chummily. 'Told me you're a safe pair of hands.'

So now I've heard it from your own lips, Captain. You're part of a military mission, answerable to your colonel, given the job of guarding the King's life, but instead you're hanging round with Topsy Dighton and running his errands just as Ed was.

As they reached a turn in the stairs and Broadbent peeled off, heading for the Stewards' Room, it finally came to Guy. He stood still in his tracks.

Toby Broadbent *had* killed Ed Brampton. Not because Adelaide asked him to – but because Sir Topham Dighton, the Master of the Household, had ordered him.

'I borrowed a bottle from the Butler's Pantry,' Guy said, plonking the whisky down on the kitchen table. 'We need it more than he does.'

'*Where's the Captain?*' demanded Charlotte.

'And, yes, some nuts for you, Charlotte. Got the glasses, Rupe? I need you to help me think this through. I'm fairly convinced I know what happened to Ed Brampton but there's one thing missing, and it's a big thing.'

'Go on.'

'I suppose I got confused, because for all this time I've been trying to think who could possibly have got within close-enough range of Ed Brampton to be able to kill him. But after I talked to Suzy Easthampton, it seemed to become clearer – stop thinking about who killed Ed, instead think about who *wanted* Ed killed. Then, when I talked to Adelaide, she told me Broadbent was secretly running errands for Topsy as well as Ed.'

Guy splashed whisky into two glasses.

'Here's where I need help, Rupe. If it was the Master who ordered Ed's killing, I don't understand it – Ed was a loyal, dutiful, obliging royal servant. What's more, he was related by marriage to Topsy. *Why kill him?*'

Rupert picked up his whisky glass and looked into it.

'Let me tell you what I know,' he said. 'Sir Topham Dighton is a remarkable man. He's nearly eighty but he runs those palaces, even in wartime, like clockwork. From what my colleagues have discovered – and we've been looking at him for some time now, Guy – he truly is devoted to the King and Queen.

'But, and this is a big but, the King is not a well man. You won't know this because nobody's allowed to talk about it at the Palace, but Queen Elizabeth is very concerned about him. He suffers badly from stress, and heaven knows there's been enough of that about since 1939. He wasn't expecting the throne and it's the old king's fault that he wasn't made ready to take up the reins if something went wrong. He smokes too much, and quite apart from that speech impediment, there are other aspects to his health which make him – if you knew the details – pretty superhuman to keep going as well as he has. Her Majesty helps carry the burden and, as you know, people say she's the one who wears the trousers – she's de facto sovereign. That's pretty amazing for someone who was born non-royal, and of course she's not popular with everyone. Those saccharine smiles disguise a chilly heart and a cunning brain.

'Take it from me, at the centre of all this is the English Mistery, the aristocratic revivalists who want to go back to the days of serf-dom and tugging your forelock. Hardly what we're all fighting for in this war!'

'Them?' said Guy scornfully. 'Aren't they rather a joke? And anyway, I thought they'd all scarpered back to the woods where they came from.'

'Far from it,' said Rupert. 'When they were founded a few years ago they had some powerful members – MPs, landowners, a few lords and their favoured sons. They're an arrogant bunch, and they're just waiting for something – anything – to give them the chance to take control and turn the clock back.'

'Go on.'

'In war, Guy, anything's possible – it's foolish to think otherwise. And that's what our lot at the GPO do – we look at all eventualities and plan against what might happen.'

'So what's the Mistery's plan?'

'They were founded by a man who cooked up this idea of the "Masculine Renaissance". He and his chums hate the suffragettes and, I think, women in general. These people are real royalists – would die for their king, but don't like the idea of a queen ruling them. Princess Elizabeth won't be eighteen until the spring of 1944. If the King should die then, she will become queen and many of them believe she'd have her strings pulled by her mother. She's a dutiful girl and would be likely to do what she's told.

'That goes against everything the Mistery stands for – in effect, *two* women at the head of the country. The men all having to bow, then bow lower still! However, should the King die before then, or become severely incapacitated, the Duke of Gloucester would sit on the throne as Regent. That would be their moment. And this is where Dighton comes in – the Mistery lost a lot of its supporters to another group, the English Array, but Dighton was winning them back with the promise of putting Harry Gloucester on the throne and keeping him there.'

'But does he have the power to do that? All by himself?'

'He knows just how to twist royal protocols and precedents – after all, he's been at the Palace longer than anyone, including the present monarch. He is, to all intents, the king-maker!'

'But everyone says Harry Gloucester would be useless as a king.'

'That's not the point. Topsy Dighton would be pulling the strings, keeping him in check, and at the same time ushering in the slow and subtle changes that would allow the Misters a big say in the running of the country.'

'Are you sure? I've never heard anything so mad!'

Rupert shook his head. 'Frankly I think the whole idea is too shaky, and its success would rely on there being a breakdown of law and order – but again I say you can never predict what'll happen in war. So it looks like we've reached a crucial point where we have to bring Dighton in for questioning. What have you got?'

'It's obvious Ed's murder – and it *has* to be murder since the poor chap didn't actually own a pistol – was an inside job,' said Guy. 'If an outsider wanted to kill him, he'd have to wait till Ed left the building and shoot him then.'

'Unless you were Rodie. Have you seen her, by the way?'

'She's coming here in a minute. I'm taking her out for supper.'

Rupert nodded approvingly at his flatmate. 'Consider it a job of work.' He smiled. 'We need to keep her sweet. You can submit the bill afterwards.'

'Don't be ridiculous!' retorted Guy primly. 'It's my thank you to her for taking me dancing!'

'Enjoy yourselves. Now, this man Broadbent.'

'I made inquiries and they're going to disband the Coats Mission. The chances of our being invaded seem to be receding, and I think the Queen is fed up with having all these chaps hanging round the family the whole time. They're gradually reducing the numbers now, and by next year they'll all be dispersed. I reckon Captain Broadbent is making himself handy to the Master in the hope of a palace appointment after the war's over.'

'Won't he be sent off on active service now?'

'Maybe, but if he survives he'll need a job to come home to. It was only when I was talking to him on the stairs today – remembering what Adelaide told me – that I realised why he and Topsy were both pestering me about my progress on the investigation into Ed's death. They were simply trying to discover if I'd found out their connection to it – Broadbent as the killer, Topsy the man who ordered it.'

'I think your Tangier flop was probably the reason you were given the job in the first place,' said Rupert laconically. 'Since the police had been kept out of it, there had to be some sort of an investigation – and it's obvious that the powers that be thought you were the one to bungle it. With almost one hundred per cent certainty you wouldn't find anything out, they could then close the case. An open verdict, they'd call it – the coroner's way of saying "we haven't the faintest idea how this man died".'

'What a compliment!' said Guy, disgruntled. 'A bungler – and I was always the clever one in my family. Anyway, it all joins up, doesn't it? Broadbent killed Ed on Dighton's instructions.'

'Can you prove it?'

Guy looked angrily at him. 'Of course I can't!'

'And can you explain why Dighton wanted Ed killed? What was the purpose, the motive?'

'I can't do that either! This whole thing has the makings of a farce, and as of this moment, I wash my hands of it. Nobody's in the slightest bit interested in poor Ed – he may have been a bit of a failure but he deserves better than this!'

'Don't give up so easily,' said Rupert. 'There *are* some people interested, including many of my colleagues.'

'When you say "colleagues", do you mean you?'

'Possibly. But what you've established so far, Guy, is a great help. We can't accuse Sir Topham Dighton of sedition, yet his involvement with the Mistery is just that. What he's doing is of deep national concern, but we can't get him.

'The Dightons are an ancient family – been around for a thousand years – and are a powerful force. I feel certain that the palace walls would circle to protect him if he were accused of political plotting – the royals do *not* want their dirty linen being aired in public – but if he could be arrested on a rather more obvious criminal charge, such as conspiracy to murder, then we have our man.

'But,' continued Rupert, 'so far I can't prove it, and neither can you. So have some more whisky – and for heaven's sake, take that scowl off your face!'

CHAPTER
TWENTY-THREE

A week passed; two. One morning, with the King and Queen at Balmoral, Guy was summoned by Tommy Lascelles, the sovereign's senior representative on earth while he was away on the moors shooting grouse.

'You made up your mind about the Duke of Gloucester role?'

'I don't think it's for me, sir.'

'No, I didn't think so either. Another pair of hands required – firmer, steadier than yours. Perhaps less sensitive. No criticism of you, Harford, you're doing well.'

'Kind of you to say so, sir.'

'Especially with handling the press, a job nobody in their right mind would want to take on. Dreadful people, Harford – vultures, Judases!'

'They're not all bad, sir.'

'You believe that if you like. But you'd better take a look at this,' he said, handing over a clipping evidently from an American newspaper.

GLOUCESTER THE IMPOSTER

ran the headline in the New York *Boulevardier.*

> Meanwhile over in London town, doughty
> Britishers are asking what's happened to
> their No 2 royal, the Duke of Gloucester

the article began.

> Remember him? He's the one with the
> nifty moustache and the rich wife
> (Duchess Alice's father the Duke of
> Buccleuch is the biggest landowner in
> Europe - though these days artful Adolf
> might seek to disagree).
>
> Harry Gloucester, 41, may be the third
> of King George V's four living sons, but
> he moved sharply up the pecking order
> when King Teddy fell for the Baltimore
> belle and tossed away his empire.
>
> Harry's critics label him petulant,
> inattentive, self-important and lack-
> ing in brainpower. Yet he's on standby
> to rule the British Empire - all 500
> million souls of it - should anything
> happen to His Imperial Majesty King
> George VI.

Wait, you say - won't Princess
Elizabeth, 15, inherit the throne?

Not till she's 18. Until that time the
Dook will front the royal show, sign
the documents, wave from the balcony.
And sit on that throne.

Whispers reach me, however, that Harry
doth tarry when it comes to hard work.
In fact he's become virtually invisible, with...

(turn to page 7)

'This is outrageous, scandalous!' barked Lascelles, waving his finger at the clipping. 'It says he's lazing about doing nothing! This is your job, Harford – you must do something to stop this kind of filth appearing! Do you have any idea who this "Caliban" fellow is? Have you come across this column before? I take it he's resident in London, but is he English or American? What can you do to shut him up?'

'I'll have to ask around, sir,' said Guy, though he knew perfectly well who'd written it. 'See what can be done.'

'*Not* what we need to see in print, Harford, just when we're trying with all our might to convince the great American nation they should throw in their lot with us. And really – the Duke . . . he's doing his best, dammit!'

'You don't think perhaps there's something in what he says? That His Royal Highness *should* be seen to be doing more?'

'Certainly not! We need to focus on people seeing the King, the Queen, the princesses!'

'But the writer surely has a point?'

'*Of course he has a point*' thundered Lascelles. 'I just don't want to see it in print, anywhere, ever again! See what you can do, Harford – let's get this thing stopped before other people decide to jump on the bandwagon.'

'I can't promise anything, sir.'

'See what you can do, I say. Have you been to Sandringham yet?'

'No, sir.'

'Rather lovely this time of year. Those endless Norfolk skies. Perhaps you could spend a few days up there taking it easy once you've got this thing fixed.'

Good Lord, thought Guy, as he walked away. They really *are* worried about Gloucester's public persona if they're bribing me with a free holiday in Norfolk. He returned briefly to his office, made a telephone call, then caught a bus from the stop next to the Tradesmen's Gate.

Half an hour later he was sitting in Ted Rochester's flat, the offending press clipping on the table between them.

'This is your handiwork, Ted.'

'Not me, old thing – not my style. Too rough-hewn.'

'Rubbish. I know it's you, no point in denying it. You can always tell who the author is because of the stories they write, the people they quote, the access they have. This has all the hallmarks of your style, Ted – but I must admit, you're a gifted journalist for hiding it so well.'

'Nice of you to say so. Sherry?'

'Look, we have to work together. It's not an ideal situation from either side – you feel you don't get enough help from the Palace. We, from our side, wish you'd write more supportively using the information we supply.'

'You're not the best judges. You live inside a palace.'

'As a matter of fact, Ted, *I* live in a cramped flat overlooking Victoria bus station – not this . . .' He waved his hand around the elegant service flat with its view of St James's Palace. 'You can't just carve a chunk of flesh out of the royal family's side and then expect to come back for more. The wounds you inflict with that typewriter over there won't heal easily in wartime, and criticising someone who could – in a heartbeat – become our head of state is doing irreparable damage.'

The journalist looked at him down the long cigarette holder in his mouth. 'When was Gloucester's last public engagement, Guy?'

'I . . .'

'You don't know. Neither do I. I gather he's spending quite a lot of time in the country just now, with his pigs and cattle. Doesn't sound like much of a war effort to me.'

'I'd remind you that he was blown up by the Luftwaffe in France only last year.'

'That was then, Guy, this is now. Since he came home he's virtually disappeared. I do think the next in line to the throne, or whatever he is, should be pulling his weight a bit more. And so do you.'

'My opinion's worth nothing. What I want to know is, where did you get this stuff from?'

'A journalist never reveals his sources,' replied Rochester smoothly. 'Everyone knows that.'

'Ted, you're a realist. I've come to you from Buckingham Palace. In the future, would you like me to occasionally give you what you call a scoop? Or would you prefer it if I never answered your calls again?'

'You have an obligation to brief the press.'

'Try me next time, see how well I do.'

The reporter looked down at his shoes thoughtfully and remained silent for a few moments.

'Let me get this straight. You want me, in my newspaper articles, to write good things about the current set-up at the Palace.'

'Yes, of course.'

'Similarly, you wouldn't mind if I wrote articles which are critical of people who bring the royal family into disrepute.'

'Naturally.'

'Would you say our friends the Windsors – Wally and David – fall into the latter category?'

'What are you saying, Ted?'

'Give and take, old chap, give and take! Under certain conditions I might tell you where the Gloucester story came from – but only in return for some griff on Wally. Foxy knows all about the Windsors, so does Hugh Sefton – they're practically best friends – you must be able to get something out of them. In return for laying off Harry Gloucester.'

Guy thought for a moment. 'No can do, old chap.'

'Well, there you are.' Rochester got up to lift a long-necked decanter and poured sherry into a single glass. He did not repeat his offer to Guy.

'I don't break personal confidences, Ted.'

'Look at it this way. Anything that's written which makes the Windsors look bad makes the King look good. Your task is to do just that – make him look good. By fair means or foul, I imagine.'

'I'll have to think about it. I daresay there are a few things I could let you have. Meantime where does this Gloucester stuff come from?'

Rochester paused only for a moment.

'Betsey Cody, your new best friend.'

'Say that again, Ted.'

'Betsey.'

Guy sat back, startled. 'OK,' he said slowly. 'This is off the record. You remember, Ted, what "off the record" means?'

'Depends,' said Ted, stoppering the decanter. 'If you're going to tell me the King is dead and brother Gloucester's now head honcho over at the Palace, I make no guarantee. In the ordinary way of things, I'm sure we can come to an arrangement.'

'It's about Betsey.'

'OK. We're off the record.'

'What she told you – and I'm not blaming you for running it, Ted, even if I wish you hadn't – what she told you is right, but damaging. I have to suppose that if she told it to you, her purpose was to dent Harry Gloucester's reputation.'

'I'd say so.'

'Then listen to this. This is the same Betsey Cody who a couple of weeks ago was pleading with me to get herself and Granville Cody an invitation to stay with the Gloucesters at Barnwell Manor. She's been pushing like mad ever since, even leaning on Foxy to get a date fixed.'

'And have you?'

'Well, yes. The Gloucesters are doing a lot of entertaining of useful people – so, you see, you weren't entirely right in your article, Ted, they *are* making a contribution to the war effort – and Betsey and Granville just about fall into that category.'

'So your point is?'

'Why, on the one hand, is she cuddling up to the Gloucesters – moving heaven and earth to get alongside them – while at the same time trying to ruin their reputation in the US? It doesn't make sense.'

'She's a woman with a lot of money. Capricious. She does and says pretty much what she wants.'

'Oh, come on – two entirely different things at the same time? Does she suffer from schizophrenia?'

'I have no idea what's in her mind. To me, she's a godsend – one of the best hostesses in London, one of the most generous, one of the nicest. She gives me dinner and she gives me stories.

Occasionally she asks me to put something in which I don't necessarily follow, but I rely on her judgement. What's the harm in a bit of the old quid pro quo?'

'Well, where the Gloucesters are concerned, it's got to stop,' said Guy firmly. 'And, by the way, Betsey's just got herself and her husband uninvited to Barnwell Manor.'

'I wouldn't do that, old chap. She's not a lady to cross swords with.'

'Watch me. I'm not having someone use their wealth and influence to denigrate our royal family – my job's to protect them!'

'She's got a pretty fearsome temper. Start throwing your weight around and she might think twice about backing your art exhibition.'

Guy hadn't thought of that.

◆ ◆ ◆

Her career as a model for Jean Patou may have been fleeting, but the look remained. Foxy was exquisitely turned out in turquoise, providing a dazzling counterpoint to her flame-red hair. Her clothes looked new and her pale skin was suffused with just the slightest hint of sunshine.

'Wonderful,' sighed Guy, shaking his head. 'I could paint you all over again.'

'Any time,' said Foxy, though she didn't mean it.

'I'd give anything to be back in Paris. As it was in, oh, '32.'

'Me too. When the going was good.'

'Ah well! I've come with a purpose, Fox. I want you to tell me about Betsey. She's stirring up trouble.'

'That doesn't surprise me. She's the most remarkable person, Guy, full of get up and go, a steely determination, lots of fun . . . but really . . .'

'What?'

'She can turn in an instant. I thought I knew her, but I don't. The way she snapped the other day when we were talking about you and the Gloucesters.'

Guy lit them both a cigarette. 'How did you come across her?'

'I've only known her since I came here from Paris. We know a lot of people in common, obviously, but we come from different worlds. I grew up in Virginia and New York; she comes from the boondocks. She's had to grapple her way to the top, there's a lot of street-fighter in her. Yet look what she did for Granville. She turned him from a boring one-dimensional figure, only interested in his business, into the figure he is today. Ambitious, yes, but I'd say ruthless too.'

Guy nodded.

'But what is it hidden inside that makes her want to feed Ted Rochester with damaging stories about Harry Gloucester,' he said, 'while at the same time wooing HRH and angling for an invitation to stay?'

'Is that truly what's happening?'

Guy explained.

'What are you going to do about it?'

'Well, I have to decide whether or not I'm going to challenge her on the basis of a scandalous paragraph by a notorious gossip columnist.'

'And if you do, bang goes your exhibition. She'll drop you like a hot potato.'

'I realise that. I realise also that what she does is buy people. Anybody – everybody. It's not the way we do things over here.'

'Agreed, that's why I like England and Englishmen. But let's change the subject – how's everything else going?'

'A few weeks ago we were sitting here in a daze after that air raid, remember? It was the night after Ed Brampton died. I told you then I had to find out if he'd really killed himself or whether he'd been murdered.'

'I remember.'

'Well, I think I've finally got there. I think I know now that it *was* murder, and that I know both who did it and who ordered it to be done.'

'Good Lord, Guy, I can't believe it – Ed *murdered*? In Buckingham Palace?'

'I just can't think of a reason why – I wish I could. Meantime, the most urgent thing is the problem of Betsey – I've got to do something to silence her. And I've got to get rid of that wretched parrot – she's driving my flatmate crazy. Sure you wouldn't like her as a wedding present?'

'Not a hope, chum. Try advertising in *The Times*.'

CHAPTER TWENTY-FOUR

They met in Soho. Rodie was dressed in her customary black trousers and top, her Eton crop strikingly at odds with the elaborate hairstyles of the other girls in the restaurant, who were all clad in floral dresses even though the summer was taking its time to heat up.

'Late again!' she said, drink in hand and a smile on her face. 'Get a move on, I'm hungry!'

Guy had spent the walk from the Palace, up through St James's Park and along Piccadilly, composing a prim little lecture on how he'd saved her once from jail but it wouldn't work twice. How she must promise to stop being so reckless, choose her company with greater care, keep a low profile, and do as little as possible to put herself in physical danger. It was a carefully thought-out piece of advice, but as he approached their table she looked too happy, too on top of the world. She didn't need his caution.

'Luigi says he's got champagne in the cellar, are you buying?'

'Certainly not. Do you know how much they pay me?'

'I don't care, anything'll do. You look lovely, Guy.'

'So do you, as a matter of fact.'

'We could go down to the Trocadero afterwards. They've got a band.'

'Your feet must recover quickly. Surely they're still covered in bruises from the last time we went dancing?'

'You just need practice, mate! Now, no more mucking about, when're you going to paint my picture?'

'Soon. There's no rush.'

'I thought you was going to have an exhibition.'

'So did I, but things have changed since we last met.'

'How?'

'Well, as you seem to know so much about my business, I may as well tell you. There's a woman called Betsey Cody . . .'

He launched into an account of how he'd been picked up and fawned over by London's leading society hostess, but now it was his duty to go and tell her off. 'Two weeks ago I was in a rush to get some portrait work done; now I have the feeling there's more time.'

'I read about her in some magazine,' said Rodie, with a mischievous twinkle. 'She's a right one, isn't she? Rich, I mean!'

'Well, yes.'

'The article was a "Mrs Granville Cody – At Home" type of thing. And I must say her gaff looked so huge it wouldn't miss a trinket or two, would it? I looked her up – Grosvenor Square, isn't it? Number 47?'

'For heaven's sake!'

'Well, if she's not going to give you the exhibition and I'm not going to get my picture done, and you're in trouble for her leaking things to the American papers, maybe she *does* deserve a visit, darling. Here's to us!' She clinked Guy's glass with gusto. 'Now tell me,' Rodie went on, 'about this Lady Easthampton. After all, I cracked open two flats for you, I found a telephone number, I deserve to know how you got on.'

'I suppose you do,' admitted Guy. 'She's gone to ground. She's being chased by people who work for the other side, the Nazis. She's of interest to our secret service as well, and as a foreigner in London she feels extremely vulnerable, so she's hidden herself away and just wants to be forgotten. I think as soon as the war's over she'll be gone in a puff of smoke. Right now all she wants to do is stay alive.'

'What's going to happen to all those clothes, those jewels?'

'She doesn't need them any more. There are more important things in life.'

'Well, I don't think they should go to waste, maybe I should pop back with my shopping basket.'

'You just can't resist it, can you?' said Guy, amused despite himself. 'I don't think you do it for the money, you just love the danger.'

'We all love a challenge. More wine please!'

'Suzy Easthampton – she calls herself something else now – wants to know who killed Ed Brampton. For a time, Ed's widow seemed desperate to know, but now I don't think that any more. But someone *does* still care about him and what happened.'

'And so do you – though you keep complaining about it. Can I help?'

'I wish you could, but I've lost all inspiration.' He explained his theory about Topsy Dighton and his soldier-assassin. 'But I can't work out why they'd want Ed out of the way, and without a motive there's nothing to be done. Topsy's far too powerful a figure.'

'Stop worrying. Eat your dinner and take me dancing. You never know what tomorrow may bring,' said Rodie with a wink.

One thing you could be certain of when you walked into Buckingham Palace in the morning, and that was, no matter the weather or the state of the war, Aggie would be in a mood.

Today was no exception. For once Guy didn't step around the puddle but splashed right in with both boots.

'I've been thinking a lot about Major Brampton, Aggie, and I want to talk to you.'

She looked fleetingly over her steel-framed glasses.

'I think about him too,' she said. 'We worked together a long time. But it's over now, best to move on. I hear you won't be taking the Gloucester job.'

'No.'

'Strange how some people don't have any time for him while others rate him highly – there's an MP who says he should be made Commander-in-Chief of the Armed Forces.'

'I'm not a military man, but might that not be rather foolhardy? If not downright mad?'

'I wonder sometimes, Mr Harford, whether your heart is in this job. I'll make some tea.'

Guy got up and walked over to the window. Outside, a trooper was wrestling with a fractious stallion, its harness half on and half off. His cap had fallen over his eyes.

'No,' he said, without turning round. 'Don't do that, just for the moment. What I'm going to do is keep looking out of the window. What you may not know, Aggie, is that I am blessed with clairvoyant powers – and I know that when I turn around again, Ed Brampton's missing notebook will be on my desk.'

There was a faint rustle behind him. 'What on earth are you talking about? It's gone. Stolen! It was taken . . . taken the night that rose appeared on your desk. And the chalked cross. On your desk, Mr Harford – whoever the culprit was that did that,' she blabbered, 'well, there you'll find the notebook, I should think!'

'No,' said Guy, 'the person who put the rose there most definitely did not take the notebook.'

'How do you know?'

'Because I asked the person concerned.'

'You *know* who broke into this office?'

'I do.'

'Did they also break into the Palace? Come over the wall, like they do?'

'I have no idea, Aggie. All I know is that the notebook was in this room, on the desk you're sitting at, that night. Next morning, it was gone – I *know*,' he repeated, 'because I asked. You were the first person in the office next morning, and while I am absolutely not saying you took it, I am also saying please put it on my desk. Now.'

Aggie, startled by his tone, slowly got up, went into the ante-room, and after a few moments returned with a sealed buff envelope. Without looking at Guy, she placed it on his desk.

'You know,' said Guy, still looking out of the window, 'I was given the job by the King, through Tommy Lascelles, to investigate Edgar Brampton's death. That is a very important undertaking, Aggie. I'm supposed to find an answer!'

'I don't think anybody expected you to . . .'

Guy smiled mirthlessly. 'I'm sorry to disappoint you. It seems I have some skills even I didn't know I possessed.'

Aggie had regained her composure. 'You weren't supposed to *find* the answer,' she repeated, shaking her head. 'You were just supposed to look.'

Guy turned to regard her sitting uncomfortably at Ed's desk. 'Sorry, that's not the way I go about things. Now, what exactly is in this diary? You'll have read it from cover to cover, no doubt – you know everything else that's going on in the Palace. It'd be a big surprise if you left this little corner unexplored.'

'What d'you want to know?' she replied sulkily.

'Does it actually name the members of the English Mistery, the ones who Ed was told to chase after for their support?'

Aggie squirmed in her seat. 'How do you know about that?'

'Does it mention meetings with Captain Broadbent? Meetings with Sir Topham?'

'I . . . I . . . I can't really say anything. The Master of the Household warned . . .'

'The Master may not be master for much longer. He's had a distinguished career, he's reached a certain age – I have the feeling he'll be tendering his resignation very soon. Now, I can sit here all night working my way through the diary, but I think, with your exceptional brain, you'll not only have read every word but remembered them too.'

Aggie opened her mouth but said nothing.

'All right, another question. Captain Broadbent and Mrs Brampton. Did Ed know about the affair?'

'Only at the end.'

'You mean just before he was killed?'

'Yes.'

'That's what made you think that somehow Mrs Brampton had a hand in his death?'

'I didn't say that!' said Aggie defensively.

'You implied it. Who do *you* think killed Ed?'

'I have no idea. Look, Mr Harford, I really have to get on! There's something urgent that I . . .'

'Not just yet,' said Guy firmly. He went over to his desk and picked up the envelope, tearing open the top and tipping out a green morocco-covered diary. He opened it and flipped through the pages.

'Is there anything in here which might lead you to suppose Captain Broadbent killed Ed?'

'It depends what you're looking for, Mr Harford, you'll have to read it yourself. But I don't think you should jump to conclusions – you've only been here a short while, you don't understand

271

how the Palace works, and you don't understand the ways that certain people have about them. I think the—'

'*I want to know why Ed was killed*,' hissed Guy. 'That's all! Do you know? Is it in these pages? Am I going to have to spend all night trying to find why Dighton wanted Ed Brampton dead?'

'What? Is that what you think? No . . . it's not that. It's not like that at all!'

Guy ran his hand through his hair. Aggie was frightened, and there was only so far he was prepared to push this interrogation. Clearly the whole day, and the following night too, would be spent trying to decipher the often-elliptical entries in Ed's spidery handwriting. One glance was sufficient to tell Guy it wouldn't be easy.

'This office comes under the command of Tommy Lascelles, correct?'

'Yes.'

'But actually its real boss is Topsy Dighton.'

'I'm not sure what you mean by that.'

'Aggie, if Sir Topham doesn't resign, he'll be arrested. He's been consorting with a group which is planning the overturn of the throne. That's an act of sedition – the blocking of Princess Elizabeth's right to sit on the throne! I imagine in wartime it could be described as treason – and we all know the penalty for *that*, don't we?'

'Yes.'

'What I'm saying to you is that, in a few days' time, the Master of the Household will no longer be with us. If you run to him now and tell him what I've just told you, he won't escape – but you will be implicated. Do you understand?'

'What do you want me to say?' burst out Aggie angrily. 'Thank you? Congratulations for being so brilliant?'

She's a tough one, thought Guy – you can never threaten a Glaswegian.

'I want you to say nothing to Dighton. His time's up.'

'If you think you've been so brilliant,' Aggie snapped, 'you'd better be sure of your facts. You seem to be saying Captain Broadbent killed Ed on the Master's orders.'

'Of course!'

'You're wrong.'

Guy picked up the diary. 'Then who . . .'

'Why don't you try looking at Major Brampton's girlfriend,' she said venomously. 'That foreign piece of work. The social climber. The Lady La-Di-Dah who swept in here and treated me like dirt when I told her to stay out of the Throne Room. The one he swanned off with.'

Jealous, thought Guy. She knew Ed's marriage was in trouble and thought, maybe, he would turn to her. Little did she realise Ed's relationship with Suzy Easthampton was sexless and that he still loved his wife.

'I now know what happened to him in those last months after Mrs Brampton went to live in the country, and I can assure you it had nothing to do with Lady Easthampton.'

'How do you know? She came from nowhere, a real nobody! Her friends, who were they?' She was angry.

'It had nothing to do with her,' said Guy firmly, his voice carrying a conviction he couldn't justify. 'But if, as you say, it wasn't Topham and Broadbent, who was it?'

It was Aggie's turn to stare out of the window. The stallion had been pacified and led away; the Royal Mews now empty and silent.

'I could never believe it was Captain Broadbent,' she said firmly. 'He's such a gentleman. An officer and a gentleman.'

CHAPTER
TWENTY-FIVE

The interview with Aggie left Guy in a foul mood. She knew more than she was saying, preferring to protect her allies within the Palace rather than see justice done. Or was it just that she was frightened? Certainly if the Master of the Household could order one killing, he'd have no hesitation in having another arranged.

It was late in the evening. For the past several hours he'd been reading his way through Ed's diary, but though the ex-soldier wrote copiously he said little. There were the names and addresses of the English Mistery members he'd met, together with a tick or a cross – apparently to signal whether they were prepared to support Dighton in the event of the King's death or capture. On the face of it, the Master was having a hard time keeping his troops in line – Rupe had mentioned that many of the Misters had moved on to join the English Array, and Dighton was having difficulty keeping the remainder under his thumb.

'Like herding cats,' mused Guy as he turned the page once more.

He'd looked first at the dates nearest to Ed's death, but the entries offered no special clue. Dotted between the various official duties the courtier performed were the initials of the men he saw most frequently at the Palace – Lascelles, Dighton, Toby Broadbent.

Lascelles was his boss, but it was Dighton's initials which appeared most often – Brampton had meetings with the Master almost twice as many times as the King's DPS. Broadbent appeared irregularly, and not at all in the week before Ed's death.

Turning back to the beginning of the year, Guy found the first few mentions of Suzy Easthampton, but shortly before the entry marked 'A leaves Mkhm St', thickly underlined in black ink, her initials disappeared.

From the many entries marked 'HrM' it was easy to see how often he was in the Queen's company – in the mornings, at lunch, at tea and sometimes dinner. Guy reminded himself Ed had been in the same regiment as the Queen's brother, and it could be that she saw in him a replacement for the favourite she lost at the Battle of Loos in 1915. There was no indication in the diary's many pages as to his feelings for her, nor for Adelaide or the children – though he noted meticulously all their birthdays and the presents he'd bought.

For the rest, even in its abbreviated form, the diary painted a picture of a man who was regular in his habits, meticulous in his record-keeping, and infuriatingly discreet in what he said.

All that fuss and bother to find this ruddy book, thought Guy, as he got up from his desk and walked round the room, and there's nothing in it.

He looked up at the clock – 11.30 p.m. – and with a sigh picked up the diary and ladled it back into the heavy buff wrapper which Aggie had handed over with such reluctance. As he did so, he noticed a slip of paper crushed down at the bottom of the envelope. He was tired and in need of a glass of whisky and irritatedly tried to jam the book back in, but the paper prevented it. He pulled out both diary and paper and glanced briefly at what was causing the logjam.

It was a coarse piece of government-issue paper, the kind used for a second or third carbon copy and usually stapled into a master folder.

While we seek to maintain harmony with
our American cousins at all times and
levels, it must be borne in mind that
not all are our allies.

The German-American Bund is a crypto-
Nazi organisation whose members wear the
Swastika and parade openly in military
fashion on the streets of many American
towns, even today. Its insignia combines
a Swastika with an Iron Cross.

The GAB's origins go back to 1933,
and its present headquarters are at
178 East 85th Street, New York City.
Membership is confined to Americans of
German origin but of these, it cannot be stressed too highly, there are
millions.

In 1939 the GAB held a rally attended
by a crowd of 20,000, echoing some of
the larger pre-war Hitler rallies in
Germany. Outbreaks of violence were
crushed by uniformed storm troopers.

This is essentially a quasi-military
group which takes pride in wearing

Nazi regalia and echoing their German cousins' denunciation of all things Jewish. Its broad base across America suggests that if the USA does come into the war, there could be civil unrest which may hamper the ambition of those on Capitol Hill who want to join forces with Britain, France, etc.

As its name suggests, the problem of the GAB remains within America; and is unlikely to reach these shores. However, government departments should be on the watch for Americans domiciled in Britain during the present hostilities who may have, and will conceal, German origins. These people present a possible threat to national security; the fact all Americans must be treated as honoured guests in Britain complicates the issue.

Please note there will be a full briefing for all departmental heads at 0900 on Tuesday in Admiralty A1/room 44B. Please signal attendance to 2/O Dimont, H., at that address.

TOP SECRET   PLMD/MT
RESTRICTED CIRCULATION   A/DZ//1941
INITIAL, RETURN, RESPOND   pp DHRTA

Guy stood staring woodenly at the memo, trying to take in its extraordinary message. How could such explosive information end up crumpled in the bottom of an envelope? It wasn't addressed to Ed Brampton, and there seemed to be no reason for it to be in his possession. Guy needed time to think.

Stuffing the paper back in the envelope, he locked it in his drawer and was going out of the door when the telephone rang.

'Guy? It's Rodie.'

'I told you never to call me at the Palace!'

'Are you busy?'

'I'm going home, it's nearly midnight.'

'I've got something for you. You'll love it!'

'Well, why don't we meet at The Grenadier tomorrow? Say six-thirty?'

'It has to be now. I'll come round to your place. I know where it is.'

'Of course you do. No doubt you've been through the contents with a fine-tooth comb.'

'Lovely parrot you've got – what's its name?'

Guy groaned. 'See you in half an hour.'

He marched briskly home, but though the walk took no more than fifteen minutes she was already in the flat. 'Kettle's on!' she sang brightly.

'Where's Rupe?'

'Out working I expect. Now look what I've got for you!'

She was wearing a one-piece siren suit with a scarf wrapped round her head – looking, Guy thought ironically, the very caricature of a burglar in a film or stage play.

'What have you been up to?' he asked grumpily. He was tired.

'It took time but I got there in the end!' she said, happily pouring hot water into the pot. 'The problem being there's been no air

278

raids for weeks, and I didn't know whether it would work. But, Guy, I AM a genius, and it did work!'

'What did?'

'Your friend Mrs Cody. I went to pay her a visit.'

'You . . . *what?* You broke into her apartment?'

'Manner of speakin', you might say. She wasn't in.'

'What a shame,' said Guy scathingly. 'If she had been, no doubt she'd have offered you a glass of champagne. Just before she called the police and had you arrested. I take it you did go round there to burgle her?'

'I don't use that word, Guy. I'm not your everyday, common or garden robber, you know.'

'How on earth did you get away with it? She has an army of staff in that place!'

'There she was, havin' a nice dinner with all sorts of smart people. The apartment's on the second and third floor – no difficulty getting to the front door, but I could hear the party going on inside. So I went away and thought about it. Like all these posh apartment blocks, there's an internal air-raid alarm as well as the public ones in the square – just to be on the safe side, like. So I went down into the basement and there it was, just like you'd expect. I reckoned that, even though there's been no enemy action recently, people are still on the kee-veeve, waiting for those German buggers to come back.'

She poured the tea, flushed with success.

'This is what I thought . . . They'll all be so anxious when they hear the alarm go off, they'll bundle out of the apartment and race down to the air-raid shelter – your friend, her chums, all the staff. It'll take time because they're always told not to use the lift, take the stairs instead. So getting that lot down there will take a few minutes. Then they'll hang around waiting for people from the other apartments to come and join them. Then there'll be a bit of a palaver about whether it's a false alarm or not, then one of the staff will be sent up to the street to see what's going on, then he'll check with an air-raid warden – when he can find one, like "Is the raid going to be soon?" – and when he discovers it truly is a false alarm he goes back and tells everybody, and they come out and have to troop back up the stairs again. I fixed the lift so they couldn't use it.'

Guy looked at her in amazement. The sheer nerve of it!

'I reckoned I'd got fifteen minutes, tops – I was in and out of there in fourteen, darlin'!'

'I'm astonished, Rodie. Appalled, but astonished.'

'So what do you think I've got for you?'

'I'm not sure I want to know. Would you prefer some whisky? This tea is dreadful.'

'Take a look at this!'

She handed over a framed photograph. Taken in summer, it featured a well-dressed couple in their forties standing in front of a road sign, smiling happily. She was looking at him; he was looking sternly ahead. Each had their right arm raised. Behind them, in the background, a handful of others eagerly copied their unmistakable gesture.

'Your friend,' said Rodie, 'your society-hostess friend. She's a bleedin' Nazi!'

'Where did you find this?'

'Where's the first place you go? Where did I go when we popped into Ed Brampton's house?'

'The safe.'

'In the bedroom, behind a picture, like they usually are. I've got an instinct like a homing pigeon, my darling, it takes me straight there – every time!'

'What's in there?'

'The usual. Top shelf, loads of jewellery. Loads! Middle, documents – I didn't bother with those. Bottom, personal stuff – letters, diaries, cash, that sort of thing. I found this in a locked box at the back – lots of other pictures in there too, but I didn't want them to know I'd paid a visit, so I left it at that. I thought it might help you make up your mind about warning her off the Duke of Gloucester.'

'I'm trying to drink this in,' said Guy, astonished. 'Let me take it over to the lamp.' Rodie came over and put her arm around him, delighted by his response.

The photo was unquestionably a picture of Betsey Cody with an unknown man. They looked like a prosperous – though not rich – couple in relaxed and happy form. But both were, without question, making the Nazi salute.

The road sign read 'YAPHANK' but there were no further clues as to where the picture was taken. Guy carefully turned the frame over, and with some difficulty levered off the back. In pencil on the rear of the picture was a woman's handwriting:

Happy anniversary!
Max & me
Yaphank
June 24th

This isn't her husband, Guy said to himself. Her husband's called Granville and I've seen his picture in the paper and he doesn't look anything like this man.

Aloud, he said to Rodie, 'Why did you do this? Why break into Mrs Cody's apartment, why go looking her safe, why choose this particular item to bring back?'

'I'm brassed off about you not painting my picture,' said Rodie vehemently. 'You were goin' to, and then this woman wasn't going to give you your exhibition, and then you wasn't going to. I want you to paint my picture!

'So I thought I'd go and take a look. Wasn't thinking I would find this. I thought I'd find something to bring back which would make you laugh, and then if you laughed you might think again about the picture. *Every* woman wants their portrait done!'

'You've got your wish,' said Guy, turning the photograph over in his hands, looking for further clues.

'I pinched this one as well, but only 'cos I liked her hat. I thought I'd have one made like that.'

She handed over a photographic print, unframed, of a group at a race meeting. Guy glanced at it quickly, noting Betsey standing at the front looking as if she'd just won a large bet but smiling directly at someone else in the group. Close by was the lantern-jawed Granville Cody, while either side of them stood soldiers in uniform.

'More recent,' said Guy. 'That's her husband. I wonder when the other picture must have been taken.'

Just then, Charlotte woke and gave a squawk from under her embroidered cage cover as a key turned in the door and Rupe walked in.

'There's whisky and tea,' said Guy over his shoulder, in answer to the unspoken question. 'Don't go near the tea. Then come and help.'

He pushed the framed photo in front of Rupe and said, 'I think we have a spy in our midst. That's Betsey Cody.'

'She's been looked over.' Rupe never gave a straight answer if he could avoid it.

'Husband is Granville Cody, in charge of the Aircraft Exchange Commission. I expect you know about him.'

Rupert nodded.

'Rodie kindly brought me the photo. Guess how she came by it. Our Mrs Cody may give splendid dinner parties and have entranced half of social London, but this picture definitely says she has other allegiances.'

Rupert grunted. 'You know where this is?'

'No idea. Strange name for a place, Yaphank. Since they're all heiling Hitler, it must be Germany? Austria?'

'Actually, it's in New York State,' said Rupert slowly, turning the picture over and reading the inscription. 'Long Island. And thereby hangs a tale.'

'Yes?'

'Rodie,' he said, turning, 'you've just done something quite amazing.'

''Course I have. I'm a genius!'

'Seriously, you have no idea how important this picture is. To start with, I'd say that the man standing next to the Cody woman is Max Kuhn.'

'How can you tell?'

'Yaphank is the home of American Nazism. There's a place there called Camp Siegfried, a kind of training ground for the US version of the Hitler Youth.'

'What? Now, in the present day? How can they do that?' cried Rodie. 'In a free country? How can it be allowed?'

'That's the point,' said Rupe. 'It *is* a free country. America isn't at war with Germany – not yet, anyway. People are allowed their rights and if they want to dress up in uniforms and form themselves into militias, there's nothing to stop them.'

'This is very strange,' said Guy quietly. 'These people are called the German-American Bund, are they?'

'Yes,' said Rupe, surprised Guy should know. 'And that man is someone that colleagues of mine have been chasing for months. He's Max Kuhn, whose brother just happens to be Fritz Kuhn – the man they call the American Führer.

'Fritz is not much admired by the Nazi high-ups back in Germany – he's a bit too ostentatious for their liking – though, mind you, he can fire up a crowd when he speaks. Thousands of 'em turn out for his rallies.

'But Max is a different kettle of fish. He's almost invisible and a very effective operator – Ribbentrop adores him, I'm told. What I can reveal is that we've been watching our Max as best we can ever since he visited a man called Walter Schellenberg in Mexico last year.'

'Your boys do get about, don't they,' said Guy, but he was only half-listening. He was looking from one photograph to the other, willing them to reveal their separate stories.

'It was Schellenberg who'd previously been given the job of either persuading the Duke of Windsor to come over to the German side or, failing that, kidnapping him. That was in July last year – when the Windsors were on their way through Spain and Portugal to the Bahamas.

'That particular caper was called Operation Willi, and the Nazis believe they very nearly pulled it off. But it wasn't the success they'd hoped for – as you know, the Windsors are now safe and sound, as far away as could be.'

Guy put the pictures down, defeated – they refused to speak to him. 'I imagine Hitler didn't take kindly to it having failed,' he said.

'Schellenberg's head was on the block. That's when he came up with the idea of targeting the Duke of Gloucester as a substitute.'

'Gloucester,' said Guy, nodding, 'who'll be Regent if the King falls under a bus. Who was criticised for his pro-German stance before the war.'

'Precisely. Now, take a look at that picture again and read the inscription out loud.'

'Happy anniversary,' began Guy. 'Oh, I see! Betsey's *married* to Kuhn. But when can this have been taken? She's married to Granville Cody, surely!'

'Well, Camp Siegfried opened up in 1936, so it could be any time after that.'

'We've got two photographs here, Rupe. Let's say this one's 1936 and the other – well, the way everybody's dressed up, it could be something like the Derby. The print looks fresh – it could almost be last year.'

'It *is* last year,' said Rupe, picking it up for the first time. 'And I can tell you why. That's the Newmarket stand in the background, as I should know – I've lost a few quid there in my time. The Derby's always run at Epsom. But it moved up to Newmarket last year because they were worried about an air attack.'

'So,' said Guy, 'it looks like Betsey's married to Kuhn in the first photo, and married to Cody in the second. Four years apart – quick work! I was asking Foxy Gwynne about her, and she told me Betsey turned up here in London in 1937 with Granville in tow.'

'So he's a Nazi sympathiser.'

'Not so fast,' broke in Rodie. 'The safe I cracked open had *her* stuff in it. Nothing male – hubby must have another one hidden away somewhere else. And the Hitler salute picture was in a locked box underneath a lot of other things at the back – as if she was deliberately trying to hide it. You wouldn't do that, would you, unless you didn't want your husband to know?'

'Or the security services,' said Rupe grimly. 'But what we have here in this other picture is a story which says Schellenberg, the Nazi who tried to woo the Duke of Windsor, met Kuhn – whose soon-to-be ex-wife has bought her way into British society and has targeted the royal family.'

'Oh!' said Guy. '*Now* I see why Betsey Cody was so desperate to get an invitation to stay at Barnwell! And why she had that story planted in the New York papers – to scare the Gloucesters into making an effort to suck up to the Americans, especially her and Granville. What I don't yet understand is how she could be Mrs Kuhn one minute and Mrs Cody the next.'

'Bigamy?' suggested Rodie with a laugh. 'There's a lot of it about these days.'

'Oh, do pipe down!'

'Anyway,' insisted Rodie, 'can I keep the other pic? Now you know where it was taken you don't need it, and I want to show it to my milliner.'

'Your *milliner*?' Guy hooted. 'Exactly how rich are you? Don't you know there's a war on?'

'Ha ha! Give it 'ere, 'andsome.' She whisked it off the table and was putting it in her bag when Guy stopped her.

'One last look,' he insisted.

The racetrack photograph had been taken in sharp summer sunlight and was exceptionally clear. Betsey was wearing a tailored suit with an extravagant straw hat and looking extremely youthful for a woman of possibly fifty. She had an animated look on her face, aimed at someone other than her husband.

'Wait,' said Guy in a low voice. 'Is there a magnifying glass anywhere?'

'Second drawer down in the dresser,' said Rodie instantly.

'You *have* been through this place, then,' said Rupe. 'You cheeky beggar!'

'I like to know who I'm dealin' with.'

Rodie returned, waving the glass in the air. Guy snatched it from her crossly and returned to the table.

'Well I never,' he said slowly after a moment or two. 'There's someone else we know in this picture.'

He pointed to a smart-looking soldier, clearly the object of Betsey Cody's close attention, standing at the end of the group.

'That, my friends, is none other than Captain Toby Broadbent. He's in this, too.'

CHAPTER
TWENTY-SIX

'I just can't understand what's going on,' said Guy, shaking his head. 'This man Broadbent is everywhere. He's guarding the King – that's his official job. Then he's running errands for Dighton and his seditious English Misters. At the same time he's hanging round with Betsey Cody, who, on the evidence of this picture, is a Nazi supporter.

'Betsey Cody, meanwhile, is trying to get close to the Duke of Gloucester, presumably to talk him round to the idea of taking the throne if the Germans invade – whether the King's still alive, or not.

'But how do all these pieces of the jigsaw fit together, Rupe? And how does poor old Ed Brampton fit in?'

Rodie, satisfied she had played her part, had taken Charlotte's cage into the kitchen and was having a lively conversation with her. Rupe lit a cigarette.

'Let's take it all apart, piece by piece,' he said. 'You think that Broadbent shot Ed Brampton, but you don't have a motive. All the time you've been assuming it must be something to do with Dighton – that Dighton wanted him out of the way and got Broadbent to do the deed. Try and look at it another way, Guy. Supposing Dighton had nothing to do with Brampton's death?'

'But he must have!' replied Guy heatedly. 'Those meetings I had with him – when he kept asking me what was happening with my investigation! They were because he wanted to know what I'd discovered. Whether whatever I knew was going to implicate him!'

'Supposing it wasn't that? I'm just saying *supposing*,' said Rupert soothingly. 'Take Dighton out of it for a minute. What we've got here on the table in front of us offers up another story. Broadbent knows Betsey, and we now know that Betsey is a secret Nazi. I go for your idea that it's not *who* killed Ed, but who *wanted* him killed. Supposing that person was Betsey Cody? Supposing she got wind of the fact that Ed knew about her and the German-American Bund? You told me yourself about that government memo you found with his diary – he knew about the Bund. He knew Broadbent.'

'But I still don't know how he got the memo!'

Rupert waved it aside. 'What would make more sense is that Ed discovered Betsey's Nazi secret, and either he confronted her with it – if he knew her personally – or else he challenged Broadbent with it. That would require Ed to know that Broadbent knew Betsey, obviously. But she's a household name, thanks to your chum Ted Rochester and his newspaper columns – if her name came up in conversation it's quite likely Broadbent would boast of knowing her. Everybody else does.'

'So Broadbent killed Ed Brampton not on Dighton's orders, but on Betsey's? Why would he do that?'

'I refer Your Lordship to Exhibit Two,' said Rupert. 'Concentrate on the way she's looking at Broadbent in that picture.'

'You mean . . . ?'

'Yes, I do mean. "The look of love", is how a cheap magazine would describe it.'

'Well, all I can say is – remarkable!' Guy gave a snort of laughter. 'There's somebody else at the Palace that Mrs Cody's been seeing as well. I wonder how she finds the time.'

'If Broadbent – a trained killer, don't forget – is besotted with her,' continued Rupert, 'how hard would it be for him to agree to bump off someone who's causing her grief?'

'That would mean, surely, that Broadbent's in on her Nazi activities,' said Guy. 'It's a lot to take in – it would make him a traitor as well. Especially since he's part of the King's bodyguard.'

'Don't worry, he'll be out of the job by the end of the day,' replied Rupert confidently. 'Even so, you can't be sure that Broadbent knew Betsey's a Nazi – look at the way she hid that photo away at the back of her safe. Her very life depends on nobody knowing her true allegiances – why would she tell him what she's up to?'

'Well, I suppose that's entirely possible,' said Guy. 'He's not very bright. And what's he doing with her anyway? She must be twenty years older than him.'

'She's ultra-rich, extremely glamorous, all the right connections. Why ever not?'

'So what happens next?' asked Guy. 'This is your department, Rupe, what's your plan? You set out to expose Dighton's activities with the Misters – have you got enough evidence to do that? I set out to find Ed Brampton's killer – have I got enough to do *that*?'

'There's a way of doing it,' said Rupe, 'and doing it all. But I'll need your help.'

◆ ◆ ◆

The door to Mrs Cody's palatial apartment was opened by a muscular young man in a tailcoat.

'Guy!' Betsey rushed forward and kissed him on the cheek.

'This is a colleague, Betsey – Rupert Hardacre. I hope you don't mind?'

'Certainly not, certainly not! A glass of champagne, both?'

'No, thanks. Betsey, we've come—'

'—to tell me you've fixed up the Gloucesters. Hooray! I think they'll find us most grateful guests. I do like to give a present!'

'Not about the Gloucesters, Betsey. Well, it is in a way.'

Betsey was bubbling with anticipation. 'My secretary said when you called that you mentioned them.'

'I'm going to let Rupert talk to you for a moment, Betsey.' Guy glanced at the manservant standing against the wall, wondering if he was likely to cause trouble.

'Mrs Cody,' began Rupe, 'I'm here on government business. If you don't mind, I'm going to ask you some questions which will, I'm afraid, require an answer.'

Until that moment the hostess had been eyeing up the new-comer in a speculative sort of way, but suddenly her expression was alert, defensive.

'Mark,' she called to the man in a shriller voice, 'get the secretary to telephone Granville. Tell him to come home immediately. I mean *now*.'

'These are official questions and I urge you to answer them truthfully,' said Rupert evenly. His tone was non-threatening but determined.

'You were born in 1890 in St Paul, Minnesota with the name Bettina Kohler. After college you took a secretarial job at the local bank.'

'Such a long time ago, one can barely recall . . .'

'You married the bank's chairman in 1912, he died in 1922. In 1925 you married Till Braben, a US citizen born in Munich who ran a large lumber business.'

'What exactly is the point of all this?' Betsey retained a voice of authority but she stood leaning slightly, her hand gripping the arm of a chair very tightly.

'Just wanting to confirm,' said Rupert smoothly, just wanting to alarm. 'You divorced Braben in 1930 after you met Max Kuhn, another German-born American.'

Betsey looked at him, immobile. Her grip tightened on the chair.

'Max Kuhn is, or was, a leading light in the German-American Bund, the American Nazi Party. I think it's probably safe to assume you were a card-carrying member too.'

'I don't know what you're talking about. Who?'

'I've been talking to our friends over the road at the US Embassy,' Rupert went on, 'and they've been tremendously helpful. Max Kuhn is the Bund's chief strategist, while his brother Fritz is its nominal leader. The Führer, I think you probably call him, Mrs Cody – am I right?'

The woman sat down very suddenly.

'In 1937 you met Granville Cody, a recently widowed and extremely wealthy businessman. By the end of the year you'd divorced Kuhn and married Cody. Each of your marriages took you further up the social ladder, but though Cody had money, he had no polish. You set about changing all that and you brought him to London, where you used his wealth to buy yourself a place in high society. Your newly acquired, powerful connections ensured that when war broke out your husband was handed the job at the Aircraft Exchange Commission, where he's made a colossal contribution to the war effort.

'Mrs Cody,' said Rupert, the charm gone from his voice, 'does your husband know you are a Nazi?'

'No.' She was shaking but remained stiff and upright.

'Are you certain?'

'Yes.'

'But you are still in touch with your previous husband, Max Kuhn.'

'Yes.'

'You are, in fact, still acting on his behalf.'

No answer.

'In June and July last year there was an attempt by the Germans to persuade, or otherwise to kidnap, the Duke of Windsor while he was in Spain. We now know that when that action, Operation Willi, failed, a similar operation was conceived by a German officer called Walter Schellenberg. In February this year, Schellenberg visited Miami at the same time that Max Kuhn was staying there at the Biltmore Hotel.

'Mrs Cody, it was there, in Miami, that a plot was cooked up to persuade the Duke of Gloucester to seize the British throne, either in the event of a German invasion of Britain, or if the King were to die. Gloucester's job would be to push aside Princess Elizabeth and reign as Regent, a useful non-threatening deputy since Hitler sees himself as the future emperor, just as Napoleon was. You were the single-most important player in this plot. You'd established yourself in London pre-war and quickly surrounded yourself with some of the most important people in the land. You bought their company and friendship with jewellery and trinkets and other acts of largesse which they found irresistible. If an English hostess had tried that on, she'd have been ridiculed for her vulgarity, but because you're American, another set of rules applies. The English upper classes sometimes look down on the Americans as savages in suits, even if you are cleverer than most of them lumped together.'

The woman remained impassive, her eyes focused on Rupert's left shoulder, her gaze never wavering.

'You had one job, and one job only, and that was to persuade Gloucester that it would be for the good of the country if he were to take over. The Duke harbours a deep resentment for the way he's been overlooked here and sidelined there – failing to take account of his own ineptitude. In other words, he's frustrated and therefore biddable. You thought you stood a good chance of success.'

Betsey looked round for the manservant but he had not returned.

I wonder if he's part of it, thought Guy, and by now he's running for his life across Trafalgar Square.

'The difficulty you faced was getting close to the Gloucesters. You managed to get the Duke of Kent to come to your table and, by the sound of it, a whole lot more than that – but it was Gloucester you wanted. That's when you heard that Guy here might become his private secretary. So you wooed Guy with the offer of an art exhibition. And you very nearly got that invitation to Barnwell Manor. But not now, Mrs Cody, not now. Now, I'm sorry to say, a slightly less palatial establishment is waiting to welcome you. We have some people outside the front door just to make sure you get there safely.'

'I . . . want . . . Granville,' gasped Betsey, looking agitatedly round for her manservant.

'He'll find you, once we've had a chance to have a proper chat,' said Rupert. 'I just counsel you to tell the truth and tell all you know, easily and quickly, and you'll be treated gently.' What might happen otherwise he left unsaid, but the threat hung in the air.

'And now,' Rupert went on, 'it's Guy's turn.'

'I'm sorry, Mrs Cody, this is about something else,' said Guy. 'While you were trying every avenue you could to get close to the Gloucesters, you befriended a Guards officer. His name is Toby Broadbent, he's part of the King's private bodyguard. You had an affair. Broadbent is a bit of a do-or-die merchant, all or nothing, and he fell for you.'

Guy shifted his chair closer to Betsey. 'He fell for you so much he even agreed to have an affair with Adelaide Brampton, just so he could find out more about what Ed was up to.'

She thrust out her chin in response, refusing to be intimidated.

'I've thought long and hard about this, and now I believe you got Broadbent to murder Edgar Brampton because Brampton had discovered your connection with the Bund. He was sent a memo – we don't know who by – about the Bund. Pencilled in at the bottom was a list of half a dozen names with question marks against them. I didn't see them first time round because the paper was crumpled up – but one of them was yours. He knew Broadbent was one of your young men – Broadbent couldn't resist boasting about how chummy you were – and Ed took him to one side and warned him you were probably a Nazi spy. From that moment his days were numbered.'

'I really won't say anything,' replied Betsey, 'until I have Granville here.'

'Will Granville want to hear about your affair with Toby Broadbent? Or all the others you've had since you've been here in London? Can he actually help you with this particular inquiry?'

She looked round the room, seeing perhaps for the first time that the riches she'd married into, the luxurious lifestyle, the servants, were over.

'Guy . . .' she said.

'You ordered Ed Brampton to be killed. I thought it was someone else, but it was you. He was a good man, he'd done nothing, and you had him killed. That is a capital offence, Betsey, which means if you are found guilty you'll go to the scaffold. What I suggest you do is help Rupert here as much as you can, and maybe the penalty won't be quite so final. That's up to you.'

Betsey Cody got up, smoothed her skirt, looked round for a hat.

'It's war,' she said bleakly. 'You take what comes. No point in complaining.'

'Why did you do it?'

'Why? I look at you, Mr Harford, and I wonder if you could ever know what love is, what love does – I don't think you do.

Max Kuhn is the most extraordinary man I have ever met. By now he should be a president or a prime minister, but he believes in achieving things a different way. Germany *will* win the war, and there is every chance the Duke of Gloucester will become Regent under Adolf Hitler – nothing you can do to stop it! He's the right man at the right time! All I set out to do is help in my small way for that to happen, with the least unhappiness and disruption to all concerned.'

'You think the Duke of Gloucester would do it? Betray his country, betray the very family he comes from?'

'All men want power. If they smell it, they reach for it – grab it. I know this. They can't resist!'

'And you think that the "least unhappiness" includes the murder of an innocent bystander? He was a decent man, Betsey!'

'He should have kept out of the way.'

She paused imperiously for a moment.

'Now, where's my carriage?'

CHAPTER
TWENTY-SEVEN

'*YOU STUPID BLOODY TANJA MAN!*'

They finally caught up with Sir Topham Dighton in the Centre Room, the ornate barn at the front end of the Palace decorated with rare chinoiserie, tapestries, and carvings by Grinling Gibbons. The ceiling-height casement doors were open, and beyond was the famous balcony where generations of royals had pledged themselves to their people with languid waves of the hand.

The Master of the Household had not been warned of their approach, and when Guy introduced Rupe, his response was to flick at his lapel as if swatting away a fly. Topsy did not deal with people he did not know.

All too soon, though, he was to learn the purpose of their mission. Marooned in this empty place, miles from his office, the all-powerful Master suddenly looked vulnerable. But he fought like a tiger.

'You stupid bloody Tanja Man!' he repeated, spitting the words out. 'You come here into this Palace, you're incompetent, can't even do the simplest jobs properly, and you dare to question what I do!'

'If you recall, Sir Topham, it was you who started it. With the constant stream of questions about how the inquiry was going. You never let up, and for a time to me it seemed you really did want an answer to Ed Brampton's death.

'Well, now I've got it, and later this morning Captain Broadbent will be arrested for murder.'

'Murder?' spluttered the old man. '*Murder?* You can't go accusing trusted royal servants of murder without any evidence!'

'Try me.'

'I wonder,' bristled Dighton, 'how you're going to convince someone in authority that anybody killed anybody. You were given the task of investigating Brampton's death and you came up with no evidence – no evidence whatever! – to point to anything other than suicide. That's you, Harford – the official investigator! Nobody's said anything about murder! And frankly it's a bit late in the day to be changing your mind and saying it was!'

You're a wily old man, thought Guy – no wonder you've lasted so long at the top. No wonder successive kings have put their faith in you, what with your aristocratic bearing, your ancient family lineage, and your military grip on their palaces. But you stepped over the line.

'It was on your instructions that when Major Brampton was found, his body was taken away before a doctor had attended the scene.'

'We can't have unfortunate deaths like that within the Royal Verge.'

'The weapon that killed him was taken away, the walls washed down, everything put back in its place. Did you never think that this was a police matter? I understand the palace force wasn't informed until thirty-six hours after Ed died, and by that stage all the evidence had been cleared away. Is that a right and proper procedure, war or no war?'

'I refer you to my previous answer.' Dighton was unbending.

'Toby Broadbent was working for you, was he not?'

'He's a soldier. Attached to the Coats Mission. Not part of the Royal Household. That's who works for me, Harford – royal servants, not Guardsmen!'

'But he came to your office daily. What were you talking about?'

'You know the Mission has organised three safe houses for Their Majesties to withdraw to in the event of an invasion. The Mission guards the houses as well as Their Majesties – what d'you suppose they eat? Who gives them dinner? Puts sheets on their beds? Makes sure the telephones work? And that the secret hidey-holes have been prepared? That's my job, Harford, *my* job. Broadbent is the liaison officer between the Mission and the Household. We talk about these things. Does that answer your question?'

Good, thought Guy, very good. But not good enough.

'Is that *all* you talk about, Sir Topham?'

The old man strode towards the balcony and turned. Behind him was the backcloth of the Victoria Memorial and beyond it the long straight stretch of The Mall. As he stood in the window, he did indeed look like the master of all he surveyed.

'I command an army of my own here,' he said. 'There are secretaries and clerks and typists. There are telephonists, carpenters and plumbers. There are gardeners, chauffeurs and coachmen, upholsterers, seamstresses, mechanics, engineers – shall I go on?'

'No need.'

'These are the people who occupy my time. Not a man with a pistol creeping down a corridor to do away with a has-been army officer who's only employed here as a kindness.'

'So you do think Ed Brampton was murdered.'

'Stuff and nonsense! What bloody rot!' said the old man, but as he spoke he was backing away through the window on to the balcony. Guy and Rupert followed him.

'Let's put to one side whether Broadbent is a murderer,' said Rupe, 'and talk about the Mistery. There's quite a lot you can tell us about that, I think.'

'I have no idea what you're talking about,' said Dighton grimly.

'The Mistery believe the country, as it's being run, is going to the dogs. They sneer at Churchill's failures, and see a better way of running things. They are a powerful chain of like-minded individuals who believe in using their underground network to force change. And they would probably prefer to see the Duke of Gloucester on the throne than the present incumbent because he better suits their taste. Am I right?'

The old man glowered. 'So far as I know, the English Mistery disbanded before the war. Whatever arguments they may have had have been packed away for the duration. They're a spent force.'

'They would be, were it not for you, Sir Topham. You've been rallying them, drawing them back together. You're an educated man and you know the meaning of the word "sedition" – but in case you need reminding, it is "conduct or speech inciting people to rebel against the authority of a state or monarch". And that is what you've been doing. Drawing together and encouraging a group of people whose idea is to dismantle the state apparatus and run things to their advantage and according to their own doctrine. Sir Topham, we have many enemies just the other side of the English Channel. It's 1941, and we are at war. Britain doesn't need an enemy within.'

'You . . . whatever your name is . . . you, and this Tanja Man, have absolutely no idea what's going on,' sneered Dighton. 'You're outsiders, you don't know how things work.'

'Does making things "work" include blackmailing needy royal servants into illegal acts?' burst in Guy. 'You got Ed Brampton a job just so you could use him for your secret activities. You saved him from being a door-to-door salesman. But you told him he was there on sufferance and if he didn't do your bidding – running round after these Mistery characters – he'd be out again.'

'He was a very weak fellow. Not really suited to palace work.'

'He was devoted to the job. Devoted to Her Majesty. And you couldn't care less that one of your underlings killed him.'

'You have no proof,' insisted the old man, turning his back on them. He occupied the position normally reserved for the sovereign on royal occasions, right in the centre of the balcony, and appeared to be gazing across the park towards a bandstand in the far distance.

'Leave me alone for a moment,' he said over his shoulder. 'I am collecting my thoughts. Go back inside and I will have something to say when I come back in.'

Guy and Rupert looked at each other and nodded. They went inside through the window and turned to look back.

Sir Topham Dighton, the 13th baronet of Baxendale Parva, Master of the Royal Household, a man whose family had served the nation with distinction for a thousand years, was no longer there.

CHAPTER
TWENTY-EIGHT

'Honestly, Guy, you're bloomin' amazing!'

They were sitting in Guy's studio in Tite Street. The last of the summer sun had saved itself for this moment and now it was pouring in through the vast artist's window.

'Not really, it was Rupe,' said Guy modestly.

'It was Rodie,' said Rupert.

Instead of whisky there was wine and a picnic of wartime remnants. It was Saturday afternoon, and for once the capital city was at peace with itself and the world. Down below on the Embankment, young couples walked hand in hand and the occasional motorboat whizzed upriver in pursuit of pleasure.

On the easel by the window were the first outlines of Rodie's portrait – sure, strong, promising. Rodie was worried that anything more Guy did to the canvas might spoil the magic of this ghostly silhouette, but Guy knew it would work; the magic of Tangier had not deserted him.

'What'll happen to Betsey?' he asked. 'Just for a moment I thought she was fun, a bit of an adornment to the social scene. How easy to get it so wrong!'

'Not what you'd expect,' replied Rupe. 'No announcements, no handcuffs, no publicity. We desperately want America to come into this war. We can't suddenly have a show trial accusing one of its citizens of ordering the killing of a trusted Buckingham Palace courtier. And of trying to murder the King.'

'Wait a minute, wait a minute . . . did you say *murder* the King?'

'Oh, Guy . . . ! Did you think these people were going to hang around on the off chance that His Majesty might fall under a London bus one day? Not ruddy likely – they wanted to win the war, and quickly!'

'But how?'

Rupert shrugged. 'It was Betsey's brilliant plan to get one of the King's own personal bodyguards to murder him – and that's when she set out to seduce Toby Broadbent. It couldn't have been easier. Broadbent fell head over heels – for her money, for the glamour and the prestige. He's a Guards officer, which to most people seems like being top of the tree, socially, but the people Betsey mixes with are way, way above that. He was bowled over by the introductions she made, the doors she opened.'

Guy looked in astonishment at his flatmate. 'But . . . *murder* King George VI? Surely the outfit he belongs to is pledged to defend the King's life to the last round, the last man?'

Rupert nodded. 'You're right. And that's where Betsey came unstuck. Broadbent didn't mind a bit of skulduggery – didn't even mind engineering Gloucester on to the throne if the circumstances were right – but kill his own sovereign? It went against everything he'd been trained to do, and I think he just told Betsey he couldn't do it.'

Guy bit his lip. 'He was still prepared to do in old Ed, though.'

'He had to. Brampton knew too much.'

'Poor man. So what'll happen to Betsey now?'

'She'll be sent back to the States and someone high up will have to make a decision about what's to be done with her. Her ex-husband Max Kuhn has been arrested, and he'll probably join his brother in Sing Sing. I have the feeling the German-American Bund is on the way out.'

'Toby Broadbent?'

'By rights he should be tried for murder. And for treason, too – after all, he knew about the plot to kill the King and did nothing to stop it – but again it's tricky . . . Just think of the court case – King's bodyguard plans to assassinate the sovereign. What d'you think *that* would do to public morale?'

Guy nodded. 'I talked to Tommy Lascelles on the telephone just now. Broadbent was whisked away from his duties with the Coats Mission first thing this morning. My guess is within twenty-four hours he'll be chosen for a dangerous mission somewhere where the chances of survival are slim.'

'No more than he deserves,' said Rupert bleakly, finishing his glass and getting up.

'One last thing – what about the English Mistery? Such a weird bunch of people, but clearly still a terrible danger in wartime.'

'Without Dighton to corral them together I think they'll quickly fizzle out,' said Rupert. 'We're keeping an eye on them obviously. But let's hear it for Rodie – if it hadn't been for her, who knows what would have happened?'

She wasn't listening.

'Are we going dancin' later?' she said, looking down from the window on to the young lovers strolling the Embankment beneath. 'They've got Joe Loss at the Paramount!'

'I want to do some more work on your picture,' said Guy. 'You go with Rupe.'

'No thanks,' said Rupe. 'Busy.'

'I'll stay with you then,' said Rodie happily, pouring wine.

Guy looked across the room at his flatmate. 'How would you feel if I said I was moving out?' he asked. 'Adrian Amberley, my landlord here, is joining the exodus to the country and I can have this place for the duration. Leave you with a bit more space in Victoria. Unless you're still spying on me.'

'It was never that. You needed looking after when you came back from Tangier. I think you can manage on your own now. Only one thing, Guy.'

'What's that?

'Take the ruddy parrot with you.'

AUTHOR'S NOTE

This work of fiction is based on fact. During the Second World War, two of King George VI's brothers, David Windsor and Harry Gloucester, both believed that in the event of the King's death or infirmity, they had the best right to the throne.

In the wake of the 1936 Abdication, the third brother, George Kent, was sounded out on the possibility of taking the throne. He had every expectation that offer would be renewed.

The English Mistery, an aristocratic revivalist group with political ambitions, supported the monarchy but were vehemently misogynistic. They would have viewed the prospect of Princess Elizabeth taking the throne with dismay.

The German-American Bund, the largest group of Nazis outside the European mainland, had supporters on the British mainland.

In 1940, the Nazis launched a secret campaign – Operation Willi – to persuade the Duke of Windsor to come over to their side. If that failed, they would capture him.

ABOUT THE AUTHOR

TP Fielden is the fiction-writing name of the acclaimed royal biographer and commentator Christopher Wilson, who has penned biographies of Prince Charles, Camilla, Diana and other members of the British royal family.

For twenty years a leading Fleet Street journalist with columns in *The Times*, *Sunday Telegraph*, *Daily Express* and *Today*, he is now a bestselling biographer and (as TP Fielden) novelist.

Most recently the creator of the English Riviera Murders featuring 1950s supersleuth Miss Dimont, he remains an internationally in-demand writer on royal matters, with regular appearances on TV documentaries and reports across the globe.

His biography of Camilla, Duchess of Cornwall, is the acknowledged source material for all other books and TV films on the subject, and his groundbreaking research on the life and family of Catherine, Duchess of Cambridge, is also a primary source for biographers and film-makers.

His biography *A Greater Love: Charles and Camilla* was turned into a top-rated TV documentary screened in the USA, UK and twenty-six other countries around the globe, and he has co-produced several major TV documentaries on the British royals. He lectures widely on the subject.

He is the co-founder of the Oxford University journalism awards, and for this work he was honoured by St Edmund Hall, the university's oldest college, with membership of their Senior Common Room.

He is married to an American writer and lives on Dartmoor, England.